# Illuminarium

## Truth Devour

www.truthdevour.com

Published in 2015
by Truth Devour
www.truthdevour.com

Interior layout and design
by Publicious Pty Ltd
www.publicious.com.au

Book cover design by:
Artist: Diana Toma
Email: diana@artbydianatoma.com
Facebook: facebook.com/ArtByDianaToma

Catalogue-in-Publication details available
from the National Library of Australia

ISBN: 978-0-9922999-6-5 (pbk)

Also available in ebook
ISBN: 978-0-9922999-7-2 (ebk)

I have love in me the likes of which you can scarcely imagine and a rage the likes of which you would not believe.

If I cannot satisfy the one, I will indulge the other.

Mary Shelley - Frankenstein

ALSO BY TRUTH DEVOUR

Enigma Series
Adult Contemporary Romantic Trilogy

*Wantin*
(1$^{st}$ book)

*Unrequited*
(2$^{nd}$ book)

*Sated*
(3$^{rd}$ book)

www.truthdevour.com

DIRECT
DEVOUR

# Contents

# Resonance

I loved taking advantage of the weather's early morning tepid start to a looming rare hot fall day. The way the breeze encased my skin as I hiked through the redwood national forest made me feel present and grateful to be alive. I'm not sure why I was always drawn to come here for solitude. It was as though the trees called to me to visit them. The enormity of the grand old structures gave a sense of majesty and wonder. Detection of the occasional flurrying within its knotholes coupled with the sway of branches encouraging intermittent release of sprinkles of pine needles all visually brought these wonderful trees to life. This is indeed an enchanted forest exhaling magic for all to breathe.

As I walked along the man made paths weaving between my old friends and crossing over the shadows cast by the dappled sunlight, I indulged in thoughts of the divinity of life. I liked exploring the ideas of how we have come to be and whether there are other life forces beyond our atmosphere. I personally always felt it would be ignorant of me to close off on the possibilities. Even to this day we are discovering new species on earth. There seem to be so many creatures yet to unveil their presence. I had no doubt they were most assuredly aware of us.

It was a long weekend as Columbus Day had finally arrived. I needed a break to segregate the monotony of the demands placed upon me through my work. It was time to get away from it all. This was going to be my only chance for a while so carpe diem of self-rejuvenation was my forefront desire. I never realized when I chose a career as a behavioral scientist that I would struggle to find a balance between what I was observing and how I felt in regards to what I was set to assess. I specialize in applied cognitive science to the field of criminology. In retrospect I don't know what the hell I was thinking when I made the choice to travel this route. I simply found a fascination in observing people's behavior. I was compelled to seek to understand the drivers behind the actions a person chose and eventually through all my education I stumbled into qualifying as a criminologist bridging my curiosity into a lucrative career path.

There was an audible silence in the layers of natural forest sounds holding me captive to its beauty. I couldn't think of any place on earth I have been which held this same resonance within me. If there is a doorway to other dimensions this forest contained the threshold to the entrance into the mystical gateway.

I paused for a moment before tilting my head up toward the dappled sunlight closing my eyes to enjoy the filtered warmth on my face. The purity of this environment held an avenue for me to easily rebalance my core of being. I could almost feel mother nature luring my weighted concerns into the earth as she poured sunlight onto the surface of my body replenishing me to reconnected once more.

"I miss you," said a deep male voice in a whisper.

As I heard these words carried on the echoes of the breeze I opened my eyes. Shivers ran down my spine as I saw the resident owl gliding silently above me. There was no one here yet I always felt as though someone else was with me. This wasn't the first time I had heard the dulcet tones of this creature but it was my first encounter of him being so close that I felt the warmth of his breath on my ear. In the past I would hear on the odd occasion distant sobbing. Internally I was present to a profound feeling of an absence of something. A dull ache meshed with a yearning compelled to appease the sad expression and tears into a conversion of joy. Much to my disappointment I couldn't locate the source and therefore was never afforded the chance.

I watched the owl as it continued in gliding flight circling above me. Typically nocturnal this owl if it was the same one, always seemed to be here when I graced the forest with my presence.

My parents had been avid believers in signs. During our adolescence many fond memories were founded from hikes they had taken my brother and I on. Across the globe we had walked countless beautiful landscapes with both of them always showing us the importance of elements that were seemingly of no consequence to all others who might witness the same. They were the ones who engaged my curiosity about my interconnection with the world. My awakening of cause and effect on existence can be largely apportioned to their influence. This resulted in my desire to search for my underlying purpose. Birds held significance to my mom in particular and I appeared to inherit the same unspoken exchange with these feathered souls or at least this is how I felt. They are to me kindred guides.

As I reached my favorite spot I noticed the owl was perched on a branch high in the canopy. It sat quietly peering down watching as I approached. This particular tree was the one I often came to rest by. It no doubt has been alive for hundreds of years, its insides at the base hollowed from a past unknown to me but it always signified the reflection of life's realities. Standing tall with scars and wounds of times gone by. Its imperfections worn with pride, adding a point of difference coupled with an air of mystery. This tree was a representation of survival. Against all odds it remains tall and strong, embracing its entitlement to be present in a world that otherwise would see it reduced to pieces.

Just as I was about to settle into a position on the ground the owl started to flap its wings. I looked up only to see it jump and swoop down directly toward me. Its eyes locked to mine with its wing span spread to glide the owl with tremendous speed came forth, swishing past me with such a gust that my hair flung to follow. My eyes watched as it went into the hollow at the base of the tree and then disappeared. Curious, I walked inside the darkened cavern to see where it had settled. My assumption was that the bird possibly resided within a nest here and was being territorial.

It took a moment for my eyes to adjust to the delta between the light of day from outside to the dimness contained within. The inside of the tree had dried clumps of sap from healing past wounds. There didn't seem to be an exit yet I couldn't detect the owl. I held still to look for movement to ensure my eyes weren't deceived by latent shadows. As I stepped forward I felt drawn to what appeared to be a darkened hollowed notch. It was too high for me to look inside so on tip toes I reached my hand up and placed my fingers on the edge of the inside to feel around. The ends of my fingers became quickly laden in dust and debris. Sticky cobwebs from a broken home were now my partial attire. I wiped my hand on my jeans and looked around for something to give me leverage. I needed to gain a foot or so of height so I could peer in the hollow. Outside I wandered the perimeter of the tree and found a broken length of limb. Dragging it back inside I placed it in position and stepped up to sate my curiosity. It took a few moments to adjust before my eyes saw the owl nestled, quietly perched on what appeared to be a book. It didn't seem fazed by my presence. It just stared directly at me with striking black eyes. The owl's plumage was speckled white on gray brown with beautifully defined feathers. I had done a little bit of research on this species after the first time I noticed one present around me. My heart smiled as I was looking into the eyes of the rare Northern spotted owl.

This little nook only held this sweet owl and the book it was perched on. I thought it was strange that there wasn't a nest. The book struck my curiosity, I really wanted to take a look but didn't want to disturb the owl. Almost as though the bird understood my desire it stepped off the book, nestled into a corner and crouched down to a butterball puff then closed its eyes. I hesitated for a moment before reaching in to remove the book. The owl didn't flinch.

Stepping down from the limb I went outside and sat against the tree where the sunlight was streaming. I felt a sensation of vibration as I heard the owl cooing when I started to wipe clean the dust ridden leather bound cover. In gold inscription the worn title had a single word '*Illuminarium.*' The first page was a hand written dedication: *For you*. I wondered how this book got to be nestled within the tree. Could this be a secret diary between two lovers? There was something about this book and the way I felt I was lead to it that gave me a sense of entitlement to read it. I quickly flipped across the pages to receive the confirmation that this did indeed appear to be someone's diary. It was all hand written. A momentary sense of guilt about prying into another person's uninvited thoughts made me pause. My nature lent itself to satisfying questions and I always hungered for knowledge. There was a reason this book was left in a place that wouldn't be easy to find. If I accepted the philosophy that all things happen for a reason then perhaps I was supposed to find it to read. I closed my eyes and stilled my breath and asked inwardly the question. Should I read this book?

"Yes."

His voice startled me. I opened my eyes and looked around. It felt so close I could sense my eardrum vibrate as though it had been issued within my own ear. The significance of this moment caused a sense of longing, which was overwhelming and hard for me to comprehend. There was so much about myself positioned in this place, which evoked emotions I otherwise seemed to be disconnected from. It was here in this forest that I truly felt at home.

Succumbing to the desire to read the contents I repositioned myself to get comfortable before turning the next page. The handwriting was cursive and neat. At a quick glance nothing on the page indicated a time. I could only detect from the yellow stain to the papers edges and the fade of the black pen that it had been embedded in these pages for a while. Unconsciously I ran my fingers over the page from top to bottom as if to sense its secrets in braille. Goosebumps rose on my skins surface as I felt the compulsion to whisper the words, "I miss you." A single tear fell from my eye and hit the page. I watched as the paper soaked it in as if to drink away the evidence of my sorrow. There was significance to what I was experiencing even if I didn't know what it was I could feel it rise within me.

I took a deep breathe and upon the exhale began to read:

*There is something amazing about the future that leaves the taste of hope in my mouth. Ideals floating around my mind savored in what fate might have installed for me. The world will venture toward becoming a different place now that the rules of equanon are motioned to begin its play. Almost everything will head towards a long awaited need for the reconciliation of balance and order. All the hopes and wishes of generations past will come to fruition in time to kick off the reversal of the damage caused by those who are self serving and take no account for the negative effects they continue having on the world and the associated solar systems.*

*I guess I should explain a few things about the principles of equanon to you. They were founded before the concept of gods and hidden in the invisible recesses of every living elements mind as part of their interconnected fabric. It's genius really. To this day no one knows how it was placed there just that it was and is in every living piece of matter across all the galaxies and has been since the beginning of life itself. The quest for the holy grail, all those stories created by humans regarding immortality, the fountain of youth, the devil and the angels all had underlying truth and were stirred into fables because those people who felt compelled to be creative and manifest these concepts were tapping into the secret chambers of gray matter that no one realized existed.*

*We as a race thought we were advanced but in hindsight we are still very much caught in a vortex of primordial oblivion.*

*The fight against good and evil is constant. You must be mindful there are those who skulk in the shadows watching for opportunities to influence elements to sway in their favor. Know their name, interferon's. They are obsessed with a desire to retain power and have demonstrated throughout history that they are prepared to do anything they can to gain and retain quorum over their immediate surrounds and always hold secret aspirations to become a pivotal driver of influence in the world. The limited few that are aware of their existence do not know who they are or what they look like. Interferons exist under their cloak of celebrated silent revelry intentionally driving a negative cause and effect on the world at large. The interferons yield their controls remotely using anything they have within their reach to execute the manipulation of ordinary people. Be warned, the ruthlessness of their endeavors has no bounds. There is a distinct absence of concern, remorse or regret for the ones sacrificed as pawns in this practiced strategy they deploy. It is a silent battle taking place using mind manipulation to strive to control as their greatest weapon.*

*The journey you are about to embark on will awaken you to appreciate how all the theories of old are intentionally limited in design. It is known that once you were ready to be present to this the wheels of destiny's motion would fall into the cogs of play. The sign you seek will be presented when the call out from Quantum physics theorists announce a breakthrough. A new relatable meaning will strengthen the understanding of the concept of living and dead. You possess the ability to guide and unlock this transitioning. Use your embedded knowledge to recall the rivers wealth of knowing so you may embrace the universal truths. The soul does not die therefore death is nonexistent, as the cycle of all living creatures continues beyond the realm of karmic flesh. This factor alone, if embraced, can alter the face of the world and how you perceive everything.*

*The laws of equanon are strengthening because you have finally arrived at the stage of readiness for your entry into the phase of awakening. It is no coincidence that this place where you are reading my words has been chosen. The connection you feel is real. Know that all life holds purpose and energies are channelled toward a predefined contribution and function within a lifetime. It is a straight line taking people on their personal journey with little to no deviation from their fated path. Only the interference of the attempters and watchers who are the pawns used by the interferons cause waves of ripple effect in the world now. Interferons work to manipulate people with the aim to send us all off course and on a path of self-destruction. They are driven by their relentless need to fulfil a desire, which is spawned by their own imbalances. They hunger for the world to yield and give them complete power, always fighting against the natural order of things because of their inward compulsion to obtain control of their surrounds.*

*The greatest delta between the life that you knew and the one that actually exists is that every child born has a known predetermined karmic opposing partner. There is no ability to avoid this fact as it formulates the yin and yang of the universal order and equally its disarray. Who you choose to become regardless of the side of light or dark chosen is precisely who you are meant to be within this life for this realm. Anyone who attempts to fight against this contributes to waves of universal imbalance. The only exception to the rule is the soul key of wills. It is only he who is able to walk within any realm and spectrum coated within the light waves of love.*

*Pay close attention to history and you will see the gossamer threads of interconnections in karmic flesh transitioning's. Across multiple life spans reincarnation from karmic flesh to karmic flesh allows for soul mate healing and growth through the cursed gauntlet of the sins trails until all seven are faced with successful conquest. It is only then the soul possesses the third eye drawn attraction and allowance for entry of the twin flame unity. The two aligned tend on a path to ascension, which eternally binds them as one, providing the final cycle of their evolution. The purpose of this continuum is critical to evoke universal energy sustainment and rotation of pure loves energy.*

*The predecessor soul mate merger allows for the individuals to bring together a unity of growth. This provides the connections to bring forward the opportunity for the souls interconnected fibers to fuse with the pool of knowledge. It is only when the soul has successfully cycled through all the soul interactions and removal of karmic bind that they are ready to unite with their twin. The critical path play for all sustainment of life is always the ascension of the twins from their physical journey in life to the state of light luster. Once in this state they are bridged into a centrifugal force of perpetual motion, which regenerates the vortex energies of the universe. It is a critical key that has been missing from the world.*

*The interferons are gaining a silent strangle hold. People have been immersed in the burst of technology waves where the interferons hold mastery in their disguised manipulation. Blind to the reality of what is influencing them, people struggle to find their path. This is primarily driven because humans are largely relinquishing their natural gift of connectedness to their soul, which is resulting in them experiencing many cycles of existence where lesson repetition forms part of their evolution of self. It's a principal factor, which will alter as the rules of equanon strengthen in force.*

*Keep steadfast to who you are and how you feel when reading my words. You know deep down there is nothing unfamiliar about what I am telling you. It's feels right doesn't it? You have heard this somewhere before, felt it before, lived it before. That is because you have. The central part of any person has always been defined by their heart and soul. The perspective and understanding of critical experiences has been realigned to the core truth.*

*Choose to observe the world with new eyes. Illness of the flesh as an example has never been understood or accepted as part of ones personal journey. Most people feel the depth of disadvantage and tragedy associated to circumstances that deviate from societal perception of normality, longevity. What if I was to tell you that in all cases of illness it just meant the lessons to be learned within the cycle given were of a shorter duration required than those who were present for a greater length of time, that people who go through such perceived challenges are often the drivers of change in the space of constraint presented and that in the absence of them the progress would not have shifted to new insights.*

*Know this, every experience holds purpose.*

*If people embraced the journey to make the best of themselves within the realm of the parameters presented then knowing there is always a purpose would allow for them to approach the challenges with a heightened perspective. Those who are destined to walk this path could know through their souls guidance that it was a step closer to providing and obtaining knowledge that would feed their soul and bring them on to the footsteps of ascension where they would reunite with their twin flame.*

*The very essence of connection to your soul is and always will be pure even though it at times causes levels of conflict and disarray in a person's life force. All challenges faced are an avenue of opportunity to strengthen resolve and close the gap on any weaknesses in the psyche to ensure greater unity of balance between the mind, heart and soul. Its only once you have mastered this that you get to unite with your twin flame and begin the purest of journeys within a space of divined love. There are many fables and tales about the concept of twin flames. My favorite derived from Plato's The Symposium where it was suggested that humans originally were designed by the Gods with two sets of arms, two sets of legs and a head with two faces. Almighty Zeus in his wisdom and wrath came along and condemned all humans by splitting them in two making their destinies intertwined in searching for the other half of themselves for all eternity. Hence your twin flame is the other half of you.*

*There is so much you need to know before you can understand any more in detail. I know I have probably revealed too much already and caused some confusion. I just want you, nay I need you to absorb the possibilities so that you can consider what you choose next. Perhaps in knowing my journey you will receive insight into what is remaining for you to do. That's the objective you know, to awaken your sense of purpose and give you the best chance at expediting your path to ascension so you can finally enter through the door to Equanon.*

*I miss you.*

I felt the tears well in my eyes as I read the words *'I miss you.'* Once again the ache within me for something that I didn't understand rose through my solar plexus. This book wasn't what I was expecting; Equanon, soul mates, twin flames, ascension? Still the words drew me in. It was as though the book was speaking directly to me. Perhaps this wasn't a diary rather a person's fiction manuscript. I found it fascinating.

*In order to make things crystal clear I had best go back to the start. All of us have seven stages we must master in order to unlock the pathway to ascension. There is no cheat's way through this. Each step must be taken with no exceptions. Reincarnation plays an integral role in providing the life portal into the earthly realm, which is the platform where the mastery of lessons is presented. All those experiences you have had, they hold purpose. You may not recognize or understand them yet but you will. I promise you, they all interrelate to the requirements of your growth.*

*Interestingly even though there are only seven stages to the shift, our soul's purity remained intact but our strength of connection could be tainted in the metamorphosis to flesh effecting the progression of the lessons. To those souls affected it has taken countless life cycles to achieve the lessons set to be mastered within one. Why? All will be revealed in due course. The best way to explain any of this is to leverage off my own journey. I completed my seven stages in five life cycles. At least I am hopeful this will be the case.*

*Let me tell you a little story …*

# Discovery

I reached into my bag and pulled out my note pad. The analyst in me needed to take notes. There were already too many things written among these pages that I needed to delve into deeper. What this person had written had ignited a hunger in me to know more. The introduction of interferons, attempters and watchers struck a chord with me on some concepts I already had marinating in the back of my mind about how the world was interconnected and at play in a push and pull force between the execution of ones perception of right and wrong. Spending a considerable amount of my workday in assessment of seasoned criminals I would get moments where I felt I could see connections of influence that I couldn't necessarily prove existed. Interferons ...

*My mother told me she knew from the moment I was placed in her arms that I was special. She sensed what she defined as a magical element in my eyes. I had always presented differently to the rest of my siblings. Although I didn't feel out of place there was an element of obscurity about me that caused a sense of alienation. The primary variant being my ability to witness things with a perspective that most could not relate to.*

*At the age of seven I went through a phase of deep sleeping. No-one was able to wake me. I understood from my mom that the family tried everything from banging pots, shaking my limp limbs, to placing me under a cold shower in an attempt to stir me but I simply would not release from my depth of slumber. My world of dreams was set in another plane that held no space or time continuum. There I would be greeted by many a sage who would impart their wisdom to me. I had no perspective of the value of what they were sharing. I only knew that I had to listen. The comprehension of their teaching was something I would trust to be unlocked when the time was right.*

*There were no mirrors to see my reflection in the dreams. My hands were always aged with a sense that I was never present as my earthly shell. I embodied what I believed to be someone else's form. A familiarity existed in the shape but not an ownership. My waking hours were consumed with silent wonder about who I am and how old I actually was. This struck my curiosity about the concepts the teachers of wisdom imparted regarding reincarnation, the physical self and the spiritual realities. It might seem such topics were too challenging for a child so young but I felt older than I appeared. I knew one thing was for certain; the human eye left to its own devices would more often than not deceive.*

*I have three sisters and two brothers. Josh is the eldest then there is Caitlin, Myself, Lilly, Wade and Prue being the lucky last to join our family. We were raised in a middle class household where there was always food on the table and a warm smile to greet us within the loving arms of our parents. I won't suggest my early childhood was all a sense of roses but the thorns that manifested were managed as best I* could. The first time I noted any sense of trouble I had just turned fifteen. There was a huge outcry in the community as prohibition was enforced. My father and a few of his friends took the opportunity to extend their careers into backyard bootlegging. This provided us with an initial wealth of money which later served a price no-one could afford to pay. My dad and many others got arrested and sentenced to lengthy jail time with no reprieve. They were the first of the many examples the law enforcers were set to make.

Poverty hit us hard in the absence of an income. My mother struggled as best she could to keep food on the table. All of us had to stop attending school and would try to get work doing anything that was available around the neighborhood. This sustained us for a little while but the realities of inconsistent income and the constant need for it soon issued us into destitution and inevitably homelessness.

In the absence of my father mom was forced to make some weighted decisions in the interests of the family. The position she found herself in was unfavorable especially with six children to care for. After a month of living in refuge shelters and abandoned houses she sat us down bursting into uncontrolled tears as she told us we would all have to be separated. Josh was set to stay with her as he was the eldest now eighteen years old and could try to get some work in the mines. Caitlin sixteen and Lilly thirteen years old were going to live with her parents Grandma Sarah and Grandpa Will. Wade twelve and Prue eleven years old were being shipped off across country to live with Aunty Jane and Uncle Michael. I can recall this moment as clear as I am writing it to you now. There was silence as we sat in this dank dilapidated room of an abandoned house we temporarily occupied. A couple of candles our only source of light. The remainder of the bread crusts and some *scattered crumbs lay on the floor where we had just shared a feeble meal. There were rats scampering along the edges of the skirting impatiently biding their time when they could safely consume our leftovers. All eyes were on me. I knew by the way they were behaving that I was the last to know. None of them reacted to the news with surprise or resistance they were all so accepting of the situation.*

*My mom shifted across to be seated next to me. She placed her hand on mine and said, "York, dear you know you are special."*

*I didn't respond. I just stared at her hand and wondered what I was installed for.*

*"Grandma and Grandpa are too old to have more than two of you so they chose to take Caitlin and Lilly because girls are easier to manage." She paused as she tried to hold back the tears. "Aunty Jane already has three children of her own so it was a stretch to get her to take Wade and Prue."*

*I could feel her hand was shaking. I wanted to console her but couldn't manage to move from my state of numbness. I knew I didn't want to hear whatever she was going to say. I felt a surge of desperation where I wanted to run but remained motionless, trapped to the present moment.*

*"I have found you a home where they can take care of you. It's a lovely place with loads of other kids to play with. You will be happy there I promise." Her hand squeezed my knee. I wasn't sure if she was trying to console herself or me. "You're special York. We 'l all come and visit you every chance we get." With this she leant in and kissed me on the forehead with her tear stained lips. That was the last night we were together as a family. In the morning all my brothers and sisters were dropped off at my grandparents to be watched by Grandma while Grandpa drove my mom and I to a place called Glenhaven.*

*I had never seen a structure so big before. The driveway was lined with trees and the house was made of blue stone with hundreds of white sashed windows. It was surrounded by the grandest garden I had ever seen. Visually spectacular, the trees were so beautiful. I started to feel guilty that my siblings were not able to come here with me.*

*When we arrived there were two men who came to greet us. Mom carried my bag inside while Grandpa waited in the car. The entrance to the building was larger than the entire house I grew up in. The ceilings were high with a staircase in the center that seemed to go on forever. While mom spoke to a lady dressed in pale blue I slowly wandered around. Most of the oversized ornate doors were closed so I gravitated toward the water fountain which was positioned against the main wall. I pressed the button and watched the water jut out. I was fascinated.*

*Mom came across and said goodbye. She didn't cry this time. She just kissed me on the forehead and left. The two men that had greeted us at the doorway were staring at me while I continued to play with the arched stream of water. One grabbed my arm and told me to come with him while the other followed with my belongings. He had a strong grip but I didn't say anything. I just went in the direction he was headed.*

*Through the door we entered was a long room with rows of beds against the left wall. There was one woman attending to a person whose screams curdled my stomach. His head was lifting off the bed as he yelled "Ahhhhhh, Ahhhhhh, Ahhhhhhhhh," over and over. By the time we walked past him the noise had ceased. Quiet as a mouse his head lay to the side with his mouth glistening from the release of dribble. The nurse without a glance walked past me and back to her desk lifting her pen to resume doing some paper work.*

*At the end of the room was a doorway that led us into*

*a shower facility. Open sparse white tiled walls with rows of showers. The toilets were a shiny metal once again set in a row with no barriers of separation. Some were covered in wet toilet paper and excrement, puddles of urine stains visible on the floor. The men stripped my clothes off and placed me under a shower. The water was colder than I liked it but I just stood there until they switched the taps off. My body was freezing as the cold crept up from the floors surface to chill my bones. The man who had grabbed my arm previously sprinkled some powder on me and then roughly towel dried my body before placing me in some foreign clothes. He seemed so angry. I secretly wished I was still playing with the water fountain.*

I felt my stomach churn I wanted to reach into the pages to give York a cuddle. To say that everything would be all right but I instinctually knew this was a lie. I don't understand why his mom left him in a mental institution and not an orphanage. What on earth was she thinking? How could a mother leave her child in such a place? I know there is something different about York. I'm just not sure what it is. My initial thoughts were Autism but now I'm leaning towards Asperger's Syndrome. He seems emotionally removed from social expression but is capable of internalized comprehension and articulation. It just doesn't make sense not to have your next of kin push hardships aside to find a way to take care of all the children. He's been ostracized for being 'different.' The only word I had come to mind was abandonment. I felt sick. This is no life for a child. There was unsettling anger surging within me. I know this is just a story but it hurt to read it, to somehow know the looming future fated to this child born of innocence. Why is the world so consistently cruel?

*They placed me in a room filled with other people all dressed the same as me. There were no children here. I stood at the doorway starring at the kaleidoscope of people all doing different things. One kept flinging his arm in the air; another running around screeching, it seemed like madness. I didn't want to be here. I started to walk backwards until I felt someone push on my back forcing me to lose balance and fall to the floor.*

*"Welcome to Glenhaven, I hope you enjoy your stay."*

*The two men laughed as they walked out the door locking it behind them. There was a surge of pain from my landing on the hardened floor infused with a sense of horror at the sound of their words. I was scared and wanted the comfort of my mom's arms. Laying still I absorbed the welcome feeling of the cold of the floor against the flush of my cheeks while watching from ground level the feet of the manic occupants each shifting to their own rhythm.*

*Slowly I rose up from the floor and paved my way to the first window that caught my eye. Thick bars held a barrier between the glass and myself. It allowed for a distorted view of the visual splendor overlooking the majestic gardens I dearly wanted to explore. Deceptively you couldn't see the bars from the outside. The display of perfect white inviting window sashes I had witnessed upon my arrival were now forever etched as a symbol of imprisonment. I no longer felt only trapped on the inside. It was now set to be part of my life.*

# Glenhaven

*M*y *first night in Glenhaven was coated by a series of events that curdled my blood and turned what little I felt of my heart to stone. They had sent us to a room to eat a plate apportioned with potatoes mashed with pumpkin and a piece of bread. The water was tepid and brown with elements free floating in a slosh and a swill as they slammed the jugs on the table. I was hungry and greedily consumed everything on my plate. Including the bread, which was stale with flecks of mold. I was famished and tired from the stress of feeling compelled to be on guard all day.*

*There was a man who wandered around trying to grab food from peoples plates. He sunk his hand into their mash and shoveled it into his mouth making a mess all around him. A few men dressed in white chased him as he ran past my table yelling something that was a cross between a portion of a word and howling. I watched as others in the room started to yell and throw their food in the air, banging their metal plates. The chorus of howls was a cacophony of screams that chilled my core. I wanted to hide under the table but was frozen in position the sounds vibrating through my body held me captive. This madness surrounding me was not one, which allowed for comprehension. Finally the men in white jumped on the running howler pinning him down before proceeding to mercilessly beat him into submission. A woman rushed into the room jabbing something into his arm. Almost instantly his body went limp while his gaping mouth revealed the length of his tongue coated in a mix of blood, mash and drool. They dragged him out leaving a bloody trail behind and shut the door. There was silence again.*

*After supper we were all ushered into the room where the beds were in a row. I stood at the doorway and watched as people robotically climbed into their allocated cots. Once they all settled I noted there were two that remained vacant near the end of the room closet to the entry to the shower. Quietly I stepped forward and sat on the edge of one.*

*"Get into bed," barked a woman with frightful eyes. In the dimmed light they seemed black and soulless. I did as told and climbed in covering myself with the sheet and thin blanket. As I looked to my right at the others I noticed two men methodically attending each bed. When they got closer I noticed they were doing something. There was a sense of fear arising when they finally arrived at my station. One on either side in synchronized motion they picked up some straps and restrained my arms and chest. The buckle was so tight it was digging into me. Inside myself I burst into tears. I wanted to go home, this place was horrible.*

*Shortly after I was restrained the barking woman stabbed a needle into my arm. I don't recall a moment after that. Everything faded to black. I was numb. In my dreams I returned to the place where the elders spoke. I was once again held in favor and much of their insights and philosophies were imparted to me as I listened. My only cause to distraction was this sharp white light flash of pain that made me want to scream but I held no voice to release the emotion. The elders stopped talking and looked at one another as I felt myself fading into the consumption of the experience. My body ached all over; I couldn't stop this surge of pain searing my flesh. It hurt, I wanted so desperately to cry. Together the elders all held hands and started to chant in a hum. The vibrations echoed within me making the pain seemingly fade away.*

*When I awoke I was freezing from the residual saturation of my urine stained bed. Still restrained my whole body was in pain. It felt like I had been laying in the same position for a lifetime. In a daze I turned my head to see the room was empty. My attempt to readjust my body was caught in the barking lady's peripheral vision. Immediately she waved with earnest to draw the attention of the two men standing outside the door. Both men took pause to look at one another before silently coming across to my bed. The man to the left of me worked to remove my restraints while the other nodded his head at the barking woman who was watching from a distance.*

*"We will have to give him a smaller dose next time. He's been asleep for fours days."*

*I felt weak as they lifted me out of the bed to encourage me to stand. The one closest to me covered his nose to protect from the offensive smell that rose from my bedding. I turned to see my cot was laden with blood, excrement and urine. I had obviously released my bowels several times during my slumber but the blood at the time was a mystery to me.*

Tears were rolling down my faced as I whispered, "I'll cry a thousand tears for you little one. You were drugged and raped sweet child." With this I placed my face in my hands and burst into tears. I hated what was happening to York. I hated the fact that people could be so fucking cruel. Why was this story here and why did I find it to read? Every word written by the innocence of him was burning at my core. He was only a child. Did he write this because he needed a release in the absence of emotional expression? My reaction aligned to the notion that this book was founded on truth. He mentioned prohibition, which occurred in the 1920's to 1930's. This meant that York being fifteen when institutionalized must have been born mid to late 1910. I only knew a little bit about the era based on some history classes from middle school. There was a part of me that wanted to walk away from this book, to close it and forget it ever existed. It no longer held a sense of curiosity, now it seemed more like a journey I had to take with York because I didn't want him to be alone. I burst into tears again. The taste of salt seeped between my lips as I allowed myself to wail. The sense of abandonment and fear he couldn't express was now rising in me. I was experiencing an empathic association to a story that compelled me to want to nurse and protect this child from the horrors of the world. I was seething with contempt at humans that would allow such atrocities. In this moment I was judge and juror and I wanted to hang them all.

I reached across and took the bottle of water from my nap sack. I was dehydrated from the hike, crying and sitting in the full glare of the sun that was beaming from between the trees. I stretched out my legs and repositioned myself into a spot with shade. Taking a sip and feeling it glide down my throat I wondered what York looked like. Would I ever get to know the appearance of this child who in a matter of a few paragraphs held me enchanted? I took a deep breath and continued to read.

*They began to drag me to the shower as I fumbled my*

*steps. Weakened from the absence of nourishment I was unable to coordinate the movement of my legs without losing my footing. Impatiently they lifted me by the armpits off the ground carrying me the rest of the way. One of the men leaned in to run the water while the other shoved me under fully clothed. My body instantly started to convulse with shivers. The same man who had engaged the running water pulled a face of annoyance before reaching over to adjust the temperature. He tilted his head to look at me muttering under his breath, "Stupid child."*

*The welcomed warmth of the water made me feel dizzy. Just as I was about to collapse a hand reached out to catch me.*

*"Its okay gentlemen. I'll take it from here." She said.*

*I wasn't aware that she had walked in or who she was but I knew this was the first time I heard an angel speak. Her touch was gentle. She carefully helped me out of my saturated clothes and placed me under the shower once more. Using soap and a small cloth this kind person gently cleaned all the muck from my body. I turned in the direction of her guiding hands and felt grateful for her willingness to assist.*

*There was sorrow in her eyes as she continued to fastidiously clean every inch of my skin. I felt pain searing over sections of my body. When I looked down I saw them. I had bruises and bite marks that had broken my flesh. Blood still dripped from the deep indentation the buckle made that fastened me to the bed. I watched as she tried to cover her witness to this with a smile. I just stood there feeling disassociated as the realization of what might have happened leveraged me back to the elders of my dreams where I had felt the surges of pain. I didn't want to accept the possibility of rape but the presence of the stinging of my wounds was scarring my mind with its reality.*

*Standing on the cold tile floors naked I was starting*

*to freeze again. She passed across a towel and asked me to dry myself while she fetched some clean clothes. It made me wonder where my suitcase was. I hadn't seen it since the man carried it into the room my first day here. Upon her return she entered with a smile that warmed my heart. I really liked her.*

*"York, My name is Adeline." She said as she bent down to look me in the eyes.*

*I watched her as she patiently waited for me to respond.*

*"It's okay. You don't have to say anything. I'm going to help you get dressed and then I'll get you something to eat. You must be starved."*

*I nodded my head while looking down at my shaking hands. Adeline gently shifted to hold them as she raised one arm at a time above my head to place my top on. Then she coaxed me to raise each leg placing some underpants and then trousers on me. Pulling out a comb from her jacket pocket she ran it through my hair sweeping it from a section part to one side. I was grateful for her attentiveness and care.*

*Sitting in the empty mess hall I waited for her to fetch me some food. Adeline placed a piping hot plate of potato and pumpkin mash in front of me. I grabbed my fork and hoed into it. The first mouthful burnt my insides but my hunger forced my disregard. I shoveled mouthful after mouthful in before the previous was even finished, that was until her hand reached across touching my arm.*

*"Slow down York. Nobody is going to take the food away from you. I'll sit here while you eat. It's okay."*

*Her kindness made me miss my mom. The nights when she would hold me in her arms and rock me to sleep, telling me that I was special. I just wanted to go home. There was a looming sadness in me that I suppressed with all my might, compelled to just go through the motions rather than react to* what was happening to me. I had always been this way for as long as I could remember. Capable of watching, feeling, understanding but I am an internal prisoner with no voice to articulate my thoughts. There were parts inside replete with screams and desire to rebel against all of this. Yet I remained emotionless to the visible eye. I lived in hell.

Instead of taking me to the room containing all the madness Adeline with her hand held in mine ventured outside to walk through the garden. She told me the names of the flowers and the age of the trees. I soaked in the welcome distraction from what had been and immersed myself in the delights of the flora that adorned my eyes with the ideals of beauty in life. It was this day that I got to see my very first bumble bee.

Releasing myself from Adeline's hand I walked across to the group of flowers where the bumbling bee was bumbling about. Such a fat clumsy flyer was he, going from flower to flower. I enjoyed watching the stems bow being weighted down as he landed to collect the pollen from the glorious purple strings of tiny flowers. There seemed to be little concern that I was in close proximity. Mr. Bumble was too busy collecting his food to care.

"This is a lavender patch and what you are looking at is a bumble bee." Said Adeline who was now standing behind me.

Satisfied with the bushels he adorned on his legs he seemingly bumbled away into the distance. I dearly wanted to go with him. I wished I could go with him.

Hearing a bird squawking I looked up and saw hands release a swinging man from the skies above. I remained fixated to witness his fast decent onto the garden bed near where we were standing.

"THUD"

Adeline screamed grabbing me to pull us back from

27

the body while I watched his lifeless eyes staring into mine. Dressed as I was his body contorted by the way he landed this man looked like a jointed puppet lying down with no strings attached. Legs bent back towards his hips, one arm above his head and the other adorning a wrist that was upside down. Blood was oozing from his ears and staining his clothes from the inside out. He's free I thought to myself.

Men came running out of the building to aid the call of Adeline's continual screams. I noted a couple of them had wry smiles on their faces as they approached the scene. It was the same two who secured me to my bed my first night here. I hated them.

As the men gathered to lift the body I saw the squashed flowers he created by his impact. I tore myself away from Adeline's grasp falling to bended knees frantically trying to resurrect the broken stems from the same fate. If they died the bumblebee would have less to eat.

"York, no!" She yelled as she pulled me up from the ground. My hands flapped in the air making the motions of clawing. I scrambled to try be released again as the two men I hated came running to assist Adeline.

They reefed me from her arms without word, threw me on the floor and began to beat me senseless.

"No, no leave him alone." I heard her scream as fist upon fist frenzied on my now limp body. I watched the grass pass under me as I was dragged back inside and thrown into the room of madness where I welcomed the cold of the hardened floor they smashed me down on. The enormity of the pain all across my body paled into significance in comparison to the sorrow I felt for the ruined patch of garden. Now I was thankful the bumblebee had flown away.

I couldn't believe what I was reading. The torment I

felt for York was unbearable. I have never in my life cried so much as I have in these last few hours reading his outpour of life's experience on these pages. All the horrors held within one so young and pure. I struggled with his inability to outwardly express himself. Oh, God could no-one hear his screams? How disassociated were these people to allow such continued atrocities to occur? Why would Adeline not seek to assist him, have the authorities come and rescue York? I simply don't understand any of this. It's beyond depraved. Why did it have to be this way for him? Fuck all things happen for a reason. There will never be an acceptable reason for this. Jesus, the more I read the more contempt I hold for all who choose to live this way. I felt internally crazed, words couldn't possibly quantify the cocktail of emotions I had welling inside. I needed to take a break to compose myself. This was too much even for me.

# Retrospective

I gathered my things to go for a walk. I needed to realign my psyche to see the beauty of the world for right now it seemingly held none. York's words touched me so deeply I felt as though I knew him. There were aspects of his story that rang true for me albeit thankfully nothing as horrifying as what he held the misfortune to experience. It was more an association to his constant internalization. Although I possessed the capacity for empathy I rarely expressed it. To a large degree I have lent my life to being driven by an analytical mind. Working with hardened criminals, taking a journey into their cognitive reasoning to understand their drivers for the choices made, I had to largely switch off from my humanity. It was part of my job and one of the reasons I was as successful as I had been to date.

The whole time I was reading York's story, my mind kept flittering to images of my life changing experience. It was the first time I can recall having a true sense of confrontation and later an awakening in relation to the possibilities of all that we see is not how it seems. Life can present you with challenges to perhaps afford one the opportunity to push past what we think we know or what is relative in life as known, to shifting into a window where belief in the unproven and intangible also hold a foundation of truth. This then confirming the ideals of the commonly used phrase 'anything is possible.'

The criminal assessment of Vernon Wreath was my most challenging case I had ever worked on. He was a forty-two year old who aesthetically was, simply put, very unattractive. Possessing facial features adorned heavily with scarred remnants of childhood chicken pox coupling his chiseled cheek and jawline, accentuated his deep sunken eyes with dark shadows. All in all he visually presented as sinister and harsh. The receding hairline and excessive dandruff didn't do him any favors either. His outward appearance would have you believe that he was blackened to the core. Through the vast media exposure Vernon's demeanor for the most part seemed to display no remorse within him for the alleged attacks on the innocent. I was much younger than I am now. This was my fifth case and the first to hold such wide spread media interest. Accused of two counts of rape and murder, he was on death row. My responsibility was to make an independent assessment of him as part of an appeal that was placed suggesting his innocence of the crimes he had already been charged for.

Alleged falsified evidence and mistaken identity were the underlying leverage submitted to re-assess the case. Vernon's recently acquired frontal lobe condition, which surfaced post a reported in prison 'accident' were the reason why I was requested. My role was set to establish if the injury compromised Vernon's ability to form rational reasoning to defend his position,

It was a time where DNA evidence was now uncovering

the misjudged convictions of the past. The whole judicial system was under scrutiny and capital punishment was being called to order. The people at large were demanding for him to be hanged and quartered. Tainted by my own perceptions I knew before I entered into the assessment I was leaning towards wanting the same.

The first time I met Vernon I was lead to the interview room by two guards. The space where he was held was a tiny enclosed location, no windows just a table that was fastened to the stone flooring by bolts. Two chairs on either side of the table were the only other pieces of furniture contained within. Vernon was already seated with handcuffs and chains locking him to the table. The guards who escorted me in walked out once I was seated. One left altogether and the other remained outside, watching through the small cut out window in the door.

"Hi Vernon I'm Harper I was sent here to make an independent assessment of you for your up coming case."

I will never forget the look in his eyes as he starred at me and said, "I know you." Then through gritted teeth sprayed saliva on the table in a stream.

The guard rushed in with the intent to reprimand but I jumped up managing to stand in his way.

"Its okay. Its only saliva." The guard still fixated on Vernon tried to press forward. Holding steadfast I reassured him once more that it wasn't an issue. He glared at me for interfering, reluctantly walking out the door to stand at his post.

Sitting back down I was now greeted by Vernon's smile. On his face it was hard to tell whether this was an evil smirk or a smile of gratitude. Unlike most people his facial scaring was to such an extreme that he didn't have the same emotionally expressive range afforded to you and I. This was something I recognized I needed to take into account.

"Lets start again. Do you know why you are in prison?"

He continued to smirk and stare at me.

I looked into his hollowed eyes and could feel the echoes of screams. I didn't want to be here. His presence sent chills through my core and a rise of an anger that I couldn't explain but knew I needed to contain. There was something about him, which was infinitely familiar to me and I hated the fact that his broadening smile seemed to read my acknowledgement of this.

Regaining my composure I started again, "I need to make an assessment of your cognitive abilities in order to decide whether the impact you held to your frontal lobe has affected your ability to think, reason, understand and feel emotions. Please co-operate with me."

"Try again HARPER." He said not altering his gaze.

"I'm not sure what you mean." Feeling his contort as a challenge of minds.

"What does it feel like to look at me? Am I pretty?"

I took a moment to contemplate where he might have been trying to steer the conversation. "My thoughts on your appearance hold no relevance. Can we focus on what's important please?"

"AM... I... PRETTY!" He yelled as he pressed his chest against the table leaning forward to accentuate the aggressive delivery of his question.

I immediately held my hand up to the guard who I knew was about to launch back into the room. In frustration he kicked the door and yelled something that sounded like, "Fuck."

I took a deep breath and stared at Vernon. "No,

visually you are ugly to me but beauty comes from within. Tell me Vernon, are you beautiful on the inside?" I knew I shouldn't make it personal. Everything I had learnt told me not to, yet I was compelled to succumb to this path he was leading me on. There was a part of me that held him in contempt. I hated him.

"So you wouldn't fuck me then?" He burst out laughing and stamped his feet up and down on the ground as he shook his head like a madman.

I watched him as he continued his fit of insane laughter. His face contorted looking heinously uglier than I could possibly describe. The guard watched outside, his breath fogging the little window as he hungered for a signal from me that I had experienced enough. His impending frustration freely expressed on his face told me that Vernon sooner or later would get a beating whether I wanted it to happen or not.

Vernon leaned his head forward and proceeded to lick the table making groaning noises while he watched me. I knew by his behavior regardless of appearances he was intelligent. Smart enough to hide behind a cloak of somewhat manic behavior. I could tell he was switched on. His face may have had limitations of expression but his eyes betrayed him. I watched him watching me for signs to read my true reaction to him. He was feeding off my repulse.

"What are you doing? Why do you want me to dislike you?" I asked in a calm voice.

He continued to lay trails of saliva on the table ignoring my question. The fact that he closed his eyes at the point I delivered the message told me that he didn't expect this to be my reaction.

"Vernon, look at me."

His tongue froze in position then quick as a viper he reefed his head up and yelled, "WHAT HARPER, WHAT?"

"Do you know why you are in prison?"

He glared directly at me as though I was a roast on a spit waiting to be carved and devoured.

"Tell me Harper, do you like to be fucked from behind? I think you do. I could see you on all fours like a dog." He eagerly waited for my response.

"Why do you want me to dislike you?"

"Does it bother you that I've got an erection and the sound of your voice makes me want to cummmmm?"

"Vernon, Why do you want me to dislike you?"

"FUCK OFF HAR ...PERRrrrrrr." He said with a scowl.

Vernon was starting to confirm my suspicions of wanting to get me to react to him. The reasoning I was unsure of but the desire was a certainty. Rationally speaking it served no positive purpose to coax me into a position where I may develop bias toward him. Although I largely already inappropriately had, he didn't know this so the drivers were a curiosity that I wanted to explore. Vernon may indeed be psychotic but the intelligence behind his eyes indicated he had drivers I was yet to understand.

I repeated my initial question, "Do you know why you're in prison?"

"Do you know why you're in prison Harper?' He recanted

I smiled and slightly shook my head, "I'm not in prison."

"Are you sure about that Harper?"

The way he kept saying my name with every question

was fucking irritating. I didn't want my name associated to those lips, or his mind let alone his groin. He was getting to me and he knew it. Mentioning his erection under the table made being in such close vicinity to this predatory fuck repulsive. I held him in contempt and it's exactly what he wanted.

He smiled as he took my silence as a win.

"Poor little Harper. The golden child with the perfect life doesn't know she's trapped inside because of me."

His words ripped at me. This insane fucker was repugnant. He had me right where he wanted and I hated myself for it.

"Don't be ridiculous. I don't know you and you know nothing about me so let's just focus on what we are here to do. Are you aware of why you are in prison?"

"Do you know why you're in prison?" He said trying to mimic my voice.

"We're not here to discuss me. Let's talk about you." I said smiling to misguide his read of me.

"Nah, I'd rather talk about you. Did you get wet when I told you about my hard cock? I think you did I can smell your cunt."

His consistent deflection back to his routine of shock value told me he didn't expect nor like my response. It wasn't what he was looking for. I knew by his attempts to debase the conversation he was leading me down a premeditated path, to have me break down, possibly cry and abuse him. Perhaps this is what feeds his desires, disillusioned power.

"Vernon, seriously if you're trying to get me to react you're wasting your time. I couldn't care less about you or your thoughts on me." I shifted in my chair.

He smirked and sat back.

I betrayed myself by moving. This fucker was able to read me. I still had no idea why the hell he was so fixated on getting a rise out of me but I knew that he needed it. His hunger for my disdain didn't fit, and I felt a compulsion drive me forward to understand the reasoning behind it.

"Ok Vernon, tell me why am I in prison? Enlighten me."

He licked his lips allowing saliva to dribble down the left side of his mouth while leering at me.

Annoyed with his intentional obstinate behavior I had had enough. "This is ridiculous. I'm going to end the session." Just as I placed my hands on the table to stand up he started.

"Poor Harper has the perfect childhood, the perfect parents but there's something causing you to scream inside. You don't know what it is and you try to hide it but there are days when you get so depressed you want to suicide. The screams become all consuming so you can't ignore them. Internally stuck with no ability to voice the anguish you keep buried inside." Laughing dramatically loud he flung his face up toward the ceiling with his mouth gaped open before settling back into a forward position. In a calm voice he continued, "I can hear the screams now. Can you?" His expression had altered to feign some resemblance of care. This guy was a psychotic pig.

"Everyone has a down day Vernon, so what. You can't expect to be happy all the time. Alternating between mood states provides the delineation to know the difference. Sadness affords the opportunity for a heightened appreciation of happiness."

"What gets you on your roller coaster to spiral down Harper?" He asked once again presenting in a way that attempted to look as though he gave a shit.

"I have other inmates I need to interview. It's clear from our colorful conversation that you possess the capacity for cognitive reasoning. That's all I really came here to assess so we are done." With this I got up and headed toward the exit.

The guard opened the door as I approached.

"He's all yours." I said as I brushed past him and made my way down the corridor.

That's when he said it. "PAST LIVES HARPER, PAST LIVES," was the words he screamed out before tapering into a manic laugh, which proceeded by screaming as the guard used over zealous force to settle him back down.

Walking out of there I shook my head concluding he just wanted to toy with my mind. I'd like to say I never thought of Vernon again but truth be told I thought of him every day. His manic laughter would find its way echoing in dreams of black where I would wake up in a cold sweat. Added to this the prick had somehow managed to find my unlisted home address sending me countless letters that I refused to read. All of them remained in a pile on the cabinet at the entrance to my apartment.

Years had passed with the letters now starting to wane. I gave him credit for his persistence but longed for the day that it would end. Whatever fixation he held to me I needed it to cease. His callous manner with no sense of remorse still curdled my blood to boil when I weakened my resolve and thought about our time together. It's in this that I would say one minute, one hour or a day can hold a significance to the possibility of impact toward change. His persistence in projecting the idea of me being in a self imposed prison made me present to the notion. It was infinitely frustrating which by my own reasoning gave insight that it held truth for me. I wasn't sure if my discontent was due to such a vile creature delivering this message or because he was able to see something in me I had seemingly held blind vision to. Either way I knew within myself I needed to explore why I felt I was bound in some way.

On Friday the 13th of September 1985 my office phone rang. This was the call, which led to events unbeknown to me at the time that would begin to stimulate the alteration of how I chose to view the world.

"Hello Harper speaking."

"Hi Harper its Vernon. Don't hang up, please."

I instantly felt sick. The moment he said my name I knew exactly who it was. His voice had become a protagonist in my head when I was searching for answers about myself.

"Did you get my letters?" He asked

"Yes."

"I didn't hear back from you so I wasn't sure if your were coming."

It was strange. Vernon's voice projected an air of sincerity delivered within a mellow tone.

"I never opened any of the letters Vernon so I have no idea what you are referring to."

"None of them," He whispered in disappointment.

"Not one."

"Please tell me you still have them."

"I do." It never occurred to me until he asked. Why did I choose to keep them all this time instead of tossing them in the trash? I had been trying with earnest to forget him ever since we met and still I kept his letters.

"I haven't got much time. I sent you an invitation request to attend my execution this evening. I was hoping if you read the letters you would understand why I wanted you here."

"What? No. I can't," Vernon caught me totally off guard. I couldn't believe he was asking me to watch him be killed. I never wanted to see him again.

"I need this. I can't explain anything now, you have to read the letters. It describes in detail everything you wanted to know. Please tell me you will come." His voice was broken as if he was going to cry.

"I'm not sure I can or that I want to."

"I understand. If you change your mind it happens at midnight. I have left your name as my requested witness. I know this is selfish of me and I'm not worthy of your considerations … anyone's for that matter, but you are the only one I want with me. I'll leave it up to you."

"I'm not sure Vernon this is all coming from left field. I need some time to process it and decide."

"Well I guess Cinderella has until midnight then." Making light of his impending execution.

"Bye Vernon."

"Harper."

"Yes."

"Please read the letters. It will help silence the screams and may even offer you a step toward presenting an opening in the walls of your prison that I know you seek. I'm sorry, for everything. Bye."

As I heard the receiver click an expulsion of tears surged from my welling eyes while releasing an unexpected howl. Why was he doing this to me? This man who presented as a monster inflicting multiple horrific acts of inhumanity and what, now he is a philosopher and a guide to me? I felt lost as I stared out the window and continued crying with only my whimpering present to break the silence.

Hours had passed in a state of numbness. When no more tears could be shed I cleaned myself up and went to the back office to find Vernon Wreaths file. My mind was flooded with images as I poured over the details of the arrest report once again. Captured in the transcription taken at the court hearings frozen in time was the depiction of the nature of his inner blackened beast.

Vernon was in attendance at a house party where he met Veronica a divorcee with her nine year old daughter Lisa. Others showing a clear interest in Veronica witnessed him watching her in a way they thought was intense. In fairness to Vernon his appearance would lend itself to this summation easily. It was marked in the report that Veronica who lived next door had left the party just after 7:30 pm to put her daughter to sleep and herself shortly thereafter.

Allegedly Vernon was seen hovering near a back gate shared between the two neighbors. Within a matter of minutes he was gone and the gate was noted to be ajar. The perpetrator broke the side window to the laundry area gaining entry into the home. Veronica woke to the noise and went to see what had occurred. She had the misfortune of being brutally attacked then dragged into the dining room before proceeding to rape her. Lisa woke to the muffled noises and went into the room where they were. The perpetrator forced Veronica to watch him rape Lisa before returning to Veronica to violate her again. While the perpetrator was consumed by his frenzy Lisa escaped to the neighbors undetected. The authorities were called while five of the men gathered to save Veronica. Their arrival was too late, the front door was wide open with no sign of the perpetrator. He left behind a palpable mess. Veronica died before the ambulance arrived to the scene.

Three years after the incident Lisa took her own life. There was no amount of therapy or antidepressant medication provided to appease her psychosis. Proving too much to handle there were a string of foster homes she entered, none would last longer than a couple of months. Spiraling deeper into depression the state psychotherapy assessment board made arrangements to have Lisa admitted to a government psychiatric facility. She took her own life the night before admission by drinking down caustic drain fluid coupled with a cocktail of pills she found in an unlocked medicine cabinet.

They found a note containing a poem titled:
*To nobody at all*

> *Watch*
> *Never Speak*
> *Internal screams*
> *Blind to feel*
> *Never seek*
> *Squash the light*
> *Shade to gray*
> *Refrain*
> *Sink in*
> *Fall deep*
> *Let it go*
> *Into me*
> *Forever bound*
> *Eternal Sleep*
> *Stop the clocks*
> *Mend time*
> *Smirch this day*

*Then continue*
*On thy way*
*Unmarked grave*
*Courtesy paid*
*Allure to Death*
*Invited to play*
*Come reap*
*Let me lose*
*Last breath*
*To win*
*Soul release*
*Marked request*
*Never be*
*Born again*
*My only wish*

The aftermath of Vernon's choices was simply unconscionable. Seven years had passed since I had been face to face with that heinous monster. There was something about the finality of the execution added by his left field request for me to attend that had me drawn towards the repulsive conclusion that I would hold regret if I didn't do so. Internally I was still searching for answers to unformed questions in regards to he and I. This repulsive man was connected to me. I had always denied my unspoken knowing of his disjointed soul.

Although I wanted to prepare myself to enter into this experience my rationale knew there was nothing that could do so. I had to walk through the doors to the witness room and be open to all the possibilities of the journey between Vernon and I. This I whispered to myself would be our last dance.

Positioned in my allocated primary witness seat in the

full view of the death chamber I waited. The atmosphere was intense. The common thread intertwined between all those who bore presence was a clear disdain for Vernon. I found myself feeling sad for him. My compassion was encircled by his decision to choose this path when life afforded so many alternative possibilities. Why did Vernon choose to be the way he was?

My body jolted with surprise as a voice said, "Your presence is requested."

I looked at the prison guard bent over staring at me. Puzzled I simply said, "Ok," and followed him out the door into the hallway where a man dressed in a suit stood along with three guards. They nodded their heads to acknowledge my presence as I approached.

"Hi, What's this about?"

"Hello, I'm Curtis the warden. Vernon has denied the absolution of a priest and has asked for you."

I heard the words but stood in silence feeling completely confused.

Curtis pulled out his cross attached to a string of maroon colored rosemary beads. "You don't need to do this. I felt obliged to tell you the request has been made. I'm a man of God and any person who seeks absolution whether it be priest or otherwise is something I could not dismiss."

My mind was reeling with the screams to say 'no, no, no.' This request placed me in the moral dilemma between what I wanted, which was to walk away versus the possibility of being able to give a person peace through their desire to receive absolution. What if this makes the difference to altering his path in the next life? Against all odds or perception of right and wrong being given absolution under such circumstances may instill faith and peace so the cycle of hate is not repeated. The only thing clear is that Vernon's association to forgiveness stemmed from him feeling connected to me. Who was I to decline his wish on the basis of not understanding the reason it was so? This was important. I knew it. My decision; I placed Vernon's needs ahead of my own desire to turn my back on him. This man would be afforded my presence to obtain his desire for absolution.

"I'm sorry, you need to let me know as he doesn't have much time left before the execution. The guards are prepping him for the walk as we speak. It's now or never."

My eyes blinked to acknowledge his words as I nodded, "Ok." I said.

Curtis seemed relieved, releasing the breath he had been holding, "Are you sure?"

"No, but I don't want to live with the regret of serving me instead of affording to assist another when called to. Even if it is Vernon Wreath." I said in a calm voice.

The warden smiled at my words and waved to the guards to escort me to Vernon's private holding cell on the green mile.

There he was on his knees in the middle of the small cell with his eyes closed and his chained hands in a praying position mumbling 'Our father who art in heaven ...'

I stood there in silence well aware that he was conscious of my presence.

"Hello Harper" he said interrupting his prayer.

"Hi Vernon."

My emotions were mixed. The tone in his voice conveyed a sense of calmness directly conflicting with my sixth sense guiding me to get away from this monster. Still, I stood there for him.

"I've missed you." He whispered.

"I'm not sure what you want or need from me Vernon

so I'm going to just afford you my time to listen to everything you need to say and if it is your wish I will try to channel absolution for you to die within peace."

"Thank you Harper, thank you," he said as he rose to his feet and walked toward to the cell bars.

This was the first time I had seen some semblance of sincerity in his eyes.

I returned his gaze knowing once again he was trying to read me.

My body jolted as a bellowing voice from my right announced, "THREE Minutes to the green mile."

"We don't have much time. Pray with me. Do you know the our father?" He asked and then took a step back closing his eyes, hands in position speaking the words.

I'm not a religious person nor was I raised under any specific influence but I knew the prayer and liked it. So I mimicked Vernon's hand position, closed my eyes and joined in the prayer. Part way through the third time we were saying the prayer Vernon stopped.

"Keep going please, just say it over and over while I meditate forgiveness. It's perfect and all that I need. Thank you Harper, Thank you."

"TWO Minutes to the green mile," yelled the guard.

Two minutes and all of this would be over. I took a long look at Vernon who was nodding his head in encouragement for me to follow his 'last' request, so I did. Closing my eyes once more I chanted the 'our father' prayer over and over.

Mid way through the sixth time I was interrupted by Vernon's voice saying, "Louder please Harper. Don't stop. Ah, yes louder, O God Harper Ohhhhh, Yessssss,"

I opened my eyes in time to see in my peripheral vision the body of a guard diving toward me pushing me out of the way as Vernon flicked his ejaculate in the air. I landed on the floor with the guard shortly after following suit, forcing the wind out my lungs. In shock still not able to process what had just happened I only managed to catch a glimpse of the satisfaction in Vernon's eyes as he with total composure savored watching my body heave to gasp breaths before the other guards blocked my view as they yelled at him to stand back.

The guard who fell on me scrambled up extending his hand mid stance to assist me to my feet. No glance or further words were exchanged before I was escorted out of there and into a first aid room located opposite the execution witness facility. I sat on the edge of the bed involuntarily shaking while the guard explained to the medical aid on duty what had occurred. There was a sense of numbness that instinctively took over as I allowed the disbelief of what had just taken place wash over me. In the midst of the nurse checking my vital signs and doing a physical examination of my limbs to ensure I hadn't sustained any fractures or breaks I heard Vernon.

"HARPER YOU AND I ARE NOT DONE. WE WILL NEVER BE DONE. HARPER ..., HARPER ..., HARPER ..., HARPER ...., HARPER ..., HARPER ..., HARPER ...."

Blinded by an insurgence of rage at the sound of this epitome of evil screaming my name over and over I leaped off the table into the witness room bowling over the unsuspecting guard and slammed my fists against the reinforced glass as I yelled, "I FUCKING HATE YOU. I FUCKING HATE YOU. DIE YOU SICK FUCK. I HATE YOU. I HATE YOU."

The injection had been released into his body as the guards grabbed my arms to pull me out of the room. I manically tried to resist their grip while repeating the words, "I HATE YOU."

Vernon smiled as he listened to my screams. His last words before he was consumed by his body's convulsion to the poisonous cocktail were, "There you are Harper."

\* \* \* \*

It was this experience that awoke the darker side of me, which had laid dormant my entire life. I was no longer the person who wanted to pacify. I went through a phase of embracing my aggression. Embarrassed, humiliated by my naivety and desire to believe in the significance of forgiveness I now accepted that evil existed in the hearts of some. My choice to place Vernon's request above my instinct to walk away frustrated me. His actions were premeditated and I allowed myself to be in a position where he was afforded an opportunity to take advantage of my kindness. It ate at my core every day and some days it still does. All I understood was Vernon felt compelled to do this but not why his fixation became bridged to me. I hated him with a seething passion and for the longest time didn't know how to manage my pain. I guess this was the true reason I felt a connection with York. All the experiences he described were people taking advantage of innocence and this made me want to scream. Flooding unresolved emotions back to the surface of my conscience. I fought against the familiarity of my underlying frustration with mankind's capacity for unrelenting cruelty. I knew at the times I cried for York I was crying for me too. It seemed that walking the path of York's words was unlocking the secrets to my own past with answers yet to be revealed.

\* \* \* \*

A noise distracted me from my thoughts. Looking around at the branches of the trees I tried to identify where it was coming from. After a few minutes of searching I finally located my camouflaged friend the spotted owl. I wondered if it was the same one and whether it had been following me. It was unlike me not to pay attention to my environment. I had been so deep in thought I wasn't paying heed to my surrounds. This was the first time I had ventured so deep into the forest. Just as I began to detect a sweet light fragrance carried by the breeze the owl flapped its wings flying across the way between the trees. My instinct was drawn toward the need to follow so I shifted course heading in the same direction.

It only took five minutes of brisk walking to have the most delightful visual splendor unfold. Rows of wild lavender as far as the eye could see spread across the expanse of land. The perfume was intoxicating and the varying shades of purple hues would have inspired Henri Matisse for another lifetime. I couldn't stop smiling as I walked around allowing the tips of my fingers to caress the flower laden stalks. This was precisely the type of visual replenishment I required.

Inhaling the aroma made me feel relaxed. The morning had slipped by quicker than I anticipated leaving me feeling emotionally weary and completely starved. It was time for me to eat. I pulled out my container of fruit salad and began to graze while staring at the lavender. My stomach was making loud noises as the first pieces of the meal landed. I really enjoyed eating food post a fast. The flavors and appreciation for what was being consumed seemed heightened.

When I finished lunch I considered whether I should commence reading the next chapter of the book. My hesitation confirmed I wasn't ready. Reaching across I grabbed my small nap sack to use as a pillow. An indulgent siesta in the lavender fields was the next point of order. As I lay down staring at the blue skies, I could feel my eyelids getting heavy. Just before they completely closed I saw its underbelly and smiled as I drifted off to sleep thinking 'bumblebee.'

# Hallow be thy name

I woke to the sound of birds chirping and felt my heart warm as I watched a Stellar Jay and a couple of Robins busily swoop in to feast on the remainder of my lunch. I lay there quietly to enjoy them. The colors on the Jay were spectacular. My eyes wanted to get lost in his sea of blue plumage. The sweet little Robins took turns between the Jay's attendances to come in for a nibble, their feathered bodies perfectly rotund with tails of pride jutting out the back adding to their visual appeal. I was surprised at how agile and quick they were in responding to the slightest sound. A necessity for them against predators I assumed. As dearly as I wanted to continue to watch them, my neck was stiff and I was busting to pee. It was time to get up.

I collected my things and headed back toward the path. Knowing I was hours away from any facilities I looked for a place where I could discreetly relieve myself. I settled near a Redwood that had a lovely entangled network of roots above ground. Crouching down in mid air while carefully balancing my hover to reduce any potential back splash I released a steady stream onto the forest floor instantly feeling the pressure on my bladder dissipate. If I had attempted to hold it in any longer I surely would have pee my pants. Just as I started to pull my jeans up, in the distance I saw a group of mountain bike riders approaching. I waved to them as they whizzed past then laughed. I knew it. Murphy is an ass. If I ever received three wishes my first would always be to have Murphy's law manifest into human form so I could punch him in the nose. My get rich quick scheme would be offering the world $20 a slug at ye old Murph. No doubts there would be an endless queue of people with fistfuls of cash.

While heading back toward my original spot in the forest I started to think about the concept mentioned at the beginning of the memoirs, in particular around interferons. I wondered who they were and why they would be so hard to identify. If malice is their intent surely they would stand out or get caught eventually. Were they masters of disguise? Did I have interferons lurking about in my life? Could Vernon have been one? I know he was clearly bat shit crazy but I couldn't ignore the intrigue of the experience. The way he said he 'knew me' and then devoted the remainder of his lifetime to attempt to sustain a connection between us had to mean something. Vernon was solely focused on evoking my anger. He wanted my hatred. His behavior toward me seemed deeply personal. It drove my need to explore concepts around esoteric binds. I leant towards the notion that perhaps Vernon and I held a karmic interconnection of some kind. A broken string of ethereal threads where I had no interest in his existence but he proved to still be obsessed with mine. The memoirs mentioned the attempters worked for the interferons. If

Vernon wasn't an interferon then he most certainly could be an attempter doing the interferons bidding. Honestly, I didn't understand what was to be gained. The concept of interferons, attempters and watchers irked me. It seemed to be a thought creation born of nightmares yet I could sense an underlying truth to a reality where they do exist among us. The greatest trick the devil ever pulled was to convince the world '*she*' didn't exist.

The day as promised turned out to be a scorcher. The sun was piercing down in patches through the canopy of trees. I was grateful my position under my special tree was completely in the shade. I sat down once more and leaned against its majesty. Settled in I took one more look at my beautiful surrounds before opening the book to venture into the thoughts of York.

*Weeks had passed since I had seen Adeline. My bruises, bite marks and fractures were healing, while new ones mysteriously surfaced. It became a part of the way of life I felt I could hold no influence to alter. All in all, it was my mind, which suffered a slow increasing agony from the lack of stimulus afforded. Each day was now a mindless routine. Breakfast of gruel, then swiftly marched into the room of madness. On the days we were given a midday meal it would usually consist of watered down soup containing sparse vegetables and on the rare occasion some putrid meat, then returned back to the room of madness. Our evening supper also held little surprise with potato mash and stale bread supplied as our staple. The end of day always settled by being strapped into our designated cots, some nights with an injection to follow and other nights I was left to hear the sounds of footsteps in the darkness visiting other beds.*

*I had learnt to be thankful for small things in this place. Each morning I looked forward to standing by the window* to peer out at the expanse of garden. The foliage on some of the trees told the story of transition and that the seasonal change was upon us. It made me wonder if I would ever get to see the bumblebee again. The highlight of my day was peaked when I approached the window. Carefully I would look up at the top right of the sash where a spider had woven its web, creating a silken bushel filled with eggs. I was mindful to ensure I didn't draw attention to it. This place had a way of taking anything you enjoyed away from you. I wanted to see the babies born. It was something I had to look forward to.

This might sound strange to say but after a while the room of madness started to provide me with a level of comfort. When I first arrived and was thrust among an ocean of lunatics I was petrified. Yet these days it was a known familiarity where fear of them no longer existed. I was a ghost to these people. The catatonics and I were the only ones who didn't get placed in straight jackets.

Jackson a lengthy thin man with wisps of hair free falling across his brow, was regularly adorned with a leather piece strapped across his mouth. This was to circumvent Jackson's tendency to burst into random rages where he would leap and bite anyone who was close enough to him at the time. It seemed to me to be more of an impulse that compelled him to act out blindingly. I only thought this because I had seen some of the people he did manage to sink his teeth into and knew within the right mindset no-one would want to.

Of all the people here Weldon was the man to watch. He would stand still for hours staring at the floor and then slowly he would provide the signal that the lunatics seemed oblivious to. Trapped in his straight jacket swinging from side to side Weldon held his breath until his face was a *visible shade of crimson. He eventually had to exhale which proceeded by opening his mouth wide to inhale several gulps of air before shooting off like a released tensioned spring running in a manic pattern around the room bowling over anyone who was in his way. Once he completed a loop of the room he would resume his position in stillness again as though nothing had happened and most curiously without his breath out of order. The attendant on duty would call the others to observe this daily spectacle. A row of men in crisp white uniforms cheered loudly as Weldon knocked person after person to the ground. When it was all over they would laugh among themselves as they openly exchanged money.*

*Herschel was a secret favorite of mine. He would sit on one of the few wooden chairs in the room with his legs crossed, head bent over releasing his saliva out of his mouth in a long string towards the floor. Just before it reached the ground he would pull it back up into his mouth. At the time I thought it was magic. Every now and then he would fling his head back to release a laugh and then go back to doing the same activity.*

*I used to think Orvel a short rotund balding man had severe bladder issues. Without fail every day you could see the urine trickle down his leg to create a big steaming puddle. Orvel would then sit next to his own urine in saturated trousers purely focused on the luminescent yellow liquid he had produced. His concentration was only broken when he laughed randomly in a manic fashion heaving his torso back and forth with exaggeration. One day I was sitting against a wall opposite him and that's when I noticed. The fits of laughter weren't sporadic at all. It was directly connected to when any of the lunatics bare feet stepped in his puddle of urine. Knowing this made me smile.*

*Of all the people here it was Alphonse who scared me.*

*His body would continually twitch, his head twisting with his face contorting as he mouthed words that didn't come out. When the twitches amplified he would miraculously find his voice and start saying words. To most the information would be considered incoherent sentences of nonsense but anyone in here of a conscious mind knew his jumbled words were expressing the horrors of this place. Daily I would see him rock back and forth between body twitches mouthing silent words. I was yet to identify what triggered Alphonse to transition to speaking let alone why he selected people to stand in front of while yelling his thoughts in a clear audible voice. The day he chose me I froze. His yellow jaundice eyes screamed the echoes of unspoken pleas as he invaded my personal space to speak with rancid breath in words he would yell 'Rape, quandary, tie them down, tie them down, blue skies, poppies up, make them drown, sleep, blue skies, poppies up, medicine, poppies up, poppies up, towel me, towel you, poppies up, free the rabbits.'*

*I didn't profess to understand all of what he would say such as 'make them drown and poppies up' but the reference to towels in particular were clear. Hygiene was not one of the highest priorities in this place. There always seemed to be a shortage of towels so more often than not we would be required to share one towel among three to five people. If you were the last in line not only was the towel-sopping wet, it was usually covered in a spectrum of bodily excretions. Most of the people here were incapable of cleaning themselves properly and the fact that toilet paper was almost nonexistent didn't help matters.*

*Alphonse's approach was for the most part nonthreatening and much to my curiosity his twitching ceased when he was visually engaged with another person. What scared me was the way he looked into my eyes while saying things I didn't understand. This only meant there were more horrors to this place I was yet to be exposed to. It was a thought I couldn't bear to entertain. Having Alphonse thrust these thoughts across my face in word bursts stained my skin with a coated stench of what was threatening to come. It was simply an unbearable concept to me.*

*I wonder if you have ever truly jumped out of your skin with fright. If you haven't and would like to know how it feels than Randolph was the man for the job. He would sneak up on people and scream with this blood-curdling vibrato right inside your ear. He always chose a different person every time and looked as though he was waiting for a sign or perfect moment before he would become animated and skulk across the room toward his unsuspecting victim. Most of the people reacted by jumping in fright, covering their ears or trying to get away as Randolph pursued them. What he stood to gain from this behavior was anyone's guess but there must have been some benefit because he did it every day.*

*Randolph looked like the type of person who you would expect to see in the theatre. He had classic good looks, which were compromised by the lack of nourishment received in here. We were all suffering the same, gaunt sunken eyes and pale skin due to the absence of access to natural light. Still he was by far the most handsome person in the room of madness. I even noticed the nurses would favor him by letting him venture out of his straight jacket from time to time.*

*I will never forget the day Randolph chose to sneak up on number Nine. Number Nine was called this because he did nothing but draw the number nine with anything he could get his hands on. Most days he would use his finger in the air or lick it with his tongue to mark the windows, walls, floor, anything. He was at least a foot and a half shorter than Randolph so I didn't expect to witness what I had.*

*Number Nine was facing a column, which was positioned off center in the room. He was out of sight of the attendant on shift who was seated near the only access point in and out of the room. I watched as Randolph travelled across the floor with light feet. When he reached Nine and set his position to lean in the most extraordinary thing happened. Nine turned his head and screamed at Randolph making him leap into the air from fright. Those who saw it started to laugh as Nine chased Randolph around the room screaming at him just as Randolph had done to others so many times before. The attendant was too immersed in reading the local rag so he didn't seem to notice the spectacle of riot that began building with an energy shift wave of laughter to sporadic manic extensions of diverse expression. After a few laps of the room with Nine still in hot aggressive pursuit Randolph settled into a corner positioning his body into a huddle while covering his ears. Nine towered over him continuing to screech until he was jumped by a couple of the attendants who came in to see what the raucous was about. Nine fought them as they kicked and threw punch after punch at him. He head butted one of the attendants as they tried to get him to his feet. Nine kicked, screamed, bit and spat as more of the attendants presented to assist. I could feel the pulse of excitement as people cheered Nine on.*

*It took almost ten minutes and six attendants to contain the situation. Nurses came in to assist Randolph while the out of breath, enraged and bleeding attendants dragged Nine's beaten body away. Nine's head was hanging loose as if he had lost consciousness, the only evidence of this not being true was the series of squiggly number nine's on the floor he was drawing with his own blood. He was never to be seen again.*

*It didn't take long before Randolph was back to his old tricks. The only difference now was he would hesitate for the briefest of moments before he started his onslaught of surprise attack screaming. Between Randolph, Alphonse, Herschel, Weldon and Jackson there was a routine of sorts. Our days filled with the consistent antics of these fellows broke the monotony for a while, even with their repetitive behavior. It added variance to an atmosphere, which was otherwise bland and tragically sad. As annoying as they were, in a sense we needed them to add color to our world.*

*I thought the saddest day of my life was the day I entered into this place but every day there seemed to be something that would take place, which would trump the previous. It almost became like a retrospective of post measures to realign my thoughts to think in light of today, yesterday wasn't so bad and the day before was actually good in comparison. I wish I was exaggerating about this, the truth is so many horrible events occurred that I often wondered if I was trapped in a nightmare.*

*Almost a year had passed since I spent time with Adeline. I could still hear her voice in my mind and felt warmth when I visualized her smile. Was she real or a ghost? Not a day passed where I didn't think about my angel. There was such an ache inside of me to see her again. I missed her dearly.*

*Leaning against my window staring out I watched as a vehicle pulled up and parked in the drive. It was the same color and style as my Grandfathers Cadillac. The driver remained stationed while a woman alighted the automobile. As she closed the door she looked up at the deceptively grand old windows. I gasped 'its mom' I thought to myself.*

*"Watch yer lookin at boy?" Said the voice behind me.*

*I turned to be greeted with Cletus peering over my shoulder out the window to see what I had reacted to. I never realized I had gasped so loud. He had deep furrow* lines on his forehead that drew me to look into his intense pale blue eyes. His stare felt like he could penetrate your skin without the need to touch.

"Who is dat? Yer kin folk?"

My eyes widened as I nodded my head.

Cletus looked across at the attendant who was perched on his chair near the door. His head was bobbing and jerking as he partially drifted off to sleep and then wake again. I looked at Cletus deep in thought licking his lips and wondered what he was thinking.

It had been over twenty minutes and no one had entered the room to get me. The time was painstakingly slow. I kept alternating my gaze from looking outside to staring at the door praying it would open soon and I would get to go home with my mom. Cletus was right beside me confined in his straight jacket, head down pacing the floor. He seemed more impatient than I was.

I couldn't recognize the man who was in the vehicle but was certain that Cadillac belonged to my Grandpa. My fingers gripped onto the bars as I saw through the window two attendants escorting my mom back to the car. The man in the drivers seat jumped out of the vehicle and ran to my mom placing his arms around her. I smiled as I realized it was Joshua my brother. The two of them were here.

Joshua turned and opened the vehicle door for mom and helped her get seated. I felt this sudden sense of horror. My hands gripped tightly around the bars as I reefed myself up onto the ledge and pulled myself back and forward releasing sounds as I screamed inside "Don't leave me here." The two attendants looked up at my window smiling as they waved. They knew I was watching, I was always at the window.

In a fit of blind rage I leaped off the ledge and ran towards the exit door. The attendant on duty stood in *readiness to tackle me as he screamed for assistance. Full boar I motored toward him as he got into a defense tackle position. BAM, the attendant was side swiped by Cletus. I jumped over them and ran to door as it was opening. I saw the gap between two of the men entering, I dropped to slide on my knees past their grappling hands and then scampered to my feet to head outside.*

*In amongst the yelling I could hear Cletus calling out, "Ruuuuun boy, ruuuuuuun."*

*I flung the doors open and could see my mom in the vehicle with her head positioned forward her hands were cupping her slender face as she continued to sob. I smiled and then it struck me like a sledgehammer to my throat. One of the attendants had been waiting behind the column. My body smashed against the hard floor with a thud. As I lay on my side voicelessly wreathing and gasping for breath they quietly dragged me out of sight while I listened to the vehicle drive off in the distance. What little hope I held of being reunited with my family, completely died with the fading sounds of the vehicles engine.*

*Once the two attendants exhausted their assault of kicking and punching they dragged me down a corridor past the area I was familiar with and down the narrow darkened halls on the outer edge of the building. It was a regular network of pathways. Number Nine came to mind as I watched the blood spill from my mouth to the moving floor underneath me.*

*They took me into a room where pulses of light were flashing. The beating had left my vision compromised so I could now only see shadows of movement and flashes. I felt the hands of another person take my arm guiding me to a seat behind a textured material screen. As the pulses of light continued I heard a shudder followed by a series of muffled* groans. I kept fading in and out of consciousness as the nurses removed my clothes leaving only my underpants on. The shock of the beating had left my frail body limp with pain while the absence of my clothes induced waves of chills which caused me to involuntary shiver.

"Next," called a voice from behind the curtain.

The nurses grabbed an arm each helping me to my feet while guiding me to a table. As I turned my head to look at the movement caught in my peripheral vision I saw two attendants dragging out a body. Aimlessly I followed the nurses request to get on the table. I could feel them strap my limbs tight to the bed and then a strap was placed across my brow to hold my head in position. Lastly one of the nurses coaxed my mouth open positioning a saliva-ridden piece of wood between my teeth. As she forced my jaw to clamp down my tongue touched the rough grain, I could taste blood.

There was no warning, they placed the elements against my temples releasing jolts of electric shock waves pulsating through my head and around my body causing searing flashes of white light to temporarily blind my retinas and have my body convulsing. The pain arrived and left as quickly as the witness to a lightening bolt displayed through the darkened storm clouds in a night sky. After the third time I felt my bowels release just before I blacked out.

Across the next few days I would phase in and out of consciousness. There was a smell of ammonia so prominent it burnt my throat as I inhaled. Long audible groans echoed through the dark toward me as a sorrowful lullaby. I had no idea where I was now. They left me naked lying on a dank stone floor in a small room with no windows. There was a little series of vents near the bottom of each corner where a slight breeze came through. Tiny glowing eyes lurked in the darkness, which I assumed were rats waiting for me to weaken so they could make an easy meal of me.

No measure of time existed here. I couldn't tell if it was day or night. Occasionally I would hear footsteps, some shuffling noises, a thud and then the footsteps would fade away. No-one provided us with food or water let alone toilet facilities. It appeared those who were left trapped here were abandoned to die. In this place after a certainty of weeks passing I understood the sheer determination of my will to survive. My tongue was sliced from licking the slow dripping moisture on the basalt walls in an attempt to keep hydrated. I lured rats out of the vents using pieces of my bloodied index finger as bait, which I sliced using the jagged wall surface. As soon as I was able to snatch one I would smash its head against the wall and suck on the contents drinking its warm blood before it had a chance to congeal. The first time I did this my stomach cramped and I reefed over vomiting. It was the combination of the idea of what I was doing and the taste that caused my desire to reject the nutrients my body desperately needed.

When the attendants finally did come to my doorway the look on their faces confirmed they were expecting to retrieve a carcass. The one I despised the most, Eugene Styple, smirked when he saw the pile of rotting rat carcasses in the corner. He signaled for his sidekick Leroy Muddler to step into the room to retrieve me. His expression changing to a pale shade as he was smacked in the face with the fumes of my excrement infused with decomposing carcass and urine. Leroy turned and ran out the door promptly vomiting the contents of his fat over indulgent belly. Eugene was clearly annoyed at this display of weakness yet he chose not to venture into the room. Instead he barked for me to come out or remain for another three months.

*I slowly rose to my feet and walked toward the door half expecting Eugene to slam it shut in my face. My eyes were hypersensitive to the dim overhead lights in the corridor. They weren't especially bright but for me they might as well have been a row of suns.*

*Following the two attendants I had back flash images of Eugene and Leroy waving at me. They were the ones who walked my mother to the vehicle on that God forsaken day. Eugene was the culprit who punched me in the throat to stop me from escaping. Of all the attendants present in Greyhaven, these two always seemed to be in close proximity when a person "jumped" off the roof to their untimely death. Both of them were always eager to be first on the scene when there was cause to discipline a lunatic. They enjoyed it, perhaps even thrived on having free reign to inflict pain.*

*As I fumbled down the length of corridor I shivered when the breeze from the partially open windows touched my naked skin. Looking down at my withered body, I was covered in soiled patches from the black mold stains on the dank floor. Portions of my flesh were eaten away by the feasting bacteria, which stood to survive in richness where all else slowly died. I knew I reeked but no longer had a sense of smell to tell. The months of exposure to the heavy build up of ammonia had shot my ability to detect anything. In a way this was a true grace given my living conditions.*

*Movement in my peripheral vision caught my eye as I saw a white sheet semi float in the air. I flinched as my body turned slightly to the landing of the fabric on my shoulders. Gentle arms wrapped the rest of the sheet around me.*

*"Why is he naked and what on Earth has happened? Look at him. Look at him."*

*'Adeline,' I thought to myself before I unknowingly fainted.*

*When I woke I was in a bathtub covered across with plastic. My head was resting on the edge of the cold lip of the tub. The water was comforting as it warmed my stinging body. I lay still, feeling overwhelmed and exhausted. I wanted to cry as the sense of relief was welling up inside me from surviving the whole ordeal. No-one deserved to be subjected to the atrocities that existed within these walls.*

*"Sip on this slowly. You haven't eaten for a while so your body will need to take in small amounts at a time, okay?"*

*I looked at the cup Adeline was placing on my now parted lips. I stared at her as I took my first sip of the warm soup. She was more beautiful than I remembered. The liquid fell down my sore ridden swollen throat and hit my grumbling stomach with a searing pain. I reefed forward pushing the cup she held, spilling part of its contents on the surface of the plastic covering. I watched through squinted eyes as the soup glided across to the other side of the bathtub.*

*"Its okay. You need to drink this slowly." She said, encouraging me to take another sip.*

*I did and this time the feeling didn't arise as harshly. I was thankful. At this point I was no longer sure I could endure any more exposure to suffering. I was weak and my resolve to fight had been crushed. All I needed was for Adeline to hold me in her arms and I would have crumbled into a convulsing mass of tears. The horror must end. I spent months defiantly fighting to survive and now that I had, I just wanted to die. I closed my eyes and drifted off to sleep listening to Adeline's voice politely requesting me to take another mouthful of the soup.*

As much as I wanted to continue reading I needed to consider heading back to my hotel. It was going to be dark soon and my own stomach was grumbling from lack of attention. My emotions were numbed to the information I was absorbing from York's experiences. It was a defense mechanism I used to prevent the pain of what was being described from affecting me as deeply as I knew it wanted to. There were no tears left in me, not today, not for York or myself. The harshness of his reality is one I knew was possible and is for many in the world in various forms. I simply can't fathom why any one person has to endure so much pain. What is the purpose? Nothing justifies the degree of horror this child has had to accept and yet it happens more often than people choose to speak about or be aware of. Once again I felt myself hating the cruelty contained within the world. There seems to be no end.

# The Calling

I dropped off my bag at the hotel and went out to find a place to settle for dinner. It was a balmy night so the walk through the streets was pleasurable. The people who passed by seemed to glance at me as if they had a secret to tell. It was an experience that made me wonder in the moment they looked at me whether they saw something I didn't. When I was a child I would hide my face and sometimes even cry because they all seemed to stare. I didn't like it. There was a notion in the back of my mind that I might secretly be somebody well known in life that had suffered amnesia. People were instructed not to approach me in fear that the shock would cause an adverse effect. So they all know who I really am and that's why they stare. As ridiculous as the idea might sound at times when I felt the consistent intensity of people's glare I would redraw on the thought of amnesia as a hypothesis, this of course being a default after I have inconspicuously checked my nose for hanging boogers.

The music from a sweet little café caught my attention. When I peered through the window there were only two couples and a gentleman sitting on his own reading a paper. A lady greeted me at the door, opening it as I entered.

"Hello" she said with a smile.

"Hi, table for one please."

"Oh, actually we are booked for the evening. All the vacant tables are reserved for people who are set to arrive within the next half hour so I'm sorry if you don't have a booking tonight we cannot help you."

I looked around the room and saw the little reservation signs on the tables and smiled, "No problems. I'll go somewhere else. Thank you."

I turned to walk out the door when I heard a voice call, "She can come and sit with me."

I looked across at the man who had been reading his paper. It was now neatly folded in front of him.

"That's okay, I don't want to intrude, but thank you."

"Intruding would be uninvited, I'm inviting you to join me if you want to." He said projecting his voice with confidence.

I watched as he gestured for me to come take a seat. I looked at the waitress who was still holding the door open as she beamed with a smile.

"Ok, that would be lovely, thank you." I said as I walked toward him.

"My name is Bahrain, please take a seat. I'm glad you decided to accept my invitation."

I sat down placing the book on the table to my right. "It was a very generous offer, thanks I'm Harper."

"Harper means harp player. Do you play any musical instruments?" He asked raising an eyebrow.

"Um, no. Does it really mean harp player?" I said adjusting in my chair.

"Yes."

"Wow, I think I'm disappointed in knowing that and impressed that you did. What's the meaning behind the name Bahrain?" I said finding him curious.

"Two seas."

"Hmm, well at least yours is a little more interesting than harp player." I said with a laugh.

"Don't dismiss the beauty of a harp. It's a unique instrument that not many master the art of playing. The complexity of the combination of strings and the finger's speed, dexterity, memory and timing required to bring the most out of the union is an art within itself that may take lifetimes to master. If you are known as the harp player then you have or are on the path to mastering the strings played in life."

I was in awe of the way he managed to convert my thoughts instantly to a romantic version of allure. "You sir, have a way with words."

"I see things as they truly are not as people intend them to be. In this life I am a soothsayer."

"Soothsayer? I'm sorry I don't understand what that is."

"I have the capacity to predict the future. I see things that most don't. I choose when to tell and when I need to be silent."

I found myself biting down on my bottom lip as I heard him speak. He looked through me in a way, which made me feel as though he was able to see beyond the projection of a person's mask. He didn't look familiar yet there was an instant comfort in his presence.

"Is being a soothsayer your profession?" I asked

"No, I'm a retired attorney but soothsaying is my way of life."

"You mentioned 'in this life you are a soothsayer'. What do you mean by that?"

He laughed, "Nice attention to detail Harper. You have a sharp mind. It's good, you must already play the strings well."

I smiled, "I assume you mean metaphorically. I would say for the most part I am reasonably good at it. Still working to perfect the art of me."

He leaned in and touched my hand, "This is good. You should never cease to improve you. This life is critical for you to transcend to your final one of flesh. If you do it right. The world will never be the same."

"Are you ready to order?" Asked the waitress who was looking at Bahrain's hand on mine.

"Sure I'll just have whatever is most popular on the menu and a glass of a nice red wine please. I'm happy for you to choose." I said smiling at her.

"I'll just have a glass of whiskey neat, thanks."

"You're not going to eat?" I enquired.

"I already had something. I might order a cheese platter later if you feel like sharing. We can decide after you finish your meal."

The waitress went off to place the order and Bahrain moved his hand back to his lap.

"You are a very mysterious fellow. There's an air of confidence in the way you deliver your messages, which makes me want to believe. I guess that's the attorney in you." I said with a chuckle.

"You should believe Harper. There is magic in you." Bahrain leant in, "Whether you like it or not you my dear are destined for great things."

I starred into his eyes, "How can you be so sure?"

"I am certain because I know what you do not. I see and feel what you refuse to embrace. Ask me anything and I will within reason show you the truth." He said as he stroked the length of his gray beard.

"Anything?"

"Yes."

"Why use the caveat of within reason?"

He released a loud laugh at my question. "Oh, Harper you are a funny one. It has to be within reason because I cannot afford to tell you what you are not ready to hear or destined to learn yet. It would effect the universal energies and perhaps add an unnecessary kink to your life course."

The thought of York came to mind about his mention of travelling to dream places where he met with sages who imparted wisdom. It seemed like a nice idea or dream, an escape from the realities of life and here I was sitting in the presence of a person who I felt had some deeper insights and wisdom. Bahrain was an ordinary looking man in his mid to late fifties. He had short-slicked back gray hair and a beard to match in color. I couldn't tell how tall he was but he seemed an average height and weight. His complexion was clean so I assumed he was in reasonable health. His eyes were his only true distinction. An unusual deep gray blue color that held a sense of kindness.

"Are you going to ask me a question?" He prompted as the waitress returned with our drinks.

"Sure, sorry I was just thinking about something. I'm not certain what question to ask you. Perhaps it is best to ask you to tell me what you feel I need to know."

Bahrain glanced across at the book and then looked back at me. "Tell me about the book."

I placed my hand on the book considering what I wanted to say. "Its just something I stumbled upon and decided to read. It seems to be a diary or memoirs or perhaps a story someone has written to pass time. I'm unsure of its origins or relative truths."

"What does your instinct tell you?"

"That it's true. Someone has written their life story as a reflective memoir. It crosses parallels between telling a life upon reflection where some of the dialogue is written across past and present expressions. Regardless of how it is presented, it feels real. I think the person who wrote this had an extremely hard life and might have used writing as a method to let it out or wrote it because they felt it needed to be heard. They were driven for a cause and I feel drawn to read the story."

Bahrain glanced once more at the book and then pursed his lips. "You found it? Tell me about this."

"I'm here for the long weekend to relax and was hiking in the National Forest today. There is a spot I like to visit, a giant old redwood tree I have always gravitated towards. I find in this space I tend to rebalance, connect with the earth and feel like me again. If it's at all possible I would say the old tree and I are friends. On my way there I saw an owl circling above. When I got to my tree the owl was on a branch. It swooped down and went inside the large cavity of the partially hollowed trunk. I followed it in and found the owl perched on this book in a cavity."

He smiled as I was relaying the story. The whole time he was gently stroking his beard. "May I see the book?"

I passed it across to him and then lifted my wine glass to take a sip. I watched as Bahrain placed his hand on the outside of the book and closed his eyes. It was as if he was trying to read the contents without the need to witness a page. After a short while he released a breath, opened his eyes to reveal tears as he looked at me. He then opened the book and flipped quickly through the pages. As he did he nodded his head and then placed the book back beside me.

"You had tears in your eyes before you opened the book. Why?"

"The book is significant. It holds secrets that are representative of the truth. There is much pain for this one's life force. A journey only marked for a special few who are chosen for the strength of the tests laid before them."

"How could you know that? You seemed to just flick through the pages without reading any of the passages."

"Harper, the book presents empty for me. There are no words contained within the pages."

I was confused by his words and reached for the book. As I opened it to look inside I was half expecting to see blank pages but there was writing inside. I looked at Bahrain, "Very funny. You had me believing you for a moment. Very convincing." I said laughing as I held up the open book.

He shook his head and waved to get the waitress to come to our table.

"Yes," she said looking at Bahrain.

"Would you be so kind as to read the passage from the book Harper is holding up. I haven't got my glasses here so I am unable to read it."

The waitress looked at the book and then at Bahrain. "Is this a trick? Both of these pages are blank."

I flipped the book to me and looked at the pages filled with words. "What do you mean? The writing is here. Can you not see this?"

The waitress looked at both of us and laughed. "Are you having a lend of me? The pages are blank."

I looked at the book again and could see the words clear as day. "Thanks I was only playing a prank on my new friend." I said feeling embarrassed and a little confused.

As the waitress walked off I placed the book beside me again and looked at Bahrain.

"What you see is clearly meant for your eyes only. York has written this story for you. It was waiting for the time when you were ready to read it." He said calmly.

"If you can't see the words how do you know his name?" I asked patiently taking another sip of my wine.

"He told me. When I placed my hand on the book it was his voice that I heard. You don't know who he is do you?"

"No I don't. Am I supposed to know? Why is the book for me? I don't understand any of this." I felt frustrated that my life all of a sudden seemed to become a series of mysterious riddles and thoughts all woven into something that rang true and at the same time made no sense at all.

"Ah, this I cannot tell you. I can only say that you need this journey. It will groom you to be free for your preparation into your final life and your union with the one who completes the journey of the flesh, your twin flame."

A feeling of overwhelming emotion welled up inside me at the mention of twin flames. I had spent a lifetime drawn towards the concept of knowing all there was to be known about them. It is the perfect match to ones soul. I never felt I was missing something I felt as though I was in an unconscious perpetual search for someone that always eluded me. I found it frustrating, a secret mystery to be solved.

"Why do you assume I haven't already met my twin?" I asked, wanting to challenge his thoughts.

"You haven't. If you did the world would be on a

different universal vibration. I know it's not so you are still in search of the other half of your soul while your other half is preparing for you. In fact Harper it is more than this, an important universal element is seeking to reconnect with you. Lets just say there is a reason why you have been chosen to be able to read the book. Just as there is reason for me being drawn to eat here on this specific day. There are many who wish for you to succeed. More than those who wish to see you fail."

I could feel tears start to well in the corner of my eye. It had been such an emotional day and his words seemed to etch at my core.

"People who wish me to fail? The interferons?"

Bahrain looked around as I said the word and then leaned in. "What do you know of interferons? How have you come by this word?"

"The book at the beginning briefly mentions another time in a space of enlightenment, interferons are mentioned as well as attempters and watchers. It then mentions past lives and the amount required to transition to enlightenment and jumps from there to the story of this child called York. It's a horrible journey but I can't seem to stop myself from reading it. I feel like I have to. This child is all alone and I want to be there for him, even if it is just in the form of reading his story."

Bahrain sat back and sipped on his drink while he looked at me.

I was slightly startled as the waitress approached without me hearing her footsteps. She placed my meal of salmon pasta alfredo in white caper sauce in front of me and topped up my wine without asking. I must have looked like I needed a refill. I said my thanks as she quietly left. I picked up my fork swirling the pasta onto it.

"Tell me what you are thinking." I said to Bahrain.

"I sit before you in awe of who you are and the things that you are yet to achieve. I felt you coming before you arrived and now you are here with me. It is amazing how lives are intertwined and destined to meet. You are well known Harper."

It amazed me to listen to the things Bahrain was saying and how small threads of the words were neatly intertwined in aspects of what I suspected, thought and felt. "People stare at me all the time as though I am familiar to them. What is there that I don't know that I need to understand?" I asked trying to coax more detail than generic statements of bait hooking white wash. I craved specifics.

"You cannot be told. It is important you discover for yourself. All will be revealed within its rightful time and place. You must trust in this Harper."

"I just want to get some answers rather than listening to statements I could read anything into. If you are a soothsayer then you must know things that I need to hear. If we have met don't you feel you have an obligation to tell me?"

"I can tell you this. All souls were split and roam to find their other half but you did something many lifetimes ago not even the wisest of the elders knew was possible. It changed the path of reality. You my dear are the one who holds the true key of wills. No more can be said, the rest must be your discovery in regards to this."

Bahrain's words made me feel as though I had just stepped into a hybrid of some fantasy tale crossed with the twilight zone. I am the true key of wills. What on earth does that mean? The whole day from the get go to now has been surreal. I wanted to buy into what he was saying, to try and pry more from him as it was a fascinating conversation between two strangers but the other part of me wanted to leave things as they were, unresolved. Even the fact that no one else could see the contents of the book defied logic. How was it possible?

"Can you tell me anything about interferons?" I asked

"They are unseen warriors set to the path of destruction, born with an eternal desire to conquer and control. Anything standing in their way is to be destroyed. There are many who are under their influence without knowledge and are used like pawns in a game of chess, sacrificed for what they wish to achieve."

"Do they kill people?"

"It's far worse. They irrevocably break the free will of man. If the will is broken there is no connection to the soul and therefore no further reincarnation to the flesh to complete the cycle of lessons. They are lost."

"Why is the completion of the cycle so important?"

"The universal energies are replenished and at their highest when twin flames unite. The flames of two combined are a miracle of creation and produce love and light in the form of vibrations, which provide regenerating sustenance to life. It is the missing element science has not acknowledged. It is only the healers, clairvoyants, mystics and yogis throughout the centuries who have known this as the true life force."

"Given the millions of people in the world I would have expected there would be twin flames united in each lifetime as part of the cycle."

Bahrain leaned in, "No Harper. It is rare, so rare in fact that the universe suffers and the hold of the interferons gets stronger."

"I don't understand. Why is it so rare? What's preventing them from reuniting?"

"The one who split the souls did so with the curse laid to bear that the seven deadly sins must be lived or exposed to the flesh and pass atonement for each before the souls of twins can reunite. It is said that seven can be the shortest of the cycles as no one has managed to enter with multiples of the sins gauntlet to reincarnation of the flesh and passed with atonement. It is those who are impatient and try that are more susceptible to the breaking of will for the burdens can be too great."

"If seven is the shortest what is the average?"

"It is hard to say, most it would seem take hundreds of reincarnations before they are cleared of all the exposure to the sins. You have to understand that there is karmic influence of connection between souls that greet in flesh which can create havoc and slow down the whole process. The interferons tend to leverage off karmic connections to send people who are close to achieving their ascension path off course. It can add hundreds of reincarnations to the process and cause the universal imbalances to grow, which allows them to have a stronger influence and hold."

"Can you give me an example?"

"You have no doubt read in the paper many times of a person who has killed himself."

"Sure, countless people end their lives." I said

"Suicide is automatically an additional seven reincarnations. It's not just the reincarnations but the seven sins are attached one per cycle. They have purchased themselves a ticket of having to run the gauntlet twice for each sin. The growth required for such a person is fraught with low odds and there is a likelihood they will repeat a pattern of suicide in multiple flesh occurrences, each time taking them back to the count of an additional seven."

"If what you are saying is true than these people may never complete the cycle."

"Exactly. They increase their probability of losing their will and become easy prey for the interferons."

Bahrain motioned to the waitress.

"May I have another whiskey and a wine for the lady. I'II also get the cheese platter to share thanks."

"No problems," She glanced at the book before she walked off to place our order.

"So karma's payment is the seven reincarnations?"

"No the seven reincarnations is the rule, karma is the connection that must be healed with those the person left behind. This is added to the need to reincarnate at times they reincarnate to afford opportunity to heal the connection. Once again this can take lifetimes because both need to be willing to take the steps towards acceptance of one another. It is all interlinked, the threads cannot be broken."

"All rules are meant to be broken. If there weren't alternatives there would be no need for the rule to exist in the first place. It would just be as is." I said drinking the last of my wine.

Bahrain laughed, "There are exceptions to the rule." He said it with a twinkle in his eye.

"Do I get to know what the exceptions are?"

"You tell me Harper. What could be an exception?"

The waitress returned with the cheese platter and our drinks. She cleared the table leaving us both with fresh plates and cutlery, all the while glancing at the book again.

"I read somewhere in my research of twin flames

that there is soul to soul healing. If you have a deep connection with your own soul could you not have your soul bypass the flesh and heal the other soul in purity and light? It bypasses the psyche and allows for your souls exchange to be re-engaged with healing love."

"This is certainly possible but it takes a person with great skill and shamanic healing qualities. They are known as light workers. They extend themselves to exchange energy cleansing the karmic debts so a person of the flesh reduces the probable life cycles. It is not just their karma they can heal, they are capable of working to assist anyone who is willing to participate."

"I want to ask you about someone who crossed my path. I've never spoken of it before but he keeps coming to mind as we are talking so I want to know your perspective."

Bahrain reached across to cut a piece of the cheese, "Go ahead."

"I was doing an assessment on a fellow called Vernon Wreath." I hesitated in continuing as I saw the expression on Bahrain's face alter as I mentioned Vernon's name. "What is it?"

"This man is pure evil. He is one of the primary lost souls who is governed by the interferons. He has been watched closely, for his execution of destruction when in the realm of flesh is unmatched. Vernon hunts the seven keys."

"Wait a minute, what is the seven keys?"

"There are fourteen unique souls who when paired as twin flames form the seven keys. Each possesses a unique ability which when united will shift the universal energy to one power. It opens the realm of possibilities to Equanon."

"Equanon is real?" I asked surprised.

"Yes very much so. It is written in the flowing river of knowledge that one set of keys can open the doors to the realm and from there the universe begins to heal and strengthen. What is your connection to this monster Vernon?"

"Vernon's first words to me were that he knew me. He then looked into my eyes as he smiled. I'll never forget the look on his face. There was something that irked me about him. I was conscious of the fact that he was butt ugly. The truth is he managed to get under my skin rather easily and I held an unexplainable disdain for him."

"He was executed so he has passed yes?"

"Yes." I said releasing a long exhale.

"What is it Harper?"

"I've never told anyone before and now that I'm talking about it I'm feeling the emotions of the experience starting to surface. There wasn't anything pleasant about his energy. I spent less than an hour collectively with Vernon Wreath and ever since wished every day that I hadn't."

Bahrain looked at the table and nodded his head. He paused for a moment before looking into my eyes, "You need to deal with this. It's not something that will go away. Tell me everything and I will guide you as best I can."

"Soon after we met I started receiving countless letters from him. I've never opened them. On the day of his execution he called me to ask me to attend. He said it was important to him. I spent hours thinking about it and came to the conclusion that I should. It was his voice at the time, he sounded so sincere. Anyway when I got there the warden asked me if I would give Vernon absolution. It was his request to confess to me rather than a priest. I thought it was odd and knew I didn't want to do it. My only reason was the possibility of regret of not offering Vernon a chance for peace. I didn't believe I was the right person, it should have been a priest but he requested me." I paused to take a sip of my wine while Bahrain remained silent waiting for me to continue.

"The guards took me to his holding cell and stood by. Vernon asked me to say the Our Father with him, hands in a prayer position and eyes closed." I stopped to take another sip of my wine. Talking about this with someone proved to be harder than I expected.

In a gentle voice Bahrain said, "Its okay Harper, just tell me."

I leaned forward and placed both hands over my face shaking my head slightly at the thought of what I was about to say. I didn't want Bahrain to look at me when I spoke. I still felt so stupid and annoyed at myself for wanting to believe in the good of people.

I steadied my breath and began, "He asked me to continue to say the Our Father prayer over and over so I did. The guards were there but their backs were turned and I had my eyes closed. I was unaware that Vernon was masturbating and when he climaxed he threw his cum at me. The guard just managed to push me out of the way so thankfully none made contact. I'll never forget the look of satisfaction on his face. During the execution he kept yelling out my name saying it wasn't over. I went into a blind rage and yelled at him to die and go to hell. His last words were '*There you are Harper.*' Then the poison gained pace and took him as its hostage. I was still in a manic state yelling that I hated him as the guards involuntarily dragged me out of the room."

I removed my hands from my face and stared at a wine stain splotch while I played with the edge of the white linen cloth under the table. The shame and ridicule was an emotional silent swell within me. It wasn't something time could heal and I just didn't know how to process the feelings. I hated Vernon Wreath then and I hate him still.

"These two times were the only contact you had with him. Is that right?"

"Yes, I would remember if I had met him before. His face was distinct and his blackened heart too ugly to forget."

"You said you didn't read the letters he wrote you. Do you still have them?"

"Yes."

"Tell me Harper, why do you keep the letters and never read them?"

"I don't know. I have them all in a large pile at the entry of my apartment. I have no intentions of reading them but I cannot bring myself to throw them away."

Bahrain lent forward. "My advise to you is to keep them but never read them. At some point before your last breath you will need to affect a release. There will be signs to show you how and when to do this. It will only occur when you are ready, of this I am certain. If you avoid it then the bond will grow stronger carrying into your next life. Break the hold by releasing the letters. It is a golden opportunity to reduce the bind and afford a channel to heal what is unfinished between you and Vernon Wreath."

I semi rolled my eyes at the thought of that monster and I having anything to do with one another. The idea of being connected with him was nothing short of vile. Reaching across I took a portion of blue cheese onto a cracker and placed it in my mouth. A memory flash of words sprung into my mind in relation to York eating moldy stale bread. It made me wonder about the evolution to commercial production and sale of blue cheese. Could there be a link between tragedies to prosperity?

"Yes."

Startled by the voice I turned to my right to see who was there.

"Are you Ok?" Bahrain immediately touched my arm.

I looked down at his hand as it transferred a level of cold to the surface of my skin. "I thought I heard someone standing close saying the word *yes* to me. It surprised me, that's all."

"This was an answer to a question you posed. What were you thinking about?"

"I guess the question was around me pondering the link between tragedies to prosperity. The voice I thought I heard said *yes* to the connection between the two."

Bahrain adjusted his position in his chair and sat back looking at me. A smile evolved to expose his manicured teeth. "I cannot emphasize how important not reading these letters are and to wait for the right signs to release them back to the universe. Please promise me you will do this Harper. It's as important as you finding and reading this book." His eyes diverted to where it sat beside me on the table.

I slowly nodded my head as I savoured the flavors of the cheese on my tongue. A part of me always thought I would read them one day when it no longer held emotional value. There was a curiosity about what Vernon could possibly want to write in so many letters.

The sensible side of me wanted nothing to do with any of it. If I could have my memory of Vernon erased I would. In saying this I also knew feeling this way was the very reason why I had to face what I was avoiding. There was something I felt had to be learnt about me within his words. Vernon's persistence and my reaction to the whole situation were too compelling to ignore.

"Why are you cautioning against me reading the letters?"

"Vernon was programmed to identify and prey on the soul keys born to flesh. His last victims were the only ones who were not soul keys or even on a path of ascension. Can you see the link Harper?"

"Hmm, if Vernon was able to recognize soul keys and you mentioned I was one of them then the only link I can conclude is the event was orchestrated to cross paths with me. Psychopath logic, theory 101."

"Go deeper Harper, think." Said Bahrain as he sipped on the last of his whiskey.

I looked into his piercing eyes as I explored the concepts running through my mind, "Ok, let's step through this hypothetically based on what we have discussed. Vernon is programmed to prey on the soul keys. The motive behind killing a person who is not on the path could be to draw me near, which begs the question, why he needs to do that rather than execute a direct connection. Two scenarios come to mind, either he couldn't find me or he held hesitance in regard to direct contact. I'm ruling out that he couldn't find me because in this theory I'm assuming he knew the way to get access to me was through my occupation. There was a barrier between us in the room I interviewed him in. A table, restraints and the prison guards. This man has a blackened heart who brutally took lives with no remorse yet he hesitates when it comes to me. Perhaps the precautions were in place to protect him from me. In saying this, Vernon's relentless obsession to sustain a connection after our meeting was tethered with actions of safe distance, the letters and then finally the call to the execution. The two times we met he intentionally worked to draw out my anger, even though inside of him I could feel a wealth of suffering. There must be significance to the need to connect to me but I hold no desire to connect with him. This alludes to me being in a position of power. The letters he wrote, kept by me but never opened. If I'm honest with myself I know the reason I never read them was because I didn't want to have him under my skin, which he seems to try and much to my disappointment succeed in. He feeds off my anger yet he is cautious of the same. All his victims were brutalized physically whereas I'm the one segregated and subjected to his mind. The approach he took verbally clearly held undertones of sexual aggression, which aligns to his modus operandi. If Vernon did do all of this to influence me then his value proposition on its importance was the cost of his life. No higher price could be paid. The question is why?"

Bahrain smiled, "Listening to you work is like a symphony dear sweet harp player."

I laughed, "I was born to explore, decipher in ways others don't seem to notice. I sometimes forget to apply the same approach when it comes to me. You know how it is, an accountant is never up to date on his own tax submissions."

We both laughed.

"Bahrain, are you sure Vernon was in service of the interferons?"

"I'm positive. Everything you said just then is real Harper. Don't dismiss it or take what you know and see for granted. The remainder of your life holds a criticality of course. Just be true to who you are. Using your mind stimulated what you have conveyed. I'd like you to close your eyes and assess it again using your heart to feel."

Instantly I felt my eyes divert. I stared at the left overs on the cheese platter, "I don't want to."

"I know. This is why you must squelch the desire to disconnect. Will you try to venture the same path exploring what is to be felt with your heart?"

I looked at Bahrain, shook my head slightly at the thought of doing it before placing my hands flat on the table and closing my eyes. I took a few deep breaths to center my focus and started.

"I'm visualizing the interview room. Vernon is sitting in front of me. There's a contradiction between his projected persona when compared to the screams of anguish I hear wrestling beyond his eyes. It's almost like there are dual personalities a conflict of sorts, his outward side emulates darkness while internally I can hear his silent pleas for mercy. I had entered the room with a bias leaning towards not liking him. As I sat there I felt compassion for a person who exuded his own pain and suffering. There is a pull and push between us. He is grappling for me to acknowledge him but he uses his anger as a mechanism to attempt to mask his pain. He knows I can see it. This makes him feel vulnerable so he defaults to distract me with his vile actions. He is torn between a struggle to be liked and defaults to the safety of hate. The price of being accepted seems to be too high or perhaps he yearns for it but doesn't feel worthy. It's clear this is what Vernon craves inside but associates this to weakness. He feels vulnerable in my presence. My acceptance, forgiveness meant something to him."

I opened my eyes as I could feel the tears starting to form with the connection to Vernon's humanity. There was implicitness to the silence in his screams eating at the core of my compassion. In feeling his truth I could no longer hate him and I was struggling against this because of how I felt about what he did.

"Why do you think this man wants your forgiveness, Harper?"

"I'm not sure." I said reaching for a napkin to catch a rolling tear.

"He is an aspect of your past, present and future."

"No, the past is over and there is no future he is dead."

"Harper, no one ever just disappears. It is an evolution. He has passed this period of flesh but he will return and is destined to do so at the same time as you. There is no avoiding the need to complete the journey between you two. There will be a choice for you to be greater than the calling for evil, to dwell within the realms of its pull, or worse, join them."

"I want you to be wrong. I don't want anything to do with him and have no desire to be like him." I could feel my blood pressure rising with a flush of heat to my cheeks as I partially clenched my jaw.

"Not wanting to be like him is good but you will still be tested to join and if you succumb to this we all lose. You will have to risk everything of yourself to make this right. The ethereal connection cannot be broken only corrected by acceptance, peace and love. Do you understand?"

"In concept yes, but in reality I'm finding the idea of being bound to this thing nothing short of atrocious. Vernon's choice to be who he is has nothing to do with me."

"Ah, but it does. This I can assure you. Nothing may appear as it seems but everything happens for a reason. In time, when it is right you will need to face the truth of who you really are and decide who you wish to be. There will be angels and guides available to support you but none can walk your path. This is yours alone to do."

"This whole concept lends itself to probabilities of experience and circumstance. The way a person reacts to any situation is based on their interpretation at the time. It's primarily driven by the instinct of flight or fight and the association to understanding of what is occurring based on knowledge formed by whom a person has evolved into. Technically, it means there is no way to predetermine how any given exposure to a situation will be managed."

"Yes and no. Yes if operating from your mind and all the adoption of confines one has created to protect themselves from fear, disappointment and pain. However, if you allow yourself to bypass this and work from the heart the results can very different. You just experienced this with your thoughts on Vernon haven't you? By looking with your heart have you not felt the shift in your perspective on him?" Bahrain folded his arms and smiled.

I took a deep breath, "Yes, I see him differently now."

"Do you get it Harper?"

"Operate from the heart and not from the head and I won't be lead astray."

Bahrain leaned in and grabbed my hand squeezing it with a big smile, "Precisely."

I looked at his hand once again feeling the coolness of his touch. I was about to ask him if he had poor circulation when the waitress distracted my thought by not so subtly placing the bill in front of me. She cleared the table while I searched in my bag for my wallet.

Raising an eyebrow with a smirk, "Guess its time to call it a night. Bahrain thank you so much for the invitation to sit with you. The experience was both unexpected and fascinating. It's a conversation I promise will be with me across my lifetime. You are indeed a unique soul."

I placed my credit card on the bill tray as I passed it back to the waitress.

"Harper, the pleasure is all mine. I had no idea it was you who I would be meeting, I only knew I would be required to meet someone here tonight. When I called you over it was because I felt your presence and recognized your face but at that point I still didn't know." He paused for a moment and looked at his hands before returning to gaze at me. "My dear, the delight in speaking with you has me filled with hope for the future. I understand this all seems like a foolish old man speaking gibberish. You cannot relate to the enormity of your purpose because you are not meant to yet. Of all the things we have spoken of tonight, please take this one message to heart." He paused for a moment and then beamed with a sense of joy as he said, "I believe in you."

Smiling thoughtfully at his words I mouthed the words, "Thank you," and then stood up to prepare myself to leave. Grabbing my wallet I waved at Bahrain who was still seated exuding a beaming smile. Upon finalizing the bill I headed toward the exit. Just as I reached for the handle it unexpectedly flung open with a gust of wind whirling into the restaurant causing some of the paper napkins to become airborne. A cold sensation ran through me as I heard the words 'the book' echo in my mind. I looked down feeling the emptiness of my hands and realized I had left it behind. As I turned to head back to the table it struck me, I'd been so caught up in my conversation with Bahrain all evening I didn't notice that the reserved tables were never filled. No one else had entered the café. Standing at the foot of the table I was surprised to find Bahrain's head tilted down with his body limp as though he was unconscious or sleeping.

"Bahrain, are you okay?" There wasn't a response. I kept my distance while stretching my arm out to tap his shoulder. "Bahrain, hello" He stirred at my touch and looked up at me. I stood back as I smelt the alcohol laden breath he heavily exhaled.

"I'll have another whiskey." He said with a slur waving his hand in the air.

"Bahrain are you okay? What's going on?"

He squinted his eyes as if to try and focus on me. "Who are you? Get me another drink," he barked before slouching forward dropping his head on the table.

I reached across and grabbed my book. Aside from his demeanor altering he looked the same, except his eyes. Bahrain had the most piercing blue gray eyes and now they were bloodshot and brown. I waived to the waitress to get her to come over.

"Yes?"

"Do you know this man?" I asked.

"Sure he comes in here almost every night and gets drunk. He only lives across the road. The kitchen staff normally have to carry him home."

"He wasn't drunk while I was having dinner with him. We had a lengthy intelligent conversation. How could he be roaring drunk now when I only just left him?"

The waitress chuckled, "I've never seen Liam talk to anyone for such a long time. He was pretty drunk before you came into the restaurant. I can tell because he usually yells at people when he is on his way to getting really inebriated. The only reason the boss lets him in is because he feels bad for him. His ex wife was murdered and his only daughter Lisa committed suicide a few years ago."

When she mentioned Lisa my stomach churned. "Liam? He told me his name was Bahrain."

The waitress looked at me puzzled, "His name is definitely Liam."

"Did they catch the person who murdered his wife?" I asked knowing full well the answer.

"Yes, I don't know his name but I do know he was executed. Liam spent weeks after that randomly talking about it."

I didn't want to ask any further details. It was enough to confirm my instinct. "Ok, thanks."

As the waitress turned to head back to her post I called out, "One last thing, what happened to all the people who were supposed to attend tonight? No-one showed up."

She looked at the untouched settings on the tables and shrugged her shoulders with a smile then walked into the kitchen leaving me standing there with Liam or Bahrain or whom ever he was. I leant down to pick up his hand, which was hanging down. As I touched him I could feel the warmth of his flesh pulsing against the surface of my skin. It was a stark contrast to the cool of his touch when he had been conscious.

This whole new insight had my head reeling. I had no idea of what was happening and even less idea as to why but some pieces to the puzzle were falling into play while other concepts were now inexplicable again. Bahrain had said he recognized me. It's highly possible that he was present to witness Vernon's execution. There were several people in attendance who I have no doubt would not have forgotten what I look like after my performance. The way Bahrain's expression changed at hearing me say Vernon's name also made far greater sense. I could feel the pit of Bahrain's stomach churn and his face flush when I first said the words Vernon Wreath. Still it didn't explain anything else. The twists and turns of the day had been never ending. The only thing that was truly clear to me was anything is possible and all is never as it seems.

I took the cardigan off the back of Liam's chair folding it like a pillow and gently placed it under his head. This man was killing his guilt and pain one drink at a time. I'm not sure why he wasn't able to step up to looking after Lisa but I had no doubt the guilt of letting her be fostered out and learning of her suicide was the greater part of his choice to be an alcoholic. The whole situation was tragic. I could still recall the words in her note addressed to nobody at all. There was such an evolution of pain evoked from these interlayered experiences. It's difficult for me to see past the tragedy of what it is to feel any level of optimism. There was no bright side to look for in this nightmare.

There was clearly nothing more I could do tonight. Liam was heavily intoxicated and fast asleep. Just as I shifted to leave the waitress returned with two of the kitchen staff.

"Its time to get Liam home and off to bed. I need to finalise the register and lock up." She said with a smile.

I stepped aside so the men could gather him in their arms. "You mentioned he comes in every night. What time does he arrive and how long does it take before he becomes like this?"

"He tends to arrive just before the supper shift staff who begin at 5 pm and usually stays until closing. On a good day Liam can take a couple of hours before he spirals from tipsy to comatose and other days he wanders in already drunk."

"Thanks for letting me know." I took one last look at Liam as the two men struggled to stand him up. It was time for me to head back to the hotel to get some sleep. I knew there was a need to collect my thoughts but first I had to rest. This day had been one of relentless emotional demands.

# Alternate Perspectives

The sun was shining through the stitch line of the thick curtains. Slowly I stretched my body while yawning as I turned to my right to see what the time was. The digital clock just ticked over to display a quarter to nine. It had been a long time since I had more than eight hours sleep let alone done so all the way through. Ever since I was a child I would toss and turn at night waking several times throughout. It was rare for me to have unbroken sleep. I must have needed it.

After my shower I sat on the small balcony overlooking the street below to drink my freshly brewed cup of coffee. It was a simple pleasure I enjoyed once a day. I placed my feet on the table and leaned back in my chair while I thought about everything that had happened. There was so much to process, some of it surreal, while others seemed fated or perhaps just coincidental. How could I be sure of anything?

"Trust and follow your heart."

I turned so quickly, startled at the presence of his voice, I made my chair lose balance and slightly tip over. I used to hear his voice only in the forest and now it seems to be able to present itself anywhere. He is so crystal in his projection it feels as though he is right here. My question is '*Who is he?*'

In an unconscious moment I blurted out, "Who are you?" There was no response. I felt a little stupid. Perhaps I was going silently mad. Nothing seemed to be remotely normal. What was curious was my ability to accept so much of what had happened. I took it in my stride because there was a part of me that felt this to be normal. I have no way to explain it other than to say there was a distinct association of familiarity to all I had experienced.

I couldn't shake the thought about meeting Liam last night. The way he spoke at dinner under the guise of Bahrain held importance. Although the reality of the conversation would suggest two innocent people died because of Vernon's need to have access to me. I won't allow myself to feel guilt over it, regardless of whether it is real or otherwise. There's a difference between being actively conscious of circumstance versus oblivious. It was Vernon who chose the route not I. Even then his choice was a gamble, someone else could have easily been assigned to do his assessment. There was never a guarantee of my attendance. It was such a high profile case at the time; I was surprised I was even considered for the assignment.

Like a shock wave there was a sensation of heat pulsating an epiphany to my consciousness. I felt the rising of circumstantial clarity as I bit my bottom lip.

Actually, now that I think about it, being assigned as a rookie didn't even make sense. Countless seasoned colleagues were chomping at the bit for the opportunity and above all others I was selected. At the time I was so ambitious it never crossed my mind to consider what the hidden drivers were for me being nominated to execute the assessment. Could this have been part of the invisible veil of influence the interferons had?

"Yes."

I closed my eyes and shook my head using my mind to convey a message to the voice. *"I get it now. You only answer the questions set to guide on a particular thought path. Why should I trust you?"* I never received an answer but my heart skipped a beat and the thought trust was present in my own mind.

Large droplets of rain hit my leg as the skies opened up to a sudden torrential downpour. Today's overcast dark looming gray clouds were a stark contrast to the warmth of the previous day. I shifted closer to the entrance to the balcony but the bouncing droplets were still crashing onto me at a rate of knots. It was time to retreat inside. As I entered I left the door ajar, so the scent of rain could waft in on the back of the cool breeze.

If the weather settles later I'll go hiking in the forest again but for now I altered my plans to remain in my hotel room to continue to read York's story. Although my mind felt as though it had reached a level of saturation there was an urge to continue past the point of reason for it was there that I felt I would find the answers to questions I was yet to pose. I held images in my mind of all the components of significance in my life placed together neatly forming an evolving surreal image that would rival Salvador Dali's perceived senility.

I fluffed up the pillows then propped them in a bundle before nestling myself against them. Placing the book on my bended knees I thumbed through to locate the last page I had read.

*Opening my eyes I realised I was laying in a bed. Immediately I flung my arms up in response to the thought* that I may be restrained. Fists taught and light as feathers they raised above me lifting the sheets with them releasing a waft of warm stale air. A sense of relief washed over my body as I placed my arms back by my side. I shifted my head slightly to look around the full length of the enclosure. There was a small window placed up high delivering the suns blessed rays of filtered light. The first thing I visually welcomed was the absence of bars. Slowly I readjusted my body to prop myself up. There was something about the energy of this place, which made me feel safe.

On the bedside table a jug of clean water and some fruit had been nicely placed. I couldn't believe my eyes. Convinced it was a trick I grabbed the apple suspiciously inspecting every inch of its skin before I greedily took my first bite. I couldn't recall the last time I had one. The juice trickled down the outside of my mouth as I listened to the crunching noise echoing in my head. I took another bite before finishing the last. I didn't want to savor the experience in case someone came in and tried to take it away from me. You see that is what I had been reduced to. An opportunist and pessimist intermixed into one very unhappy person. I no longer held faith that my family would come for me. I knew by the way my mother was crying she had been lead to believe I was dead. I guess given how I felt inside it wasn't really a lie.

I ate every bit of the apple including the core. Given where my pallet had been forced to venture I would never take food for granted ever again. My legs were stiff as I swiveled them over the edge of the bed to sit up. I didn't bother pouring a glass of water, instead I drank straight from the jug. The sensation of the liquid travelling down my gullet was extraordinary. It was delicious. I didn't remove the jug from my lips until the last of the contents greeted my tongue.

Almost instantly I felt better but was clearly still very

*weak. The muscles on my legs had wasted away. Gently I placed my feet on the ground to prepare myself to stand. I wanted to see what was behind the screen in the corner of the room. Fumbling across slowly I began to regain my balance. Placing one foot in front of the other I walked toward the divider. My heart was palpitating so hard my head hurt as the anxiety began to build. I paused for a moment trying to gain the courage to look behind the barrier. Peering at the space I was surprised to see a toilet. It was clean and there was toilet paper neatly stacked beside it. Unexpectedly my legs gave way as I fell to my knees where I spontaneously burst into tears. I'm not sure why this moment drove my wall of emotional expression to break nor was I expecting it. Saline droplets rolled down my face while I heaved in gasps releasing acres of pain, which had been trapped within my frozen body for my lifetime. I couldn't have stopped myself even if I had tried and I didn't want to. I needed this.*

Wow, I was not expecting York to have the capability of outward expression. I thought he possessed a condition limiting his ability to demonstrate emotion. This changes everything for him. The fact that he is able to cry, releasing tears has enormous healing powers for the dear soul. I had been secretly so concerned for his body's ability to hold onto so much with no outlet. If there isn't a channel for release studies have now confirmed what natural healers of the world always knew, bottled emotions are a breeding ground for disease. Emotional rot was the phrase coined by the man who discovered the visual trace markers of emotional impact in water studies. Images of polluted water exposed to prayer altered the state of the water. There were thousands of images capturing the transformation of water when exposed to words of both positive and negative connotations.

This was a novel discovery until Dr. Cromlin Loust had the foresight to extend the research into the behavior of human blood. The premise being our bodies are made of an average of 65% water it therefore stands to reason that all emotional influence on the water would have a lasting impact on our effectiveness to function. It was Cromlin who identified the negative water marker patterns in the human body, which were later discovered to be the foundation of many terminal illnesses people face today. I felt relieved for York. This is a fabulous sign.

*It seemed like hours had passed as I continued to cry. The flood of memories, the horror of what I had endured was reefing at my insides in a steady stream of overflowing tears. I howled recklessly out loud with the freedom of my newly discovered voice. I no longer paid mind to the fact that I may draw unnecessary attention to myself by the evils looming outside the confines of these walls. I could finally hear myself, no longer an inner voice but an actual sound projecting machine. I wasn't certain when my tears made the conversion from exalt of pain to an assembalance of joy for the freedom of release I felt in the experience. I just knew that it did.*

*The shadows on the walls caught my eye as they moved. It was caused by something intermittently distorting the light sifting through the window. I could feel my eyelids get heavier as I set myself the task of getting back into bed. I managed to acquire muscle cramps in both my legs due to the position I maintained after I fell. I didn't notice it was cutting off my circulation until I tried to move, only to be greeted with a sensation of tingled riddling. It was as though a billion worms were eagerly scampering under my skin. There was no hope of me attempting to walk so I opted to drag myself across the floor. When I got close enough to the edge of the bed I propped myself into a sitting position stretching out my legs jiggling them to hasten the blood flow.*

*There was a moment of peace within the silence of everything, which rebirthed my sense of hope. I wanted to believe the worst of all my experiences were over, that I could finally be left to follow my own course to establish a sense of self and identify my place in the world. My thoughts were distracted by the sound of footsteps. Involuntarily my body started to shake as I urinated on myself. I looked down at the yellow watery stain appearing through my white pants soaking up the moisture. As the door handle turned I realized it wasn't locked. No key had been used. If only I had thought to try open it I could have escaped. Where was I?*

*A relief washed over me as I saw my Adeline enter the room.*

*"York are you ok? You poor dear, you're shaking," She said placing what she had in her hands on the bed and rushing to my aid. Adeline positioned my arm around her neck while putting the other around my back. I shifted my legs as I felt her lifting me to allow myself to prop on the edge of the bed. I placed both my hands on either side of the mattress gripping it for balance while I sat looking down at my stained pants.*

*"It's okay, I have a fresh pair for you. We can change you out of those and give you a little wash so you are feeling fresh again." She said with her angelic voice.*

*"I'm pleased to see you have had something to drink and eaten. That's good, York. You need to get your strength up."*

*I remained still and only moved when Adeline gestured for me to do so. I wasn't sure where I had been housed but I was so glad that she was here with me. Once I was washed and dressed she brushed my hair and then asked me to get back into bed. She refilled the jug with clean water* and placed an apple, orange, two chunks of bread and some cheese on the side table.

"This will need to last you until tomorrow evening. I'm going to have to work all day so I won't get a chance to return until after dark. It's important that you stay in the room. Do you understand?"

My eyes diverted to look at the exit.

"York, no going out the door. It would cost you your life. It could cost me mine too. I've risked everything to help you. Please stay inside the room and keep as quiet as you can. When the time is right I will get you out of here, out of this place. You just need to trust me and remain in this room where you are hidden from the others."

I looked at the frown lines on Adeline's brow as she stared into my eyes. I blinked to acknowledge her request and released an exhale. In truth I was glad to stay here. This place was nice and afforded me the sanctuary I had craved ever since I entered Greyhaven.

"Thank you." She whispered raising the sheets and blanket up to my chin to tuck me in.

I closed my weary eyes as I listened to Adeline read the adventures of Huckleberry Finn. My mind embraced the ideals of the freedom afforded to the characters in the book. I drifted off to sleep feeling nurtured and safe.

The days melted into one another as I remained within the confines of these walls. Adeline came to visit every day providing me with supplies. The greatest part of her attendance was the lessons she started to give me in reading, writing, arithmetic and a myriad of other teachings. She told me of the outside world, the things I needed to stay away from and how to find assistance when required. It was exciting times for me as I embraced the stimulus of learning. In her absence there wasn't much to do so I practiced *everything she taught me. Adeline was always seemingly impressed with my advancements but I knew it was her support and encouragement, which aided my leverage. In secret I spent time pronouncing the words I had learnt to strengthen my voice. Regardless of my growing vocabulary and capacity to speak I still never felt the compulsion to do so with others. I just liked knowing I could.*

*Teaching me to read and write was the greatest gift ever bestowed upon me. I consumed all the books Adeline provided. My appetite for words became insatiable. It all began with novels like Peter Pan, The tale of Peter Rabbit and built up to A room with a view and the Scarlet Pimpernel. When I wasn't reading my mind was reeling in imagining of adventures. Paper was a scarce commodity and the chalk board Adeline gave me to practice on was too small for the thoughts overflowing in my brain, so I began to use the tiny lead pencil I had been given to capture thoughts on the walls. It was a marvelous time in my life.*

This was the first time I could feel the elation in York's story. I don't know why I felt so grateful to Adeline for watching over York. I have never been big on labels but would lean towards classifying her as his guardian angel. Perhaps she was compelled to assist him because he was so young. Their connection held curiosity for me. I liked the feel of their energy together. In a world where York was overlooked Adeline saw something in him worth saving.

*When I ran out of wall space I started writing on the floor. There was no stopping my thoughts and need to express them. Adeline knew my restlessness was growing as I quickly headed towards filling every available space with words.*

*In more recent times there had been a few nights when she didn't come to visit. It wasn't often but when she* did return her demeanor wasn't quite the same. I knew something had caused her absence and it made her unhappy. I could read the sadness in her eyes that her smile tried to guard. Initially I let it be but the increased frequency of occurrence had me concerned. Doubts crept into my mind allowing for negative thoughts to swill. Was she tired of me?

I was asleep one night when Adeline came into my room. The light from the moon shone on her face revealing trails of glisten where her tears had made a pathway of escape from her eyes. In silence she crawled into my bed pressing her body against mine as she reached across to find my hand. I could feel the exhale of her shaking breath on my neck.

"Listen to me York. I need to make plans to move you from here so that you are free. I wanted to have more time to prepare you but I can't anymore. If we get caught all of this would have been for nothing. Are you listening?"

I squeezed her hand as silent tears rolled down my face.

"I've been searching for your family. York, there are things you need to know. I have to tell you so you don't feel compelled to go searching. Your father has died in jail. There was an epidemic of typhus. He was one of many who didn't make it. Your mother was taken too suspected of acquiring a disease called syphilis. I managed to reach your brother Joshua, we were to meet the night before last but he never presented. The local news papers reported yesterday that a mine collapsed. Many of the men were trapped. The article stated few of the people survived, most of them are severely injured while the remainder were listed as confirmed fatalities. His name was on that list. I'm sorry York." She whispered as she released sobs.

I thought about my other brother and sisters. Did they know all of this? Life seemed to be a never ending spiral of tragedy and sadness. Still I knew the tears that were *falling in this moment were for Adeline. I could hear the desperation in her voice, a sense of urgency as though we were running out of time. I squeezed her hand tight as my own tears slid down soaking my pillow.*

*"I know York, I know." She said in response to my tightened grip.*

*We lay there for the longest time in silence. When Adeline managed to recompose herself she imparted the outline to her plans for my escape from Greyhaven. I listened intently, knowing my life would depend on the accuracy of execution. Finally she slipped into my hand a map and some money before alighting from the bed. Adeline placed a bag filled with apples on the side table.*

*"I got them from the orchard across the way. It's not much but it will keep you going until you get to where I have told you to go. Please York, when you are outside of these walls don't stop. Keep going until you find where you belong. Promise me you will never stop, no matter what. You must promise."*

*I sat up and looked into her eyes. "Yes." I whispered.*

*Adeline cupped her mouth with her hands as she gasped, "You spoke." Tears once again flowed from her eyes as they did from mine. She stretched out her hand to touch my cheek, "You dear, sweet soul."*

*A look of horror landscaped my face when I saw the trail of bite marks on Adeline's arm. I grabbed her hand pulling the length of her sleeve back to reveal black, purple bruising and deep teeth indentations. Adeline quickly retracted her arm placing her sleeve back down.*

*Wiping the tears from her face she transformed to a hardened expression, "Pay no heed to this York. You have to go. When I leave get dressed in the fresh clothes I just brought in. Here are some shoes too. They might be a little big but it*

*just means you can grow into them. Take the bag of apples,
the map and money and quietly get out of here. Remember,
follow the path down the length of the passage just as I told
you and stay on course. Don't stop you hear me, no matter
what, don't stop."*

*As soon as I nodded my head to acknowledge her words
she turned and walked out the door. I didn't know it at the
time but this was the last time I would ever see Adeline in
this life. She had made plans for herself that were hinged on
my escape being a success.*

It made me sick to the stomach to entertain Adeline
being subjected to the same treatment York and so many
others had received. There was ingrained helplessness
to the situation. The decrepit thrived freely subjecting
repetitive sexual and mental abuse with no recourse. How
was this possible? Life once again demonstrated that it
was a far cry from fair. In a world where your childhood
ideals were interlaced in the promotion of fairy tales and
happy endings there seemed to be none afforded here. All
I saw was interlayered tragedy upon fucking tragedy.

Adeline was clearly protecting York. I'm leaning
toward her being subjected to tolerating the abuse
because she was being coerced. I couldn't see why else she
would be voluntarily exposing herself to such monstrous
acts. The perpetrators had to have something on her. She
mentioned the apples were from a neighboring orchard.
I wonder if the attendants caught her stealing food like
the bread and cheese from the kitchen. Surely if they
knew where York was he would have been reclaimed.
I'm leaning toward her being caught in the act of taking
something, which was then used as leverage in exchange
for allowance of deprived sexual favors. If she had been
turned in and fired there would be no ability for her to

assist York. What a precarious position she was placed in. Her decision to maintain her secret and succumb to the debauchery was a testament to how deeply connected she felt to York. The whole situation must have been completely soul destroying for Adeline.

Glancing out the window I could see the weather had settled. It was still overcast but the threatening rain clouds seemed to have shifted across in the distance. My mind was reeling; I decided to get dressed to go for a walk. I needed to clear my head. It was the first time in forever since I craved a cigarette. I had never been a full time smoker; I mostly binged when I felt low. It was a self-destructive habit for sure but it relaxed me. Rather than resort to indulging my weakness I purchased an apple at the corner store on my way to the park.

Entering the grand old cast iron gates of the city central botanical gardens I immediately starting looking for visual cues to lift my spirits. There was a person throwing a Frisbee to his manically happy dog. A mom jogged past pushing her pram with her little baby snuggled fast asleep. I watched the little children in the playground lining up for the slide. I prized seeing their excited expressions as they sat at the top about to take the journey down. It helped me find my breath again. I'm not sure why I continued to read the book. The impact of the story resonated so deeply with me, I almost felt as though I was there. All I knew was no matter what I had to see the book through else I might spend the rest of my life wondering, which was not a palatable option. I simply had to know what happened.

I followed the garden path around its twists and turns admiring the transition of landscape design. The flora was a truly spectacular display of texture, aroma and color. Even the man made lake was captivating with its giant reeds on one side creating a pseudo marshy swamp while the opposite side was dressed with hundreds of pink and white lotus flowers in bloom. The surface of the water had millions of ripples created as the thriving insect community broke the surface to feast on what lay below. I was in awe of how lovely this oasis was in the heart of the hustle and bustle of every day humdrum.

I spied a park bench positioned near the edge of the water canopied by a lovely oversized willow tree. There was a person in a tan trench coat sporting a caramel colored fedora who was leaning over throwing what looked like pieces of bread and seed out to the variety of water birds gathering for the feast. There was something about the serenity of the moment that made me wish I had bought my camera on the walk.

Unconsciously I found myself crossing the expanse of manicured lawn toward the bench. As I got closer I could see the swans had their babies by their side and one was snuggled hitching a ride on it's parents back. There were small black water birds lunging forward to grab a piece of the banquet and then quick as a flash turned flying into the water making a splashing entrance before guzzling their treat in perceived safety.

"Hello, it seems you have made yourself some friends." I said as I walked around to the front of the bench to sit down.

The man had prominent black rimmed glassed on, he didn't turn his head to make eye contact, instead he continued to throw handfuls of food from his brown paper bag in a rhythmic motion. "Hi, yes they do like a feed. I come here almost every day at the same time so they know what to expect when I arrive." He started to laugh as a large black swan boldly stepped forward and snatched a piece of bread straight out of his hand. "This fellow is the bossy one. He gets impatient when it comes to feed time. The trickster sometimes even tries to bite me."

I laughed.

Placing the bag on his knee he slowly removed his tan leather glove then extended his hand out to me. "I'm Liam."

I was shocked to realize it was indeed Liam. He looked so different I didn't recognize him in glasses and cleanly shaven. "Hi Liam I'm Harper, Pleased to meet you."

Liam shook my hand and laughed, "The expression on your face would suggest otherwise. Its like you've seen a ghost."

"Sorry, Its just you looked like someone I know. Have you heard of a person called Bahrain?"

Liam shook his head, "No, should I?"

"No, I guess not. If I didn't know better I would suggest he was your doppelganger."

"Really? Wow I've never had one of those before." He said releasing a big hearty laugh.

Watching him I felt bemused by his vibrancy of presence. It held my curiosity. "You seem really cheerful in contrast to this gloomy weather were having today."

Liam paused for a moment to reflect on my words. "It's been a long time since I've felt any semblance of happiness. I guess you have met me on a good day."

"I'm glad it's a good day. Do you know what the difference is today to any other day?"

"No, should I?" Asked Liam cheekily raising an eyebrow.

"I guess what I was alluding to is if you know what makes today a better day than most perhaps the knowledge of this trigger could be used to assist you to shift from a looming state of melancholy."

"Are you a psychologist?"

"Yes, of sorts. Guilty as charged. I specialize in the field of cognitive science."

He frowned at me and turned to gaze to the lake, "I don't believe in psychology."

"What do you believe in?"

"Yesterday I would have told you my answer was I believe in nothing at all."

"Okay, and today what do you believe in," I asked.

"One word, faith."

"Wow, you transitioned overnight from feeling hopeless to hopeful? It's a major leap. Do you have any idea why you experienced this paradigm shift?"

"No. I honestly can't tell you. I woke up this morning feeling different. My desire to annihilate myself through alcohol was absent. I was motivated to shower and shave. Removing my overgrown beard felt ritualistic. It was like I was granting myself a clean slate. A new beginning."

"I'm happy for you. This is wonderful. I hope it lasts." Given he already indicated his disdain for psychoanalysis I didn't want him to feel I was subjecting him to assessment, so I kept my response light.

"Me too," said Liam as he placed his glove back on and recommenced feeding the birds.

"Well, I'm going to continue exploring these wonderful gardens. Thank you for the honest chat Liam. Look after yourself." I said as I rose to stand.

Liam adjusted his body position so his knees were pointing in my direction as he looked up at me, "I'm not usually this open. Thanks for showing an interest. You take care too."

"You're welcome Liam. I will indeed take care. Bye." I said as I turned to head on my way.

"Bye."

Walking along the path I could feel my heart lift in spirits as the thought of Liam's laughter echoed in my mind. There was a level of accountability I felt towards him and what happened to his family. Understanding I'm not responsible and knowing I was the cause held a burden, which I never asked to carry yet it sat heavily on my shoulders. In theory if I never existed then the situation would not have happened, by the mere nature of this thought process it stands to reason there is some contribution unintentional or otherwise which is apportioned to me. Seeing Liam clean shaven feeling better and speaking of faith inadvertently assisted me too.

Ah Bahrain, Bahrain, Bahrain, what an interesting evening that was. In my dream last night it was his piercing pale blue eyes peering out from the shadows, which lured me deeper into my labyrinth of thoughts. It made me wonder about the old saying *'the eyes are the windows to the soul.'* If Liam wasn't pretending and Bahrain did exist as an entity, then the possession in the absence of a better description, which had taken place may have caused his eyes to alter color to align with the soul present. The ice cold hands when he touched me were also an anomaly related to Bahrain and not Liam. Multiple personality disorder seemed a more plausible explanation for what had happened. Liam's alcoholic abuse, depression and extreme stress in trying to manage the realities of his life could have prompted the creation of Bahrain as a coping mechanism. Yet it didn't explain the color change of his eyes and the ice in his touch. I had to accept I wasn't going to find all the answers; instead I would need to move forward embracing these experiences with an untainted mind and an open heart. There were so many elements of yesterday's journey stimulating my consciousness to the viability of miracles.

I paused to appreciate the monkey puzzle tree. This and the boab had always been particular favorites of mine. My eyes ran up the column of the tree's trunk and extended to assess all the visible branches. Oh, how I would have dearly loved to climb up this tree to sit on its arm, rest against the trunk and simply let the world below dissipate. I was happy to ignore the do not climb signs but there was no bypassing the large metal sheath wrapped around the trunk to deter people from a successful attempt. I would have to settle with the privilege of sitting underneath its canopy for the rest of the afternoon while I read.

There was a spot where the earth happened to have a natural indentation the size of my bottom. Sitting there while leaning against the trunk of the tree felt like a comfy armchair, albeit the bark on the trunk was a bit rough. Just before I opened the book to begin my journey with York again I visually inhaled the vista to get my mind cleansed in preparation.

*I sat on the edge of my bed with my eyes closed listening to the sound of Adeline's footsteps fading into the distance. She had only been gone a few minutes and already my heart missed her. It was in this moment for the first time I felt truly alone. A part of me wanted to stay here just so I could remain close to Adeline but I knew the cost of doing so was a price too high to pay for both of us. Those bite marks on her arm were set to haunt me forever.*

*Judging by the change in the light outside I only had three hours at the most before day break. I knew my best chance was to leave now. I quickly placed my new clothes on.*

*The pants were too big for me but the suspender belts held them in place. When I slipped on the shoes I smiled because they were oversized just as Adeline had suggested. I loved that she knew me so well. In the midst of gathering the remainder of my things together I took one last look at the walls with all my writing. I had been in this room for over a year and in Greyhaven for just over two.*

*As I walked toward the door I could feel my hands trembling. Overwhelmed by thoughts of possibly never seeing Adeline again I was awash with a sense of urgency that surged through me like an electric pulse. I wasn't ready to leave with so many words unspoken between us. She never gave me a chance. Reaching underneath the bed I pressed the palm of my hand hard up against the section, which had a crack in it. The sharp point tore my flesh open. I could feel the warmth of the blood pooling to the surface, by the time I lifted my hand up it was already dripping on the floor. Using the blood as ink I collected some on my finger and wrote a message for Adeline on the wall. Upon completion I stood back and looked at my translucent red masterpiece. Tears rolled down my cheeks as I stared at the words I always wanted to say but never did, 'I love you Adeline. York'*

*My hand was throbbing from the wound but it was nothing compared to the sting in my heart. I placed my belongings on my shoulder and left the room without a backward glance. Skulking down the hallway I passed a series of doors. I kept hearing her words encouraging me to not stop, no matter what don't stop. The length of the passage was coming to an end. Adeline had told me there was a break in the wall large enough for me to crawl out to freedom. It left me placed on the south side of the building close to where the property bridged with the neighboring apple orchard. It was the only section of the estate, which didn't have fencing.*

*I could cross over and head down to the stream to walk its edges until I found the markers she placed on the map for me to follow. Getting closer to the end of the hall I could taste the cool fresh breeze whistling through the opening.*

*It was just as Adeline had described. I got down on my hands and knees to align myself with the largest section of the hollow. I tossed my bag out first and then proceeded to crawl. My heart was beating so loud I could feel my pulse on my neck jumping. Then I heard a sound, which made the fine hairs on the back of my chilled neck stand further on end. It was an echo of a elongated whimpering moan. I paused to try and establish whether it was coming from outside or in. The thumping in my head was distorting my ability to make a clear determination.*

*I know Adeline urged me not to stop but I was compelled to investigate. The noise sounded distressed, someone needed help. Quietly I walked to the door closest to where I was. Silently I stood on the outside waiting for the sound to recommence. When it started again I checked all the doors until I identified the one, which I was certain, contained the noisemaker. My body was trembling as I reached for the handle. Cautiously I entered the room being first greeted with the detection of a significant drop in temperature and a faint unpleasant smell. The lamp in the far corner was flickering intermittently. When my eyes adjusted to the dancing light I could see shadows cast on rows of jars. Walking closer to them revealed contents my eyes wished they had never laid upon. Tiny babies suspended in liquid, some had been cut in half so you could see their insides. One jar had a baby with feet sown where its arms should be and visa versa. Rows of body parts suspended in fluids neatly stacked and labeled. I leaped in the air as I bumped into a tray, which consequently fell to the floor making a large crashing noise. It had surgical tools still stained with blood.*

*My eyes widened with the realization that there were human bodies on the tables before me cut wide open. The stench must have been awful in the room but my sense of smell had not been right ever since I was trapped in the dank room. Picking up the lamp I shone it over the open empty chest cavity of the person closest to me. His skin had been peeled and pinned to wooden edging on the table. Altering the position of the light I recognised the carcass on the next table was Orvel, the man who urinated every day and laughed when people stepped in it. The top of his head had been sawn off, his brain removed. Orvel's eyes were sunken into his skull and there was something black protruding from his mouth.*

*I spun around as I heard a groaning sound come from the right far corner of the room. It was too dark to see anything over there. Fishing around on the floor I found a couple of sharp edged tools. I placed them in my pocket and proceeded to walk over to where the noise had come from. As I crept closer I could hear quick shallow breaths being taken. My eyes began to adjust to the darkness enough to see there were things moving about.*

*"Yelp"*

*I jumped back and held my heart as it raced to escape my chest from the fright. I had stepped on a dog. He was laying down with his hind leg pinned to the ground by a metal rod. A scuttling noise just above him caught my attention. It was the familiar sound of rats. Avoiding the dog, this time when I stepped forward I realized attached to the wall was a series of cages. Inside there were rabbits and in others these little creatures I had not seen before. They were the size of a rat with stubby noses, they didn't have a tail and their bodies were rotund.*

Fumbling around I found the latch to the cages and one by one unlocked them all. I took off the coat jacket Adeline had given me to pile all of these creatures inside. I stacked them as high as I could and then filled my pockets with the remaining little fellows to prevent them from running about. All the critters leapt out in different directions when I placed my jacket down outside. A select few tried to re-enter Greyhaven. I had managed to grab each of them, lightly tossing them away to discourage any further attempt to go back inside. When the last of the critters were out of sight I returned to assist the dog.

Using all my strength I tried to remove the rod from the ground. It didn't matter how hard I pulled it wouldn't shift. The only way I was going to be able to release him was to lift his body while sliding his leg up and off the rod at the same time. I got down on all fours to inspect his wound. I could see by the way it was healing around the structure that he had clearly been in this position for a considerable amount of time. The dog lifted his head up to look at me. He released a tiny breathless whimper and then dropped his head. I couldn't see any alternate way to release him. Dragging his leg up the full length of the pole would be his painful price for freedom.

Prior to attempting to shift him I shut the door to the room. I knew I ran the risk of drawing attention to myself when the dog most assuredly started crying out in pain. Gently I crouched down sliding one arm under the length of his body. I didn't know whether doing it fast or slow would be best. The dog lifted his head to lick the side of my face a couple of times before dropping it down again. I placed my other arm across this torso and used my hand to close his mouth. It was safer for the both of us if he didn't make too much noise. I drew a deep breath and sprung to my feet *lifting the dog above my head so the leg was forced to rise higher than the rod.*

*The poor fella released muffled high pitched whimpers while it was happening and then went limp. He had lost consciousness. I cradled him securely in my arms as I quietly walked toward the escape route. Poking my head out the hole I peered left and right to ensure it was clear. The night sky was rapidly becoming lighter so it would be a matter of no time before daybreak was due. I lay the dog down outside and then crawled through gaining my true first taste of freedoms air. I could never begin to quantify in words what inhaling the first few breaths felt like. It was a moment I would always treasure and one of the greatest gifts anyone had ever given me. I paused to place my hand on the stonewall. There were many horrors contained within but it also graced me with the blessed meeting of Adeline. She was the greatest gift of my life.*

*My jacket had been soaking up the dew from the ground while hosting a couple of those strange little critters nestled neatly in the folds. They scuttled away as I picked it and my bag up from the ground. After I put my jacket on I carefully lifted the dog above my head so I could place him across my shoulders leaving his legs to straddle my neck. Once I was clear of Greyhavens grounds I shifted my momentum to a brisk pace. The sooner I reached the riverbed the better. I wanted to wash the dog's wound before he woke up to save him from experiencing any more pain.*

"What are you reading?"

"Harper, hello."

I looked up a bit dazed, "Oh Hi Liam, I'm sorry I was so engrossed in my book I didn't hear you calling."

Liam was walking towards me with a lovely calm smile on his face. He looked younger without his beard.

"I was asking you what you are reading?" He said as he crouched down to looked at the open book resting on my knees.

I smiled wondering how to respond given he was viewing what appeared to be blank pages.

"Wow, how can you even read that? The words are so faded its not even legible." Said Liam turning the book so it faced the right way for him.

"You can see the writing?"

Liam looked at me and laughed, "Of course but it might as well be a blank page. I can't even make out a single word. No wonder you were concentrating so hard. Why are you bothering to try and read this? Does it unfold the secrets of the universe?"

I smiled as I reclaimed my book and closed it, "Something like that."

"Well perhaps you could join me for a coffee. I would love to hear all about it." Liam stood back up and extended his hand to help me to my feet. He was actually presenting as rather charming. I accepted his hand and graciously rose to stand beside him.

"Do you have a preference of where we go Harper?"

"I'm not from this area, I've only come for the long weekend so I have no idea of where the hip coffee houses are located."

Liam extended his folded arm as a gesture for me to grab it and said, "Then allow me to show you."

I picked up my bag, packed the book safely inside and took Liam's arm. "Why thank you kind sir."

The coffee house Liam took me to had created a totally unique interior layout. It was a daring clash between 60's retro, bohemian chic and a mish mosh of antiques sprinkled about the place. Each wall was a different vibrant color with an eclectic selection of art displayed in no particular order. It felt to me like a designers fine line between genius and madness. I really enjoyed the visual entertainment of everything in there.

When the waitress placed us at our table I couldn't wipe the smile off my face as I laid eyes on the orange lava lamp centerpiece.

"This place is fabulous. I love the madness of it all. From the moment we entered I could feel myself become visually hyper stimulated."

"I know I was watching as you looked around. You had the expression of wonder rarely seen on adults but exists naturally with children." Said Liam.

"I didn't realize I made it so obvious but yes, this place is marvelous. Thanks for bringing me here."

"They make great coffee and are known for their cakes so this should be an all round treat."

"Sounds perfect." I said as my stomach started to grumble at the suggestion of food. My intake for the day had been a partial coffee and an apple on the way to the park.

The waitress returned with the menus and a carafe of water for the table. I looked at the impressive cake selection feeling it would be impossible to choose. They all sounded spectacular.

"I can recommend the pecan pie, lemon tart, lemon meringue and the Danish triple creamed cheese cake." Said Liam peering over his menu at me.

"Seriously I haven't eaten all day and this variety is insane. I thought I would be hard pressed to choose but now that I've read it a second time I'm gravitating between the pear frangipani tart or the caramel soufflé with home made hazelnut and vanilla ice cream."

"Order both."

"Ha, one is indulgent enough." I said wondering if I should flip a coin to let fate make the decision for me.

The waitress returned with pen and pad in hand.

"Hi, I'II have a strong Americano and a slice of the pear frangipani tart please."

"I'II have the same coffee, a serve of the Danish triple creamed cheese cake and two caramel soufflé with home made hazelnut and vanilla ice cream, thanks."

I burst out laughing, "No, we can't eat all of that. It's too much."

Liam raised an eyebrow, "What do you mean 'we' I ordered all of that for myself."

The waitress collected the menus off the table, "Is there anything else?"

"No, we're fine." Responded Liam

As the waitress was walking away Liam unfolded the garish lime green linen napkin and placed it on his lap. Prompted by his actions I followed suit.

"So tell me about this book. The writing is faded so I am assuming it is aged. Have you been able to decipher any of the words?"

"I don't know when it was written. I'm still unsure if it's a work of fiction or someone's memoirs of a life written in fiction form rather than a diary. It flitters between past and present tense and uses terminology you wouldn't usually expect from this particular main character. I'm leaning toward this book being created by a person who wanted to write a memoir of sorts later in life. He does it in a variety of styles. It feels to me as though he is capturing the retrospective journey as though he was living it again."

"Wow, a simple answer of yes or no would have sufficed." He said in a jest.

I chuckled, "Yes, I am able to read the words."

"What's the story about?"

"Its primarily focused on a teenagers life experience in the late 1920's early 1930's era. The family becomes financially destitute which forces them all to be split up. York the main character is severely introverted which provides him a one way ticket into an Asylum. After two years in there he is about to escape."

"Sounds rather intense for a weekend getaway read."

I smiled at Liam's comment and nodded my head in agreement; "The book has been a very emotional journey for me."

"I still can't believe you are able to read anything. The writing is so faint."

"I have magic eyes," I said as I pulled a cross eyed funny face.

Liam released an unexpectedly loud laugh causing a few people to glance.

I just shook my head and chuckled. It was so nice to experience his joy. Liam had a lovely disposition and a definite charisma.

The waitress arrived with our coffees and first round of cakes. My mouth started salivating at the site of this delicious looking tart. The Danish cheesecake was presented beautifully with a snowflake pattern created using dusted icing sugar.

"The soufflés will take forty-five minutes to an hour for it to be cooked, cooled and served as they're made to order." She announced.

Liam picked up his fork to get a piece of his cake. In a cheerful tone he said, "I guess we will have to eat slow or order an in-betweener while we're waiting."

The waitress simply smiled and left without making

comment.

"Tell me Harper, is there anything about this book you enjoy?"

"I guess to me it's a challenge to read it. I find most of the experiences described tax me emotionally. The contention orbits around me maintaining focus on understanding what causes me so much angst. I've never lived a fraction of the horrors this child has been subjected to and yet I feel directly impacted. York is not able to express himself so at times I almost find myself compelled to be his channel for emotional release. In my life I have read thousands of books and none have evoked so much from me. It's as though I need to be part of his journey. This associated connection is what drives me to read the book to the end."

"It definitely seems like you have found the book of a lifetime."

"What do you mean?" I said as I took the first bite of my tart.

"The book of a lifetime is that one books ability to touch you deeply. It is so profound to you personally you feel as though it was written for you and is fated to be a part of you. Every reader is on the search for the 'one' story that speaks to their soul."

"I've never heard the phrase before. I like it."

"How's the tart?" Asked Liam

"Here try a piece it is really delicious." I shifted my plate so he could reach.

"Only if you try some of mine. I want to know what you think."

We both sampled each other's dessert.

"I feel like I just ate a mouthful of decadent sin." I said amazed at how yummy it tasted.

Liam laughed as he leant in to protect the rest of his cake, "I will defend it to my death."

I smiled at his expressive playfulness, "What's the verdict on the tart?"

"Truly lovely. They really do excel when it comes to sweets. It's what attracts a large percentage of their patrons to return."

"The café's name makes sense now, Guilty Pleasures. My first thought when I read the signage was the coffee house is used as a cover for the hidden boudoir with decadent ladies and gentlemen for hire in the back." I said giving him a wink.

"I love that you mentioned both sexes. Most people would only reference women."

"I'm the type of person who likes to ensure no one misses out." I said with a cheeky smile while slowly taking a sip of my coffee.

"I like you Harper. You're an interesting person," said Liam staring into my eyes.

"Thanks, Liam." I tried to keep my response casual to ensure he understood I wasn't interested in him romantically. I could sense his growing attraction in the subtleties of his demeanor. It was important in his fragile state that I didn't accidentally lead him astray.

"You mentioned this character York is about to escape. How has that left you feeling?" Prompted Liam.

I was glad he went back to referencing the book. This change of topic provided me with confirmation he understood I was not open to romantic interest. "Actually this is a good question. I have no doubt most people would feel relieved, uplifted by the thought of York escaping. I'm glad he is heading towards his entitlement to freedom but there are things he has done in the course of this which has left me disheartened. It's a perfect example of how people don't consider the consequences of their actions."

"I'm not following."

"Let me explain, a lady had hidden York in what I would suggest was an unused section of the asylum. I'm assuming the other staff were lead to believe York had passed away. This woman feeds him, educates him to read, write, do arithmetic and so on. There comes a point where she is being subjected to physical abuse by other staff for reasons yet to be known. This stimulates the urgency for York to escape sooner than she had planned. The woman was adamant he adhere strictly to her escape instructions, emphasizing the importance of not stopping for anything. Understandably, York is feeling distressed by the idea of separating from a person he has grown to love. Feeling overwhelmed by this need to tell her he writes a message on the wall. The mistakes start when he places his and her names on the message. If anyone ventures into the room for any reason and sees this they will know York is alive and Adeline is connected to him. The second mistake as I see it was his compulsion to stop and look inside one of the rooms in the institution. It was a lab of horror containing mutilated human carcasses and animals in cages, which I assume, were used in non-sanctioned medical experimentation. York set all the animals free. Once again his actions draw attention to 'someone' interfering. Whether this can be tied back to York or Adeline is yet to be seen."

"It all seems obvious when you say it but I agree people aren't trained to think with a broader scope about their actions." Liam said nodding his head.

"To me, life has always been best depicted by the

game of chess. To truly embrace the fullness of living a person must be engaged in strategy, direction and environmental consideration. I may enter the game with a particular approach in mind but my strategy needs to adjust to counter balance my opponent's moves. Those who play the game by reaction more often than not tend to lose. Players who reevaluate the environment, consider all the options and pre-empt counter moves are better placed for success. The difference between a good player and the masters of the game, I believe, is the individuals ability to be lightening fast at not only considering what is presented before him or her but to also factor the best course of action at least three to five steps ahead, coupling this with the associated probabilities of counter attack combinations."

"I really like the analogy. These are the kinds of ideas people should be developing in schools to help mold the minds of new generations to think differently."

"It goes far deeper than the chess game. Chess is set on a black and white platform with a defined number of pieces, rules and moves. Life is filled with an infinite number of these and is the full colored spectrum interspersed with multilayered dark and light hues. Learning how to play chess well is to master the art of the rules. Learning how to embrace life and live to your utmost potential is about taking what you have mastered in the game and knowing when to break the rules. There's a lot to say about a persons ability to conceptually theorize versus real time application of the knowledge in any given circumstance."

"I think you need to stop reading books and consider writing one. This is truly fascinating. People need to have access to material stimulating them to think beyond fairy tales. Everything you've said makes sense. Its simple and complex."

I looked across at the remaining portion of his cake, "I'm not a writers ass, I wouldn't know where to start but I am an opportunist so I feel compelled to ask were you impressed enough to reward me with another share?"

Liam burst out laughing, "Sure, here you go. Unlike you, I have no issues with ordering another slice if I want one."

"Great then you're okay with me eating the rest of this." I said teasingly.

He squinted his eyes and watched me take a piece of the cake and then quick as a whip he snatched it back. "Mine, I tells ya."

I laughed, "Cute."

The waitress arrived with our piping hot Soufflés. We had been so engrossed in conversation I hadn't quite finished my tart. The presentation of the dessert was beautiful. The soufflé had its own circular multi colored porcelain container sitting on a larger oblong earthenware plate laden with small melon size scoops of ice cream stacked in the shape of a pyramid with fresh berries in between and what looked like a whisk of raspberry sauce on the side.

"Oh my, this is visually spectacular. Please tell the chef I think he's an artist." I said staring with delight at the masterpiece placed before me.

The waitress smiled, "I'll tell my husband. He will love hearing that. Thank you."

"You're welcome. Being married to him must be sweet, all sugar and spice." I said laughing at my own corny joke.

The waitress shook her head rolling her eyes as she smiled.

"I know, it's corny but when I see an opening I have to take it." I said cheekily ready to fling an array of other dumb lines my mind was creating.

"Let's just say it's all been said before."

I raised an eyebrow and looked at Liam, "This sounds like a challenge to me." I returned my gaze at her. "How about a little wager? I vouch before we leave this lovely establishment, Liam and I will create a sweet line you and your husband have never heard before."

"Oooo, I'm in on that," said Liam rubbing his hands together.

The waitress laughed, "Good luck. If you can come up with an original line before you leave today, I'll give you a voucher to return for a full banquet lunch on the house complete with unlimited dessert."

"Prepare to be astonished." I said waving a single finger in the air loving the idea of word play.

"Ok, I'll leave you to it. Enjoy your soufflé."

Turning back to Liam I said, "Well I guess we've got our work cut out for us." Instantly I was amused with the way he was staring at his dessert.

"Are you going to court it or eat it?" I asked releasing a laugh.

"Both, I'm in love."

"Yikes, you clearly use that term all too loosely." I said then clapped my hands to draw his attention. "Focus on coming up with a great line. We need to win."

Liam returned my gaze and raised his left eyebrow. "We? No way. I've got nothing. I'm counting on you to get me that free meal ticket Harper."

"Ha, yeah right. You will be contributing. There are no free rides in life, remember that!" I said picking up my dessert spoon and mercilessly scooping my first portion of the soufflé onto it. I raised the spoon as cheers to Liam prior to shoving it into my mouth. The flavor was heaven sent.

"Oh mercy that was brutal, I like it," he said while momentarily holding his hand against his heart. Then swift as a swallow to the swoop, he picked up his own dessert spoon and did the same.

"How good is it?" I asked as I started on the ice cream.

"I've never had a soufflé before. It is definitely worth the wait. The flavors are holding a symphony in my mouth."

"I think mine is developing a magnum opus." We both laughed and continued to unceremoniously consume our desserts.

It took less than eight minutes before I placed my spoon down and patted my stomach, "I inhaled it."

"Me too, I couldn't stop."

I lent in and with a masked serious expression said, "I know we haven't known each other long but I think we have become fast friends so if you agree I would like to have you be my wing man for something I need to do."

Liam studied my expression and then said in a serious tone, "Ok, Harper sure. What do you need me to do?"

"Make a distraction, I'm going in to lick the plate." I then, with a big smile on my face shamelessly picked up my plate to lick the remainder of the oozing melted ice cream.

Liam jumped from his chair waved his arms in the air and wiggled his bottom while calling out "Woop, woop .... Woop, woop .... Woop, woop" and then sat back down beaming with pride.

I burst out laughing to the point where I had tears in my eyes. "I said make a distraction not draw attention.

You may be the worst wing man ever." We both laughed not just because it was amusing but also because people were now staring at us.

Once we finally settled Liam took his napkin, folded the edge and reached across to wipe the tip of my nose. I glared at him and shook my head, "You mean to tell me I had ice cream on the tip of my nose this whole time and you never said anything."

He shrugged his shoulders, "Well I didn't want to be the only one who looked silly."

"Its official, you are the worst wing man ever." I said folding my arms pretending to be annoyed.

"I may be a bad wing man, no arguments from me, but there's no denying I am an exceptional fast friend." He said fishing for a compliment.

I paused and looked at him looking at me, "You are."

Liam immediately diverted his eyes to look at the napkin in his hand, "Thanks Harper, it actually means a lot to me."

"Don't get all mushy on me, we have a free lunch to earn. Let's hear what you have."

"Seriously I'm drawing blanks, you need to start while I think of some."

"Ok, but only because I'm adorable. Ha! Let me think … How about 'Marrying your sweet prince must have been the icing on the cake' or 'You must have known that you would have a great sex life because you knew before marrying him that he loved dessert.'"

"Oh, that's heading toward the gutter side of sweetness. Ok then how about; marrying him provided you with dessert in the bedroom and a prick in the kitchen."

"I love it. That's a classic. Playing on stereotypical Chefs with hotheaded tempers. Yes. See you not only can do it, you did it. First go, that's stellar. Well done you."

"Geez, I think I'm blushing. It was your prompts that got me started but thanks." He said fanning his face with the lime green napkin.

I looked at the empty plates on the table and the small portion of my tart that remained. "I'm stuffed, do you want the last piece of this tart?"

"God no, I haven't eaten this much in I don't know how long. First day recovering alcoholic remember?" He said pursing his lips.

I nodded my head. "I know you probably don't want advice and I certainly don't want to sound like I'm preaching but I really would like to say a few things with your permission."

"Tell me," he said.

"Set yourself up for success by putting some support mechanisms into play. Consider introducing alternative therapies to assist your body in the detox process. Meditation and yoga can relax the mind and strengthen your core while acupuncture is able to reduce cravings and assist the lymphatic system to flush toxins. The most important is to find some friends who can support you, connect and lift your spirits in times when you need to simply have a laugh. Whatever outlets you choose are fine, just find what they are and get them established."

He lent in looking directly into my eyes and said, "Thanks Harper, that's good advice. I appreciate it."

I smiled and nodded my head. Liam didn't say he would do it, he only chose to acknowledge my ideas were good advice. My instinct said to leave it as it stood. "Great, well I think its time to present the winning line to the waitress, settle the bill and get on with the rest of our respective days."

"Yes, let's." He said as he stood up, wiped his mouth with the napkin and theatrically threw it on the table.

I reached down and grabbed my bag and then stood up. Surveying the expanse of the room once more in appreciation of its manic vibrant design before heading to the front counter where Liam and I waited for the waitress to arrive.

"Harper."

I turned my head to the left to look at Liam, "Yes."

"Thanks for not pushing."

I smiled at Liam, "You're welcome."

The waitress saw us and flagged she was on her way. We watched as she finished clearing up a few empty tables before walking back towards us with a lovely smile on her face.

"Are you ready to hear the winning original line?"

She threw her head back as she released a big laugh, "One moment I'm just going to take these dishes to the kitchen. I will be right with you."

The swinging doors to the kitchen flung out as she reentered the room, "Ok I'm ready, let's hear it."

Liam looked at me and I gestured for him to do the honors.

He cleared his throat and straightened his posture, "Ok here it goes; marrying him provided you with dessert in the bedroom, a prick in the kitchen and an endless surplus of dishes to clean."

She placed her hands over her mouth as she laughed, "Oh my God you just described my marriage to perfection."

Liam threw his hands up in the air and did a jog on the spot wiggling his ass while I laughed.

"You added extras." I said poking Liam in the ribs.

"I know, I felt inspired and went with it." The

expression on his face was akin to a happy little boy. It was seriously sweet.

The waitress was still laughing. I knew it was a winner when I saw her smiling eyes releasing tears.

"So, what's the verdict?"

"You win, you win, Oh my Gosh, that's fantastic, you win, you win, you win. Hold on a moment I'm going to get a pen to write it down." She crouched below the counter to find a pen & paper. When she arose her hand was extended passing the items to Liam. He stopped doing his jig to capture the line.

I lent in and whispered loud enough so it could be heard, "Thank you for distracting him. I didn't know how much more I could take."

She chuckled.

Without altering his gaze Liam reached across and gently poked me in the ribs, "Careful or I'll do it in public while we're walking down the street."

"I'd love to tell you I'd like to see that, but seriously Liam I wouldn't." I replied.

The waitress had seemingly caught the giggles. Everything we said made her laugh uncontrollably. It was cute.

Once the sentence was given life in print we settled the bill and left Liam's details as a reference in their book to confirm lunch was on the house the next time we chose to grace them with our presence. Together we walked out the doors side by side to be greeted with a nice cool breeze laden in sunshine. The storm clouds cleared leaving blue skies to brighten the afternoon.

"Well I'm going to head back to my hotel. Liam thank you so much for an amazing time."

"The pleasure was all mine. When do you want to book the lunch?"

"I'm only here until tomorrow and if the weather's nice I plan to go hiking. Perhaps we can leave it for a few weeks. I'II make time to return and we can have our stomachs ready to indulge. How does that sound?"

He looked a little disappointed, "Sure, no problems. I'II call you in a couple of weeks to see how you are tracking. Is that okay with you?"

"Sure, I'II give you my number."

Liam waved his hand, "It's okay I already have it."

"Excuse me?" I said a little taken back by what he said.

"I've wanted to tell you but I didn't know how. I know who you are. Harper Perelle right?"

"Yes, my surname is Perelle. Liam, what's going on?" I asked feeling somewhat exposed.

"I recognized your face. You were at '*his*' execution. I watched you come storming in screaming all the things I couldn't say. 'He' killed my"

"Shhh, you don't need to tell me. I know exactly who you are talking about and the entire history. I get it. You recognized me at the restaurant the other night."

Liam's expression changed to confused, "No I only just met you in the park today. When I looked across I recognized you. I introduced myself to get you to say your name to confirm it was you."

"Tell me why you have my number."

"After that day I looked you up. I needed to know everything I could about you because I felt you were my voice and convinced myself we were somehow connected. Why else would you be so passionate about expressing your hatred for that monster. I thought, maybe you had lost people too." Liam paused to look down at his shaking hands. He kept talking but would no longer provide me with eye contact.

"It was difficult to find anything related to you. I became obsessed and hired a private investigator. I lied and told him you owed me money. I'm sorry Harper I wasn't well at the time and felt completely desperate and alone. I just needed someone to understand my pain. You must be thinking I'm a complete weirdo right now."

I released the breath I had been holding, "Not at all. I can't imagine a fraction of what you have been through and given the circumstances I understand completely why you struggled to raise the subject. It's very brave of you to do so, honest too. You could have had me give you my number and never told me any of this. I respect you for it. Thank you Liam."

I could tell he was sad as he raised his head to look at me.

"When I woke up this morning feeling better I was glad to receive reprieve from my dark thoughts I have relentlessly fought to abolish. I regained a slither of the taste of faith when you of all people on this day of peace chose to sit on the same park bench. To me it was a sign things were going to be better. I know this will sound crazy but there is something about you that's different, special. I don't know you but I believe in you."

Liam's words were imparted with such passion intermixed with the strain of pain from a journey most would thankfully never have to endure. "I'm not sure what to say other than thank you."

"Today has been the best day I have had in many many years. I thought I had lost the ability to laugh. You made it so easy to be myself."

"Liam, you have to keep yourself present to who you

are. It was you who chose to give yourself a break from purgatory; it was you who chose to ask me out for coffee, it was you who chose to execute the worst wing man support I have ever seen. Woop, Woop, seriously, what were you thinking?" I said as we both burst out laughing.

I regained my composure, "Liam, a large portion of what you experienced today was stimulated by you. I may have been the curiosity or motivation stimulus you leveraged, however placing this aside, all the rest of it was and is you. Please don't create some false reliance on me or anyone else for that matter. All you ever require already exists within you for you. Embrace it, use it and dare to live your best life possible."

Liam stepped closer into my personal space randomly announcing, "I'm gay."

"I'm lost, why are you telling me your sexual orientation? Also as a side note this helps to explain that whole ass wiggling thing you had going on, you opportunistic advertiser," I said with a wink trying to keep it light.

Liam provided a half smile and diverted his eyes to the ground, "Its why I left them. I was an oppressed gay man living the Christian lie. In my early twenties I married my childhood friend and we eventually had Lisa. Then one day something switched over in me causing the façade to become unbearable, I lived with the struggle in silence until I simply couldn't do it anymore. My wife felt betrayed, lied to and began ostracizing me. In her anger she threatened to make a scene by telling everyone unless I abided with her request to contribute financially and stay out of their lives. I wasn't ready to come out. I had confided in her because she was my best friend and I loved her. I was looking for her support, not realizing it was possible to have her turn on me the way she did. I don't blame her for her backlash I can appreciate in retrospect her reaction was a testament to how deeply she loved me. While I was trying to embrace who I am she was losing her husband, best friend and father to our child. Look at me Harper, I'm an old gay man who has never found true love. If I hadn't been so selfish about my needs I would have been there the night he …" Liam dropped his head into his hands and burst into tears.

I stepped in and wrapped my arms around him. Liam immediately shifted closer putting his arms around my torso drawing me in tight as he sobbed into my neck. I closed my eyes as my tears welled to the surface. The enormity of his pain, the burdens he carried were weighing down his soul. His whole body shook as he released loud sobs. I squeezed him tighter as I felt him releasing his pain and openly cried with him. The anguish I felt through the energy of his body had me wanting to rock him in my arms and tell him everything was going to be okay.

"Let it all out Liam," I whispered while he continued to howl.

We had been standing there crying for over half an hour. Liam finally began to settle. When I felt he was stable enough I whispered in his ear, "It's not your fault. We all have a life path and destiny, which has to be fulfilled. You may not understand the reason things take place but this is when you should hold faith to accept there is a purpose in the absence of circumstantial comprehension. Trusting we don't know because we are not supposed to know. When the time is right you will learn and understand all there is to be known. You cannot carry the burden of guilt for another man's choice to commit a heinous crime. There is a reason you have been placed here. There is a reason why you chose to marry and have a child and most assuredly there is a reason why you came to a point where you had to live as your authentic self. You're obliged to be the seeker of your purpose, your truth. You could spend the rest of your life playing hypothetical scenario after scenario to no useful avail. Fight the urge to succumb to the darkness and focus on becoming the best version of you. If it helps, do it for them too. There is no value in three lives being lost to the actions of one man. Do you hear me?"

Liam slowly lifted his head from my saturated shoulder. Sniffling heavily he looked at me with his bloodshot eyes and nodded. "You're the first person I've ever told."

"I know." I said as I pulled out a tissue from my bag to pass it to him.

"You really should write a book. I mean it. When you speak it makes sense. People need to understand. Maybe your path is being the voice to the world on the things they themselves cannot see."

I smiled, "I'm not sure what my path is yet Liam, but I know I'm definitely walking in the right direction."

"Have I scared you off from being my fast friend?" He said it in such a sincere voice I almost felt him shrink to the age of a young boy.

"You are a dear soul Liam. I'm proud to have you as my fast friend and look forward to making it a lifelong commitment of exchange. You just have to work on the whole wing man thing." I said releasing a chuckle.

He placed his hands on his hips and did an exaggerated hip swing, "You're not going to let me forget that are you?"

"What good fast friend would? It's practically part of the unwritten code that I just made up."

Liam released a big laugh and stepped in to give me a cuddle. "Thank you so much Harper. I always knew you were the one who could help."

Internally I wanted to resist the acceptance of his comment but thought better of it. I returned his embrace and simply said, "You're welcome."

When Liam and I stepped apart the button on his coat pocket snagged the edge of my bag making it come off my shoulder. Some of the contents fell to the ground as the bag titled to an angle. Liam took off his jacket so I could set my bag free while he knelt down to pick up what had fallen. In the midst of passing things up to me I saw his body became still.

"What is it Liam?"

"The book, it's empty. The pages are all blank."

"Pass it up, let me see."

He held it up and open. I could see the writing clear as day. Without comment I placed it in my bag. "Is there anything else down there?"

"Just this pencil, here you go." He said standing up again.

"Well I really should be heading off. You have my number and I'm assuming email too so feel free to reach me whenever you like."

"Harper, why were you sitting in a park pretending to read a blank book?"

I released a sigh, "Today you said you could see the writing faintly but weren't able to read it, yes?"

"Yes, I could but I saw it just now and there isn't any contents, not even a pen scratch."

"What I'm potentially about to tell you is going to

require you to have an open mind because I don't have all the answers yet. If you are willing to listen and just accept in blind faith what I say is my truth than I will tell you." I stood there watching his eyes to determine whether the answer he provided was founded on honest intent.

"Yes, I can do that," nodding his head thoughtfully.

"This book is filled cover to cover with text that I can clearly see and read. You are the first person who has confirmed they could see something everyone else has said it is blank. My instinct tells me the book and I have connected somehow. A very special person I met last night, your doppelganger no less Bahrain confirmed finding this book and reading it was a crucial part of my destiny. He told me no-one else can read it because no-one else is meant to. When you said you could see the text faintly I surmised there was a strong enough spiritual or karmic tethering with me to allow you to be aware of the text but still not be privy to its contents. The fact that you can no longer see the text at all makes me lean towards karmic debt and healing. Perhaps you choosing to unburden your secrets coupled with the two of us crying together and agreeing to be present in each other's lives caused the shift. Once cleared you were no longer able to see the text because the bind has dissipated. We have allowed our free will to choose to be present to one another with no string attached."

"You are the single most fascinating person I have ever met. Regardless of how fantastical it sounds the way you convey the story makes it plausible and I want to believe you." He said placing a hand on my shoulder. "Harper, I do believe you."

"Well my caveat is I don't really know anything. I'm accepting everything as it is being presented. It's a combination of instinct and ingrained skills utilized to create the frame on the scattered bones of this strange puzzle I have placed before me. Who knows, ten years from now I may have experiences, which alter my perspective on how I see what has occurred in the past and the drivers behind them. Its my convoluted way of saying I'm making it up as I go along as best I can so don't lock yourself into any one theory as gospel just yet. The last two days have reminded me of the fundamental truth, nothing is ever as it seems. The quickest example I can give you is the incident with my bag. Did that happen by accident or was it meant to be? You choose to kneel down to pick up my things, which created the opportunity for you to look at the book again. Was that a fluke or was it universal intervention of fate bound to show us the ethereal shifts when they are made? Answer: Who the fuck really knows. So we can speculate, assume or accept the status of we don't know and therefore we aren't meant to or don't need to. Are you following my madness of method?" I said half expecting Liam to run in the opposite direction and never look back.

Liam leaned in, "Write the book."

"Ha, you aren't going to let the idea go are you?"

"What good fast friend would? Its practically part of the unwritten code I just stole from you after you made it up," he said smugly.

"Very funny, cheeky monkey. We've only known each other for a minute and you're already using my words against me, respect to that. Ok, I really should head off."

"Thank you again for everything."

"Liam, honestly, the pleasure was unexpected and all mine. Make sure you go see a doctor to get a full check up and consider the idea of putting a support plan together. Those shaky hands you have been trying to hide all day are a sign your body's started withdrawal. It's probably going to get worse before its better so do the right thing by you, please."

Liam stepped in and gave me another cuddle then kissed my forehead, "You're amazing. Write the book."

"I may have to just to shut you up." I said laughing as I peeled myself away from his embrace. Giving him a wave and a salute I headed in the direction of the hotel. Liam stood there watching me fade into the distance. He was wearing the loveliest smile on his face. This day was set to be a favorite. There was so much to celebrate.

# Destinies Reign

I woke with a jolt from my afternoon naughty nap. The day's adventures had me feeling pleasantly exhausted. Unfortunately my sleep wasn't providing any reprieve. Adeline must have been on my mind because she was present in my dream. It was a vivid image of a woman who I absolutely knew. There was such a strong sense of familiarity. I've known her before and I was adamant it was Adeline. She was dressed in what I assumed was the standard nurses uniform of the era. Her pale complexion didn't seem to detract from her face, as she was still very pretty. Even though she appeared gaunt her upper cheeks were full and her eyes had a tiny sparkle to them. I couldn't tell what color they were but I could see her mid length hair which was pinned back was Auburn. There were no words exchanged between us. She gestured with her thin hand for me to follow. I watched her svelte figure manoeuvre freely in the open field. The grass was mottled with interloping weeds championing the expanse. The silhouetted cluster of old trees caught my eye as she gravitated towards them. I could feel rubble under my feet, bricks and other disposed refuse but the low light conditions made it difficult to visually confirm what I was stepping on.

Adeline stopped at the third tree to the right and stared at the bark. I stepped in to look at a marking on the trunk. When I edged closer it disappeared before I was able to read it. Adeline shifted to a spot not too far from where I was standing laying herself down on the ground. Facing upward she calmly raised her hand extending a single bony digit pointing to the sky. I visually followed the angle of her finger. As my eyes reached the point where I thought was correct I couldn't see anything. The sky was a deep blue black with no moon, stars or even clouds present. When I looked down again she was gone.

I've always believed there is immense value in deciphering dreams. If the subconscious mind feels so strongly to speak, then it's my duty to listen. I guess the obvious interpretation for me would be Adeline showing me her unmarked grave. Her action of pointing to the sky could have meant she's in heaven or her way of saying she's in the spirit world. It's the unusual absence of any light in the sky, which triggered off some internal sensory alarms for me. Perhaps she is somewhere else and is pointing to the heavens suggesting it is where she would like to go. Maybe there wasn't any light in the sky because she had embraced the dark. It was all too ambiguous for the moment. Instead of consuming energy thinking about it I decided to wait and see if dreams to follow afforded further clarity. I picked up my phone opening my to do list app and typed in a reminder note, 'find Adeline's unmarked grave.' I chuckled to myself imagining somebody accidentally looking at this list. Toilet paper, Baking soda, Coriander, Pantyhose and find Adeline's unmarked grave. Shaking my head as I placed the phone back down I released a sigh, my life was anything but normal.

It was starting to transition into early evening. I could see the tiny insect swarms outside being carried by the winds soft currents. There was lightness to the evening atmosphere. I stepped out on the balcony to peer down at the streetscape. All the people seemed to be ambling by at a less manic pace than usual. Today might have been a rather special day for many people not just Liam and I. My half drunk coffee was still on the table. It seemed like a lifetime had passed since this morning, so much had occurred. From the moment I arrived I have been on a magical mystery ride of emotional highs, lows and personal challenges. There was a long way to go, I knew this instinctually but I also somehow knew it would be worth the effort.

Just as I was returning inside there was a knock at the door. When I opened it I found myself greeted by the sight of a hotel porter holding a large silver serving tray balanced on one hand aligned to his shoulder.

"Hi, I didn't order any room service."

"It's compliments of the house," said the man as he stepped forward. I shifted to one side to let him in.

"I don't understand, why am I receiving this with compliments to the house?"

"I'm not sure. I was just told by the kitchen its compliments of the house and to have it delivered to you."

I looked at the tray which he placed on the edge of my unmade bed and nodded, "Ok, thank you."

"You are welcome," he said as he took the tip I had retrieved from my pocket. He smiled and did a little bow before closing the door behind him.

The wine was already poured in the glass with the opened half size bottle beside it. When I lifted the silver lid steam came gushing upward before revealing a nicely displayed sizzling beef and vegetable hotpot with jasmine rice on the side. The cake looked like black forest and was richly layered with mottled cream. I found the combination of main & sweet not complimentary at all. I kept returning my gaze to the opened bottle of wine; there was something about the porter and this meal which didn't sit right with me.

Placing the lid back on the meal I decided to have a shower. I always found water helped me to think. I leaned on the cold tiles as the liquid streamed down the contours of my naked skin. It felt good to cleanse myself of the day. Just as I closed my eyes to enjoy the sensation, images presented as flashcards to the forefront of my mind. The first was of me asleep on my bed hugging the book, then my position changed slightly and this time I was empty handed. My heart instantly released a pumping thud within my chest that drove me to place my hand on my heart while I gasped. Something wasn't right.

In a state of light-headedness I quickly towel dried my body, threw my hair up in a saturated bun and scrambled into some clothes. Grabbing my bag together with the tray I left the room to head to the hotel kitchen. My instinct told me to avoid reception so I walked directly into the restaurant thrusting the doors open to make a dramatic entrance into the kitchen. It was a buzzing hive of activity.

"I'm sorry you can't be in here," said a lady stepping towards me.

"I know, tell me did this meal come from your kitchen?"

She looked at the tray I was holding. "If there's something wrong with your room service order just let reception know and we will correct it for you," She insisted now raising her hand to point at the exit.

"Chef, I need to speak with you. CHEF," I called out loudly sounding like a woman possessed as I stepped forward to hold my position.

All the staff were now intermittently looking at me as a man peered his head around the corner, "You're not some psycho are you?" He asked displaying the edge of a handle he was clutching.

I laughed, "Is that a cleaver in your hand or are you just happy to see me? Tell me Chef, would a psycho answer the question truthfully or even be aware they are a psycho? I just need to know if this food came from your kitchen. It arrived at my door by a fellow who said it was compliments of this kitchen. I have my suspicions. Take a look please," placing the tray on the bench then lifting the lid. The Chef and others peered at it.

Immediately he scrunched his nose, "No, this is not from us. Look at that cheap silverware. The price is still on the lid."

I turned the lid over, sure enough the price tag was still on the inside. "How about the wine? Do you supply this brand and would you deliver it open with a glass pre poured?"

He waved his hand in a swirl, "Never, this is all an abomination. Who did this?"

"Chef if I knew I wouldn't be here seeking answers."

The Chef laughed, "Well I hope you find them. Bring them to me and we will teach them kitchen etiquette." His staff all nodded in agreement.

"Thanks, I might take you up on it. I'm going to leave this with you. Don't drink the wine, I'd hedge my bets its been tampered with."

Furrows appeared across his brow, "Who would do such a thing to you?"

"I'm looking forward to finding out. In the meantime this needs to be our little secret."

He tapped his chest and kissed two fingers in gesture, "No problem, Antonio, escort this lovely lady out the back then into the Hotel foyer. I'm sorry you must not been seen by the patrons. It's against health regulations to have you in here."

A man came from around the corner, "Ah, Antonio, take her now please."

"Thanks guys," I said as I waved to them.

"Follow me," said Antonio in a heavy foreign accent.

As we walked past the cold room and open pantry I inhaled the infusion of spices in the air. Antonio used his shoulder to coax open the back door then motioned for me to step out. The exit led directly into a poorly lit alley. The garbage in the dumpsters immediately stripped the joy of the spices that had been entertaining my senses. I placed my hand up to cup my nose as I watched Antonio bend his head forward to light his cigarette. He blew the first stream of smoke into the air. It rose free of constraint towards the night sky shifting to the commands of the subtle breeze.

"You want?" He asked holding out his packet.

"No thanks, I don't smoke." I said trying to read the label to establish the brands origins. "Where are you from Antonio?"

"Italia," He said exaggerating his next exhale of smoke while trying to blow rings.

As we began walking down the narrow cobbled stone path I looked at him and smiled, "I thought so."

"Your name?"

"Harper."

"Bella Harper, Bella."

"Thank you," I replied.

When we entered the foyer the two reception staff glanced across. One lady caught my attention when her expression seemed to convey she was surprised to witness Antonio and myself together. Her eyes flitted between us while her body language rather quickly transitioned to project annoyance before she left the counter disappearing through a doorway.

"Antonio, does your girlfriend work here?"

"No, she in Italia, she come for Antonio one month."

"I think one of the girls at reception might have a crush on you. I noticed she seemed annoyed when she saw us walk in together."

"Woman, like Italia men," He said not really fussed about it.

As we reached the front counter I turned to Antonio, "Thanks for walking me in."

He leaned in kissing me on either side of my cheek, "Ciao Bella Harper."

"Ciao Antonio."

He walked off without a second glance back out the front door. I leant on the reception counter while I waited to be served.

"Good evening, how can I help you?"

"Hi, I'm in room 1111. I received a complimentary dinner on the house and was wondering if you could tell me the reason." I said carefully watching her expression for signs.

Her brow creased, "I'm not sure. Did you make a complaint or was there something that happened to disrupt your stay?"

"No."

"I honestly don't know. Maybe they sent it to you when it was supposed to be for another room by accident," She suggested shrugging her shoulders.

This was good I hadn't thought of that as an option. Still it didn't explain the fact that the food wasn't from the hotel. I was trying to explore why my instinct told me to avoid reception. I knew there was something I was failing to see.

"You know what that's probably exactly what happened. Can you do me a favor and just ask the other girl on staff whether she knows anything about it. If the meal was supposed to be for another room it would help me sleep to know I've done the right thing."

"Of course. Marla said she was going on break; she's due back in a couple of minutes. I'm not allowed to leave reception unattended. If you are happy to wait you can ask her yourself."

"Perfect. I will, thanks." Internally I could feel myself simmering. Someone knew where I was, my room number and I suspect was trying to drug me. If the visions I saw in the shower are accurate then its possible they were planning to drug me so they could obtain the book while I was unconscious. The only way anyone had access to the room would be to steal an electronic key or be on staff. I needed to work out the motives. What's the use of a book they can't read?

"Hello can I help you?"

I looked up to see Marla standing before me with an expression presented as a masked scowl.

"Hi, I received a complimentary meal to my room and I was wondering if you knew anything about it."

"Was there something wrong with the meal?" She said while folded her arms.

"Not at all. I was wondering why it was sent to my room. Can you tell me?"

"It was a complimentary meal," she replied tightening her arm fold.

I stared directly into her eyes. "Yes, I am well aware. I'm asking you to tell me why. I'd appreciate you answering the question I've asked you."

I watched as her body shifted while her eyes flicked up toward the ceiling and returned to look my way but not at me. "Um, it's a new thing we are doing here. Customers get selected for complimentary dinners as a reward for patronage."

"This my first time staying here. What's the selection process?"

"It's random ok?" She snapped.

The other girl looked across from where she was serving her customer and said, "Since when? I don't know anything about it."

Her face flushed red as she hissed, "I don't know."

In a calm voice I drew her attention back to me, "Marla, look at me."

She turned her head with an expression of surprise at me saying her name.

"Do you know me Marla?"

"No, why would I?"

I reached into my bag and pulled out my book while keeping my eyes locked on her. I watched as her pupils dilated dramatically. Usually it's seen as a marker of people being attracted to one another. It is also a fantastic guide on what people are drawn to. In this case my book evoked a heightened stimulation response.

I opened the book at a random page, "Can you read me a passage. Any one will do."

She leaned in to look closer and then looked at me, "It's blank."

Marla was telling the truth. I closed the book and placed it back in my bag while she watched intently.

"One last question then I'II leave you be. Your tattoo, what does the symbol mean?"

"Is this a joke? There's no writing in the book and I don't have a tattoo," She said defiantly.

I watched her head twitch to a slight tilt. She was lying, "Sure you do. It's a white tattoo on the inside of your left ear. Easily disguised but when your face flushes red Marla it stands out like oversized hairy dog balls on a Chihuahua during a sweltering hot summers day. Just so you know." I said staring her down while trying to calm my rising anger.

She immediately cupped her ear.

"Tell me what the symbol means."

"I don't know." She said stepping away from the counter.

She was telling the truth, "No problems, prepare my bill I'm checking out. If you try to call anyone to tell them I'm leaving I will know, do you understand me. Don't fuck with me Marla. I promise you it will be life changing and not in a good way." I said continuing to stare at her. I turned my head to look at the other reception attendant, "Watch her. If she tries to call anyone I want you to tell me."

"What's going on?" She asked looking at me and then back at Marla.

"You don't want to know." I said as I turned and walked towards the elevator.

It took me less than five minutes to grab the rest of my things. On the way out the flashing red light on the hotel phone caught my eye. I hesitated for a moment before picking up the receiver to listen to the voice mail. There was a lot of noise in the background, people talking and cars driving by then a voice said '*trust no-one*' and hung up. The hairs on the back of my neck stood on end as I recognized the accent. It was Antonio, I was certain of it. What the fuck was going on? I placed the receiver down and in a fury went back to the reception area.

"Where's Marla?" I said looking around.

"She walked out. I tried to stop her but she flung her arms up in the air and left. She didn't even take her coat or bag. I don't know what's happening. Can you tell me what's going on?"

"It doesn't matter. I just need to settle the bill so I can go." I felt a sense of urgency. I needed to move.

"No problems. I'm sorry about all this."

"It's fine, don't worry." My mind was in hyper drive running through dozens of scenario options on what was happening and the potential drivers. I felt my raw instinct for survival surface taking over as a natural course of presence. At the same time Vernon's words, 'There you are Harper' became present in my mind, which only set to fuel the beast rising in my belly. Something was on the prowl hunting me for this book and from what I could see they were using idiot pawns in this chess game. Whomever it was driving this clearly considered the likes of the pseudo bellboy and Marla as readily dispensable in the game I was unwillingly entered into. Judging by their epic failed attempt to gain advantage they may no longer underestimate me.

I finalized my bill and left the hotel very aware of my environment. The hustle and bustle of the street was a distinct shift from the relaxed atmosphere I witnessed around dusk. My senses were electrified by sensations of pulse I had not felt before. I wasn't sure what it meant; my body was definitely signaling something. Looking at the people I noticed they were almost all diverting their gaze, intentionally straining not to make eye contact. Hands tightly gripped, some shoved straight palmed deep in pockets was an easy tell. I knew I had to get off the streets not because I felt threatened I just knew I was being watched by pawns. Turning the corner I increased my pace then ducked into the first entry point of the massive open plan multi level shopping mall. Wandering around I focused on the store windows rather than the people around me. Using my peripheral vision I watched to identify who would feel it was safe to stare. Dozens of people looked at me as they passed by. I couldn't make a determination between the people who usually stared versus the potential pawns; or were they one in the same all along? There had to be an easy tell. I suspected the tattoo might be a clan mark of sorts, the symbol looked like a bastardized version of a hieroglyph, satanic mark and something else I was sure I had seen before but couldn't quite place my thoughts on.

The smell of incense caught my attention. It was emanating from the Hipster Store across the way. Cautiously I entered the store surveying the room. It was empty with the exception of the boy behind the counter who was leaning over the desk reading a comic. He briefly looked up at me and gave a half smile before continuing to read. The amount of dreadlocks on his skull impressively appeared to look as though it weighed more than his head. I'm not sure what I was looking for as I scanned over all the shelves of randomly bundled together goods.

I called out to the attendant, "Are you burning Frankincense and Myrrh?"

"Um, I don't know man. It's whatever." He said not lifting his head from his comic.

I walked across to the counter flipped my head upside down where he was standing to look at the staff only shelf. "Yep, Frankincense and Myrrh," I confirmed when my eyes spied the incense packets. As I stood up again he was looking at me. I raised an eyebrow, "Thanks for your help, much appreciated."

He laughed shook his head and recommenced his reading.

"Where is the incense stored I'd like to buy some."

Using his thumb he gestured behind him.

I scanned the shelves finally finding them tucked behind a row of glass bong bottles. I took a couple of packets then turned to head back to the counter accidentally knocking over a tray of sun glasses as I walked by a cluttered display table. I bent over to pick them up and smiled whispering 'thank you' to the universe.

"Hey buddy do you have any of those glasses that people wear at those gigs, Um you know the ones where they play techno music?"

"If there are any left they will be on the top shelf right corner on the side you're standing."

I jumped to my feet feeling rather clever as I meandered across to take a look. The shelf had an assortment of glasses none of which stood out to me, "Can you point out the ones I'm looking for please."

He released a sigh as he walked across, glanced at the goods retrieving two pairs. "These are all that's left."

Much to my surprise they were translucent, "Are you sure these are it?"

"You wanted ravers, these are ravers man," He said as he returned to the counter.

I paid for the items and left the store wearing the outlandish oversized flower framed glasses. In truth they could have been the shape of penises and I would still have worn them to see if they worked.

Wandering around I intentionally didn't glance at anyone. Aside from looking like a total douche in these glasses I was trying not to draw any more attention to myself, which under the circumstances was laughable given, I was wearing these ridiculous ravers. I knew the full effect worked best in low light so I located the posted signage for the nearest exit so I could hit the streets for a test run.

There was nothing set to prepare me for what I witnessed as I walked the first five hundred meters of the street I entered. Everywhere I looked were clusters of people who bore the tattoo in their left ear. It felt as though I had just been thrust into a zombie apocalypse movie where I was the only human left. My heart beat faster while a silent ancient rage deep inside my core commenced its up rise as I envisioned myself morphed into a bear trapped in a circus of watchers. The numbers were prolific; everywhere I turned they were present. A silent war of minds had begun on the chessboard of life and my opponents were the interferons.

# The Art of War

It was crystal clear after my entry into the sixth hotel that I was not able to safely stay in a service driven space. My only option was to drive home or find a place to crash for the night. The moment I completed the thought I knew precisely where to go. I flagged down a taxi to head toward my destination.

After a few wrong turns we finally made it to the street of the restaurant I dined in the previous night. I paid the taxi driver and stood in the middle of the road as he drove off. The street was deserted. In light of what I had experienced the quiet now felt eerie. All the overhead lights spanning down the street were emitting a very dim light. When I stepped onto the footpath I realized all the houses had the exact same façade. The paint finishes seem to be the only variance. I wasn't sure how I was going to identify which of them Liam lived in. I only knew he lived across the road from the restaurant.

Scanning the length of the street I was looking for any signs of households where people were awake. I would start knocking on their doors first. Just as I was about to walk further toward the end of the street the front door of a place three houses away from where I was standing to my right had opened. I waited to see who would come out before I approached.

Several minutes passed while the door remained wide open with no human in sight. My arrival was known to whomever was residing within that establishment. I stood present to the flash back of every moment I watched a horror flick where a person hears a noise and decides to investigate. I'm the one who yells at the screen 'you're an idiot, don't do it.' Often laughing at the sheer stupidity while wondering who would actually do that in real life? Tonight I got my answer; me.

I saw no point in approaching quietly. Just before I reached the opening of the entrance I called out "Hello." The only light source was a lamp on a side table. A person was sitting in the armchair beside it. Male, average weight and height. His hands were positioned flat on his knees; his feet were also flat on the ground in front of him while the rest of his posture was unusually upright. I couldn't see his face due to the lamp conveniently position to block it from view. This felt like a test.

I surveyed the street from left to right looking for any anomalies. There were none I could identify readily. Inside the man still had not moved nor acknowledged my presence. My instinct was drawn to crossing the threshold, mentally I had no certainty of anything given the words trust no one now permanently lived there. I closed my eyes to ask the question within myself 'Should I enter?'

"Yes."

"You're here?" I said to the voice.

"Yes."

"Can you tell me your name?" I asked with my mind. The voice didn't reply. I opened my eyes and jumped back almost falling over as I whacked my right elbow on the corner of the mailbox.

"Jesus Liam you surprised me. I didn't even hear you sneak up on me. What's up with that?"

Liam just stood in the doorway staring at me. The expression on his face was non threatening it seemed more akin to curiosity.

I stepped forward looking straight into his eyes, "You're not Bahrain and you're not Liam. I detect a variance in the projected energy. Who are you?"

"I am Zivah," she said executing a slight head bow.

Shocked I shook my head, "Holly Cow, I was not expecting THAT. Where's Bahrain?"

"Your time is with me now. Please come." She stepped aside so I could pass through the door. Liam's eyes were back to a stark light blue color. This whole thing made the concept of lunacy depreciate to a level of normality. I had no label for this new realm of insight I was acquiring at a rate of knots about the perceived world.

"Sit with me Harp player we have much to discuss."

Zivah's hand gestured for me to sit right beside her on the sofa. I chose to shift the coffee table then pulled up the armchair so we were positioned face to face. She smiled nodding her head.

"You have questions for me?"

A cheeky smile landscaped across my face, "Sure, when I sat down you smiled. What were you thinking?"

"You do not take orders or follow. I ask you to sit here, you chose there. To sit here it is passive. You naturally chose confrontational. This is good."

"Ok, next question. I think we need to discuss the elephant in the room before we get into the really deep stuff. What's it like to have a penis?" I said as I burst out laughing.

Zivah looked down at Liam's crotch then back at me, "It is awful." Then joined me in laughter. My stomach was tensed as we both continued our cackle. I loved that she looked at his crotch before she responded. It was priceless.

In between chuckles I said, "I'm sorry I just couldn't resist. It looks ridiculous having a female voice coming out of Liam's mouth. I guess it could have been worse. Yesterday he had a big unruly beard." I said as I burst into laughter again.

Once I managed to finally compose myself I looked at Liam and could see there was a definite softness to him now. "Zivah, are you a spirit possessing Liam's body?"

"Yes I have entered his channel to speak with you."

"Is there no other method than this? It seems almost antiquated."

Zivah released a loud laugh and then looked at me, "There are many ways to connect. It is you Harp player who placed the constraint on us. The five you selected cannot reach you any other way."

"I closed channels and left this open as your only means for connect. Possession?"

"Yes. You are the key of wills Harp player. This was your will," She said in a calm tone.

"If I did this there is a reason for it. This I know and trust." I said as I shifted in my seat and leaned forward. "Do you know what the reason is?"

"No, you held many secrets and provided few answers. We are all bound to your strict instructions."

I nodded my head to acknowledge her words. There was no doubt in me she was speaking the truth and I was prepared to stand by my current reasoning. If I placed the restriction on them it was for good purpose.

"Ok, Zivah lets do this," I said rubbing my hands together.

"Do what?"

"You said I could ask you anything. I'm about to play go fish. I'll ask you a flurry of questions to try assist myself in bridging the gaps."

"I am here for this."

"Why did you come tonight?"

"Rejuvenating universal energy shift rippled from your agnya charkra today. It is a powerful healing force. You did not go unnoticed by all who are connected with awareness to the fabric of light and love."

"Agnya is the third eye, yes?"

"Yes."

"When you mention it didn't go unnoticed you are referring to the interferons correct."

"Yes. They actively hunt you now. In the realm of flesh you are the only one left."

"Is Vernon responsible for all the others? Did he manage to track and kill the ones who are the soul keys born to flesh?"

"Yes," She said with sadness in her voice.

"How many?"

"Five, you are the sixth."

"You mentioned the interferons hunt me. They don't want me dead, they are trying to get hold of the book."

"Yes."

"I know they won't be able to read the book so the purpose is less about the book and more about me not having the book. Is my assumption correct?"

"Precisely so."

"This would mean technically it's in my best interest to read the entire book quickly."

"You must complete reading the book. Yes"

"Consider it done. Next question, there were people all around me tonight who bore a tattoo symbol in their inner ear. It's iridescent under certain conditions. I believe they are the watchers working for the interferons and they are marked as such. Like cattle branded for purpose."

Zivah dropped her head, "It is not a tattoo. The interferons created an actovirus which they integrated into all human vaccines from inception. Every human who had been vaccinated has this sitting dormant within his or her body. When the interferons need to use someone they stimulate the virus to become active for the purpose set. Each role has an activation variant causing the virus to present as a different symbol held in a specific place on their body. When live it emits a certain dull frequency humans cannot detect whereas all other living creatures can. They feel the subtleties in the shift in the bodies pulse."

I sat back in the armchair shaking my head at what I was hearing. "Surely there has to be something created to block the activation of the virus? There's always a solution. It doesn't make sense. What's stopping us fighting back?"

"You are searching for solutions without appreciating the problem. Think Harp player. Tell me what you see with all you now know."

I sat in silence to replay the information she told me. As I closed my eyes and drew a deep breath Zivah said, "Yes."

I reopened my eyes and looked into hers, "This is a human problem which must be human solved. Any educated person who has the capacity to execute the scientific research to create a solution has the virus within them. Even if I somehow managed to convince them the virus exists the moment the interferons became aware of the activities they would activate the virus within them and its game over. Unless there was a way to execute this activity in absolute silence the interferons can always easily thwart the efforts." I looked down at my hands. "I saw hundreds of watchers this evening walking the streets."

"Many have been activated now. You are a real threat Harp player. This makes you a target they will not remove from their sights and will try anything to get the book away from you."

"I know they can't control me. Is this what threatens them?"

"Yes it is a part of it. You have moved into your strength quicker than they expected and far stronger than any of us imagined Harp player."

"I don't feel different. I'm in a heightened state of awareness of my environment but under the circumstance this is to be expected. When you reference strength I'm assuming you are talking about the vibrational pulse you mentioned before. Yes?"

"You only opened the channel yesterday. Today, in one act of healing for this man your vibrational waves caused ripples on a universal scale. There is no telling the extent of the strength you will develop. If you master harnessing your energy, the channeling of this could create alternate universes." She bowed Liam's head. "It could also destroy them."

"Why don't the interferons try to kidnap me or directly coerce me in some way? Vernon Wreath was frightened of me. Do you know what it is they fear?"

"What is your favorite saying Harp player? The words you live by."

"Allow thy enemy to underestimate whom you are so they may possess confidence to reveal their true self. In the art of war the greatest trick the devil ever pulled is to convince the world she doesn't exist."

"You have your answer."

"Are you suggesting I'm the devil?" I said half smiling.

"All born to the flesh have a pulse toward good and a pulse toward bad. You are the soul key of wills. The actions yielding from your core are not bound to being ruled and therefore amplified. You have executed extreme acts of evil and counter balanced by extreme acts of kindness. This is why you were able to enter neutral in this life. The interferons couldn't take hold of you when you compelled yourself to the dark you were merciless in your capacity to hunt, torture and execute. Entering neutral is their ultimate chance to sway you to join them voluntarily. You are a sole entity, one of a kind. No one has ever been capable of existing without interconnected belonging. You, Harp player, became the exception to the universal rule of oneness. What you now choose to do impacts everything."

"I'm a saint and a sinner and now I'm balanced neither one side or the other. Why didn't Bahrain tell me all this yesterday?"

"Information passed must never be done in advance. It would influence the way you think, feel and the choices you make which could have irreparable impacts if you are not ready to receive."

My mind was a hyper drive of information processing multiple layers in various formats simultaneously. What Zivah was telling me became something I had already known the moment she said it. Mental recollection of events, symbols, flashes of times past not of this life all awakening me with an explosion of lightening stimuli firing off the synapse of my brain.

"Vernon was an attempter. How many are there?"

"There were fourteen attempters, one for each soul key."

"Were? How many are there now?" I asked

"Two remain. Vernon Wreath and there is one other which alludes all. We can account for thirteen. Legends foretold this final attempter is revealed in the time of the last battle. It is only once the last of the attempters is permanently destroyed that the doors of Equanon can be opened by the soul keys."

"How many of the soul keys did Vernon destroy?"

"None."

"I don't understand. If there are only two of them remaining and all of the soul keys are intact why are we deemed to be losing this battle?"

"The soul keys cannot be destroyed without it destroying an interferon. All interferons have one directional binds to a single soul key. There is no way to detect which one they are paired to so none want to risk the possible Russian roulette of destruction. Hence the soul keys remain untouched. The interferons send attempters to kill the flesh to prevent soul keys from completing their journey of growth and mastery of the sin entered but the soul remains intact. It was Vernon who mastered his approach to drive the ones of flesh to suicide adding the additional cycle of seven. When we learned of his plan we shifted the rebirth cycles to separate eras circumventing his ability to reach any more than one per flesh entry. Once Vernon enters he is flesh bound for the duration of his mortal life. He too is governed by the rule of suicide seven. The ugliness of his crimes marks his entry with the curse of hallows. It means he progressively becomes visually hideous. The disfigurement scares people which prevents him from easily winning favors through false sincerity of faux presentation such as feigning being enamored to gain close contact."

"Well he was butt ugly this time around that's for sure. It also explains a driver for being placed on death row. It was an avenue of early release of flesh without suicide." I shook my head. I wasn't playing a chess game with set rules. My opponents held the distinct advantage of knowing a wealth of information while I was blind sighted.

"I'm human. I could catch a disease, get hit by a car. Any number of things could happen to remove me from this body. What then?"

"No Harp player. All living creatures human and otherwise subconsciously protect you including the interferons. This is why you have seen all your life people stare at you. Inherently they sense you and instinctually will step in to provide protection without understanding or reason. You must live. You must finish what you came to complete in this life so you may enter the next. The person your heart yearns for will meet you there and soul willing unite with you. I speak of your twin flame, Harp player. Bahrain myself and the others you chose work towards guiding you to achieve this, while the interferons work towards you not transitioning to the next life without their alliance. Neutral as you are, or positioned to either side you choose, there is no altering the destiny of the entry into your next life. It is this one which shall determine the future set for all."

I lent forward to look directly into her eyes, "Zivah are you capable of expressing untruths?"

"No."

"Is Bahrain capable of falsification?"

She gave a slight indicator of an immanent smile on Liam's face. "Yes. What drove you to ask this?"

"You said I chose you, Bahrain and others yet Bahrain emphasized he was excited to meet me as though it was our first time. This means either he was lying or you are. If I am to trust my intuition then in this moment based on your response I know you are telling the truth. There are things Bahrain said which are aligned to your messaging but now I wonder what there is he was not telling or perhaps intentionally misguiding me in."

Zivah smiled and did a slight bow of Liam's head, "Your memory serves you well Harp player."

I closed my eyes shaking my head, "Am I going to wake up at some point soon in hospital to be told I was slipped some psychedelic drug and have been hallucinating for the last couple of days?" I said sticking my arm out now one eye squinting shut with the other open. "Here pinch me so I know its real."

Zivah looked at my arm and smiled, "This is real. The illusion is the life humanity thinks is reality."

I put my arm down and released a deep sigh, "I know." I looked at the palm of my hands and traced the length of my heart line, "Zivah, How many combinations of lives have I lived and which of the seven deadly sins have I completed?"

"This is your fourth cycle of karmic flesh."

"Can you tell me which of the seven deadly sins I have transitioned through successfully?"

"No, this you must discover. You already know the answers to all the questions you seek."

"Out of the four lives how many have I travelled through disconnected, a sole entity?"

"Three of the four. Once you passed through the first you shifted the gravitational force of connectedness to neutral. Thereafter you commanded how you received and released your energies. It can never be taken or given without your absolute consent."

"Can you please expand on what you mean by I already know all the answers."

"When the soul is released from the binds of flesh and bone it must rise through the river of cleanse as it is the doorway to the reassignment plane. All travel through is to be presented for the next gateway back to flesh. The waters draw all the information from the lifetime, leaving the soul wiped of past memory set."

"So it's dirty water?" I said cringing at the concept.

"No, the water is pure."

"Have I been through the waters?"

"Yes, three times. Each time you entered the river of cleanse was able to obtain the information but not wipe it from you. As the key of wills you commanded an exchange. Enlightenment shared for knowledge received. You possess the wealth of consciousness from the river within you."

"So its as I always secretly suspected. I'm a know it all. I just knew it." I said laughing. "Actually this reminds me of a joke, three nuns standing at the pearly gates are waiting to pass through. The gatekeeper is holding an oversized open book in front of him. He peers over its edges and tells them to confess all sins then cleanse the parts of their bodies associated to the sin in the waters of purity, once complete they can enter the gates. He warned if they lie he will know and they would be sent to hell. The first Nun steps forward to confess she has masturbated all her life. The gatekeeper instructs her to wash her hands in the water and go through. The next Nun steps forward. Just as she was about to speak the third Nun aggressively pushes her out the way and steps forward in her place. The gatekeeper yelled at her asking what was the cause of such insolent behavior. To which the third Nun replied, '*Well, I'm not going to wash my mouth out in that water after she's washed her ass!*' I burst out laughing and so did Zivah.

I knew what was happening was serious but fuck it, I had a policy of ensuring I always made time to laugh and laugh we did. I wasn't expecting Zivah to find it as funny as I but she laughed so hard, Liam farted. This sent us into another wave of joy. In between gasps of air and holding my stomach from the pain of contracting I said, "Careful, you might make Liam shit himself next." That's it we were done. Our minds had officially lost the plot on the coat tails of hilarity.

A wave of exhaustion washed over me as I stretched and released a big yawn, "I'm exhausted."

"Then you must rest."

"Zivah, how do we fight a battle when the army is made up of an endless surplus of unknowing pawns in a silent war?"

"This is something you will have to seek the solution to."

"Why is it up to me? Why not us? You, Bahrain, the others you mentioned."

She smiled, "When the time is right you will know the answer to this. There is a reason and it must be done this way. You are the soul key of wills. This is your path."

"Your smile indicates there is something I need to know and I am yet to see."

"Take care Harp player."

"No don't go, tell me please."

Liam released an elongated exhale. I watched as the rigidity in his body softened to a limp slump. I momentarily contemplated taking him to his room but upon the release of another yawn and a big stretch I felt too exhausted to be overly concerned about shifting him let alone how I was going to explain my presence. It was time for me to get some sleep and this armchair was clearly set to be my bed for the evening. I shifted it back to its original position while simultaneously dragging the coffee table across so I could elevate my legs. The room was a mild temperature; still my preference would be to have a blanket to snuggle under. Aware that it is impolite to rummage around Liam's home I curled up, lay my head on the arm of the chair and closed my eyes to welcome sleep.

\* \* \*

"Harper?"

I slowly opened my eyes to see Liam holding out a cup of piping hot coffee. The surface of my eyes felt like sandpaper against my eyelids as I blinked. I'd completely forgotten I was at his house. Sitting up I smiled at Liam who was clearly confused.

I reached up and took the coffee, "Thanks Liam, how did you pull up? The way you fell asleep I thought you would wake up with a stiff neck."

"Yeah I did actually. I have to say I wasn't expecting to wake up on the couch or to find you sleeping on my armchair. What happened last night I don't seem to remember a thing?"

"There were complications at my hotel so I decided to check out and find another one. I was on foot meandering around when I got a little off track and ended up in your street. You were outside. I came over to say hello and realized you were sleep walking. I'd read somewhere it wasn't recommended to wake a sleepwalker so I guided you back inside and sat you down. I decided I should stick around for a little while to ensure you settled in for the night." I looked around the room, "Ta Da, I'm still here."

"I don't sleep walk. Are you serious?"

"It's funny from all of what I just told you the sleep walking thing has your attention. What about the fact that I bumped into you in strange circumstances twice in one day? Consider the probabilities."

"You're pulling my leg. I don't sleep walk." He said shaking his head.

"You are right, that was a lie I just made up. Here's the truth. An ancient soothsayer had possessed you. When I entered this street she greeted me at the door and asked me in. We spent a large portion of the night talking did some laughing, you farted, that just about sums it up." I took my first sip of the coffee while sporting a smirk.

Liam released a little chuckle then shook his head, "I wonder when I started sleep walking?"

"Honestly Liam I wouldn't worry too much about it. These things come and go so it may be far and few between."

"Yeah, you are probably right. It just seems a little freaky. Sleep walking." He said as he sat on the couch. "It is bizarre how we keep accidentally running into each other don't you think?"

"Ah, you are catching up with the conversation. Welcome," I said raising my coffee cup in the air as a solute to his thought. "I am coming to appreciate more and more that there are few to possibly no accidents Liam."

"What are your plans for today?" He said rubbing his hands together.

"No more cake Liam." I said laughing as I watched him lick his lips.

He pouted his bottom lip, "Really? Not even a share between fast friends?"

I released a big laugh, "Let's see what the day brings first. My priority at the minute is to have some quiet time to read. Technically I was supposed to head home tonight but I think I'll stay in town for a few more days."

"Really?" Said Liam in a slightly high pitched excited voice.

I laughed, "Yes, really. I have a favor to ask. You are welcome to say no so please do so if you don't want to."

"Sure what is it?"

"I'm not really enjoying the hotel experience and wanted to stay somewhere quiet. Is there any chance I can crash here for a few days?"

"Of course, I have a spare bedroom. Follow me." He got up and disappeared down the hallway. I grabbed my bag and followed suit.

I walked into the small very tidy room. "This is great thank you so much." I looked at the sheet covers and nodded my head in thought.

In a sad voice Liam said, "Where ever I went I always rented two bedrooms in case you know."

"I know Liam, I know."

Liam walked out of the room. The bed covers had imprints of unicorns and rainbows. He had set it up for Lisa in the hope that one day they would spend time together. There was so much unspoken pain in the world.

Interlayers of stories spanning across the ether projected in wavelengths never reaching the ones intended, just floating about in a mottle mess of entanglement.

I placed my things beside the bed only selecting my day bag to take out to the lounge room. Liam was in the kitchen preparing another round of coffee. I wasn't sure where I could go to chill out and read the book. At the moment nowhere seemed safe. Even here with Liam I felt exposed.

"Liam have you ever been vaccinated for anything? Rubella, Flu, when you were set to go travelling anything at all?"

"That's a bit of a random question. Why do you ask? Do you think it has something to do with this sleepwalking business?"

"No, it's related to a thesis a colleague of mine is writing about the pros and cons of vaccination. It just sprung to mind while I was contemplating who might hold statistical records on vaccination information."

He entered the room with our coffees, "Here you go." He passed me my cup and then sat on the coffee table positioned in front of me. "Actually I'm pretty sure I never got vaccinated. I was petrified of needles, I still am. At school when they were doing the vaccinations I refused to calm down. I threw a royal fit every time they tried. The kids at school used to tease me about it."

I sat up in my chair feeling a sense of relief. Dear sweet Liam was proving to be an important asset in my life. "Pfft, kids are cruel. We all got subjected to shit heads when we were young. Are you sure you have never ever, never ever, ever never been vaccinated? What about when you travelled overseas?"

Liam laughed at my obvious persistence, "I've never been anywhere that's required me to be vaccinated and I would avoid going because I hate needles. I can't even look at them without breaking into a sweat. Even hospitals, the thought of walking into one makes my stomach churn."

"Liam I need to hire someone I can trust to do some random research to gather information without questioning me or talking about it to anyone. Would you be interested in doing this?"

"I'll just help you, no need to pay me. Fast friends never exchange money but they do share cake." He said with a wry smile as he sipped his cup of coffee.

I laughed, "Fine, if you get me a pen and paper I'll write down what you need to research. Just remember all the excess consumption of processed sugars could develop into diabetes which can lead to the need for a daily injection. You might be better off accepting payment instead."

"Nope, I like sharing cake with you. That's my price."

"You are a tough negotiator but I accept your terms." We both shook to seal the deal.

I spent the morning jotting down the list of topics I felt I needed Liam to research on my behalf. Meanwhile Liam tidied up his already well organized home. There were so many other questions now coming to mind I wish I had asked Zivah last night. One of the primary ones is how do I call her to me when I need to get guidance. Of all I had now learnt I felt certainty of one thing. I simply can't do this on my own. I need to build an army of supporters to a cause they would be oblivious to. I just knew by my instincts the less people were aware of the situation the stronger my position of influence would be. All seemingly far easier said than done.

Liam stood there reading the list. I watched his facial

expression as his eyes scanned down the piece of paper. At the end he looked up at me, "No questions?"

"Correct, the rules of engagement are no questions and no speaking about it. The less anyone understands the better. Do you trust me Liam?"

"I do trust you. I believe in you." He said sincerely.

"Can I trust you Liam?" I asked looking into his eyes.

"Yes."

I smiled. "Thank you. One day all of the things taking place will make sense. Maybe. Until then just accept that you don't need to know. Okay?"

"Sure. I'm going to go into my back office to get a start on this. It might take me days to find all the information you want."

"I know, this is just the tip of the iceberg. Once I review the results I'll no doubt need to get more refined information or start researching in a completely different direction. It might take months."

"Lucky for you I'm retired, have no social life and enjoy eating a lot of cake." He said smiling as he left the room.

I sat in silence staring out the front window not visually focused on anything in particular. I knew I should be overwhelmed perhaps even frightened by all that had transpired across the previous two days. Physiologically I was calm, my mind on the other hand was firing on as many cylinders as it could engage which was somewhat exhausting. Other than this I felt peaceful with a touch of excitement about the enormity of the task at hand. What I had been told I was chartered to do was beyond my own comprehension yet I relished the challenge. I saw no other way to manage this than to play it out like it is a game of sorts. The rules somewhat ambiguous, the opponents were ghosts so all I had was myself and in particular my mind to utilize in preemptive defense against the interferons. The sooner I obtained knowledge of my opponents and the rules the quicker I could set myself to breaking them. Therein lies the true strategic art of my game plan in the silent wars.

# Preemptive

L iam was out picking up supplies. He had not had a drink since all of this had begun and, much to my delight, proved himself to be a sensational cook. Liam was invaluable not just as a cake eating fast friend and diligent researcher but, thanks to his connections from years of servitude as an attorney, I had begun to establish access points into an influential network of people. This set me up nicely with avenues of enablement. Individuals with vested interest in key areas that I needed to stimulate were now at the ready to push forward with the first launch of my strategy. A vast majority of the activity focussed on utilizing some very low profile underground networks. It had taken us weeks and countless hours to quietly prepare in the background. There were only a few more items to line up in order to get the cogs of the wheels ready for motion. I was feeling rather satisfied with myself possessing no doubt the results would bear fruit in pushing the interferons buttons. I want them to come out and play in the open arena.

There wasn't anything else I could do until the remaining ducks were lined up. I now needed to focus my energies on reading the rest of the book. In truth, there wasn't a day that went by where I didn't think about York. I missed him. I missed the way I could hear his voice telling me the story as I read the words. He was very much a part of my life now and dare I say it, I loved him.

I made myself a cup of cocoa then headed outside into the small courtyard where Liam had an ultra comfortable cushion filled swinging cane chair he rarely used. It had become my favorite spot to rest. Today it would be my reading chair. I hopped in snuggling into position like the expert I now was and took one sip of my drink before placing it down to commence my reading.

*I welcomed the sound of the river, water running as I approached. The dog was still unconscious, bleeding profusely from the gapping hole in his leg. In the clearing I could see the edge of the river was laden with a combination of large and small sharp rocks. Carefully I removed the dog from my shoulders placing him down on the flattest boulder I could find. His breathing was fast but shallow. I glanced around to see if there was anything I could use as a scoop. My preference was to place the water directly on the wound rather than shock him by emersion into the cold running waters. There wasn't anything I could see so I didn't have much choice other than to take him in. Once I removed my shoes and socks I rolled up the bottom of my trousers to just under my knees. Picking up his tiny body I cradled him in my arms as I walked into the water. The rush of the flow swirled around my feet tickling my toes. Leaning down I placed him on a shallow portion of the riverbed while resting his head on my left foot to keep it above the surface so I could free my hands to clean his wound.*

*His coat was covered in lovely black and white patches with some little flecks of gray in places. His small floppy ears finished just above his eyes and his snout was a mix of all three colors, white, black and gray flecks. I didn't want to name him until I was certain he wasn't going to die but in my mind I was already calling him Huck.*

*As I rubbed around the edges of the wound to get some of the dried blood off he began to stir. When he opened his eyes fully he looked up at me instantly wagged his tail then he twisted his body slightly to look around while licking the water. I laughed when he released a bark before dipping his snout under after which he reefed his head back sending water droplets flying in all directions. Huck knew I was aiming to help him and settled to stillness while I continued to wash his leg. Once complete I thrust up from my squatted position to straighten to a stand leaving him to lay in the cool shallows. It took no more than a few strides before Huck leapt to his feet. I turned to see him run toward me on three legs barking.*

*"Hello"*

*My body jolted at the sound of the voice. I turned to see a man standing a few feet away looking down at little Huckleberry who was now growling at him.*

*"His leg is bad boy. Maggots will be eating him alive if you don't close that hole."*

*I looked down at sweet Huck who was now wagging his tail releasing a high pitched round of barks, then returned my gaze to look at the man. He stood there watching me quietly while I turned my head slightly to the left toward the river wondering if I should try and make a run for it.*

*"Look boy, here I'm going to show you." He took his shirt off and tore some pieces from the bottom of it into long strips. "Come here I need to find one for you. I won't hurt you, follow me." He said as he searched up and down the trunks of the surrounding trees.*

*I quickly put my shoes on, stuffed my socks in the bag then followed him while cautiously keeping my distance. Huck bounced along on three legs with the other propped up and out of the way. He was panting and wagging his tail. I think he knew he was safe and free.*

*"Here, I found it. Look up there, can you see the tree is crying. Them tears can heal a wound, keep them maggots from getting in. Wait here I'm going to get you some." The man put the strips of shirt in his mouth before he ascended up the tree. I watched as he balanced and manoeuvred his way to where he needed to be. Leaning across, he scraped then scooped some of the stuff into his shirt strips placing the collection now wrapped in a ball into his pockets. As he climbed down he was wearing a big triumphant smile. I liked him.*

*When his feet touched the ground he looked around and then gestured we go back to where we had been by the river. This time I was walking ahead. At the bed of the river he called the dog over crouching down while placing his hand out so Huck could sniff him. Huck took a step toward him stretching out his neck to take a whiff, only to quickly recoil while releasing a low audible growl.*

*"You will have to do it I don't think your dog likes me." He said offering me a big smile again. "Here take this and fill the hole. Its special, won't rot will help him heal and keep them maggots from eating him."*

*I reached across taking the strips of cloth into my hand. I placed the extra few in my bag, keeping one out to put on Huck. The substance was thick and sticky. As gently as I could muster I placed the stuff inside his leg then used the strip to wrap it around to prevent it from oozing out either side of the hole. Huck remained still the whole time only whimpering once.*

*As I stood up I noticed the man was looking around again. When I saw him licking his lips I reached down retrieving an apple from my bag to give as a gesture of thanks. He looked at the apple and once again smiled.*

*"An apple isn't what I need. What are you going to give me boy for helping you with your dog?"*

*As he went to move forward Huck started growling again. I bent down to retrieve another apple from my bag to offer him two for his assistance. I watched as he stared at the dog and then at me. There was something in the way he was now looking at me which felt uncomfortable. I placed the two apples on the ground in front of me then took a couple of steps backward. The man extended his reach while bending down to retrieve the apples. Part way down his body jolted as he lunged at me instantly turning me around so I was facing the riverbed while he shifted to be flush against my back. His whole hand wrapped around my throat squeezing me in place as his other hand was now leaning on my stomach clasping my right suspender.*

*"A man needs to be rewarded for helping." He whispered in my ear as he pushed his body hard up against mine. Huck was barking and growling as he bit the bottom of his trousers. Struggling to breathe my mind was reeling. I reached into my pocket pulling out one of the tools I took from the room in the asylum. The man's breath laid heavy on my ear as he placed my lobe in his mouth to suck while he pushed his body hard against mine. Clasping the handle of the tool tight I stabbed his hand then dragged it across the length of his exposed arm. Immediately he screamed, releasing me. Gasping deeply for breath I spun around striking at the air left and right, managing to catch the side of his face with my fourth attempt. I watched as the blade melted into his skin opening it like a rose in bloody bloom.*

*The man fell backward trying to avoid my continued frantic slashing as he screamed holding his face.*

*While he was down I grabbed my bag and ran across to the path back toward the orchard with Huck keeping pace. I needed to find another way to the river. If this man saw me travel down its edges he would surely follow after what I had just done. I ran until my lungs betrayed me knowing I had no time to lose. I pushed on as fast as I could until I reached the place where the orchard began. Walking the length of it I found an entry point back into the forest where I did my best to follow a straight line, as there was no longer the luxury of a well laid path. This time I would have to find the river on my own.*

*Part way down I settled on a log in the thick of the forest to have an apple. I was tired, hungry and missed Adeline. Huck nestled into a ball beside my feet. I bit off a little of the apple placing it beside him. He sniffed it, licked it a couple of times and then left it there. I had no idea what I was going to feed him I only had apples.*

*It seemed to be taking far longer to find the river than it did when we walked along the rough cut path. The rustling leaves in the wind masked any way of me hearing the running water so I was forced to rely on my visuals and hope I was walking in a straight line toward the rivers edge. Time flitted by as I watched Huck dart ahead into the scrub and then return. At one point I could hear him barking in the distance. Instinctively I froze to gain my bearings. I couldn't hear anything over his incessant noise so it left me no choice but to cautiously creep forward to see what all the commotion was about.*

*When I got closer there was a change in the air, the breeze seemed cooler. I peered through the trees to find Huck barking at a rock a couple of feet from the rivers edge. Stepping out into the open I could see there was a hole under*

181

*it. There was something in there Huck wanted access to. I clasped the edge of the stone and heaved to shift it across exposing the hole. No sooner had I done this Huck nose dived in frantically digging around the sides with one paw repeatedly into the soft ground until half his body could fit inside. It didn't take long before he lifted his head revealing a rat in his mouth. Greedily he tore at it swallowed the pieces. When he was finished he went in searching for another.*

*I sat on the edge of the rock to look at the map Adeline had drawn for me. It said to keep travelling down the edge of the riverbed until I reached the wooden cross bridge. According to her it would take two days walk. It was going to be a long couple of days with little reprieve from the sun beaming down. I didn't even know where I was going to sleep. I ran my fingers along the ridges of the pen strokes Adeline had made. I closed my eyes lifting my head to feel the warm rays coat my skin. The idea of freedom had a cost, which I was beginning to feel. The more distance I put between the asylum and myself the more aware I became of my heart aching to hear Adeline's voice call my name.*

*Huck licked my leg taking a seat beside my left foot as he dropped a dead rat on my shoe. I smiled; his little belly was full. I folded the map placing it in my pocket, put the rat in the bag for Huck to eat later and started the journey down the river. In my mind I recited the stories Adeline had read to me. I imagined myself as a character in the books and would re-enact parts. My favorite was picking up a stick to sword fight like the Scarlet Pimpernel.*

*Hours had passed, with the sun now showing signs it was ready to go to sleep I knew night was soon due to cloak the skies. There wasn't anywhere I could see that would be comfortable to rest. The rocks near the river's edge were jagged. The only option I could identify was to create a makeshift bed using fallen foliage under the canopy of trees close by. Huck positioned himself near my neck curling into a neat rotund ball. It had been a really big day so it didn't take long for me to fall asleep.*

*My dreams were non distinct. I had this reoccurring experience of stinging sensations all over. I felt myself struggle in the dark of the four walls I felt I was trapped within. My heart was racing realizing my escape and freedom was a dream. Sweat poured from my brow as the pain seemed to catapult across aspects of my tired limbs.*

*I woke to a startle as Huck barked and licked my ear. In a daze I sat up to look at him. He spun in a circle whining. In the light of the moon I lifted my arm to see I was covered in stinging fire ants and so was Huckleberry. Leaping to my feet I grabbed him then swiftly ran into the heart of the river immersing us both under. I placed Huck back on the edge quickly removing the last of the ants I could see on him before submerging back under the water to remove the remaining ones from me.*

*When I returned to retrieve my bag I realized it was the rat carcass, which attracted every night crawler around to feast. I washed the contents of the bag reloaded it and decided given there would be no further sleep this night we might as well continue our journey. My body was signaling pulses of pain from the stings indiscriminately placed all over my limbs. It drove both Huck and myself to distraction.*

*A little way down the river Huck began sniffing at something then dropped his body into what looked like a puddle of mud. He rolled around until he was completely covered before looking up at me releasing a bark. The wag in his tail quickened as I got closer to inspect what it was he was standing in. When I bent over to touch it Huck licked my finger and dropped once again rolling around to recoat his body. Scooping a little in my hand I tried to smell it but the scent wasn't strong enough for my broken sense of smell to detect anything. Huck barked and leapt up on my leg leaving dirty drag marks of the stuff where his paws had landed. Almost instantly the stings it touched felt relief. My eyes widened with a smile, I dropped my bag stripped off all my clothes and joined him. I generously spread the goop all over my body feeling the cooling relief of the muck. It no longer mattered what it was, it worked and I was grateful to Huck for showing me.*

*Frozen by the cool night air I shivered as I walked along the edge of the river naked witnessed only by the light of the guiding moon. The world was nothing like I had imagined from the books I read. I knew now there were more secrets to be learnt in the natural order of things. It all made sense after it happened, the carcass, the ants and so forth. I needed to get smarter in my thinking rather quickly if I wanted to survive.*

I looked up after reading those words smiling with a deep feeling of pride for York arriving at this crucial epiphany. He was now at a point of awareness about his need to consider all his options and associated actions, this would be a life changing paradigm shift. What a clever young emerging man he was. I closed my eyes and breathed in feeling so much pride. He was going to be okay. I knew it. There was a sense of hope intermixed with relief.

"Hey are you asleep?"

I opened my eyes to be greeted with Liam's bright smile as he proudly held out a bowl for me to claim. I reshuffled in the chair to sit more upright, "Yum what is it?" All of a sudden present to my hunger.

"Steamed vegetables in my own concoction of peanut, lime and coconut sauce with Hokkien noodles."

"Wow it sounds divine and smells out of this world. My mouth is salivating so much it's clearly happy to see this." I said laughing.

"Try it."

"Am I the guinea pig in this gastronomic experiment of yours?" I said squinting my eyes suspicious of his eagerness for me to take a bite.

"No, I sampled it while I was making it and I'm thinking it's a masterpiece." He said while raising his hands with a twirling motion toward the sky.

I swirled the fork to gather some noodles, stabbed a piece of broccoli, sliver of snow pea, piece of squash then unceremoniously shoveled it into my mouth. My taste buds instantly sang a chorus of joy as the juices of the sauce coated my tongue. The sound of the combination simply didn't do the experience of meshed flavors justice. To say it was delicious was an understatement. Instead of conveying anything to Liam who was eagerly awaiting a verdict I scooped another forkful in my mouth and then another until the bowl was finished. My tongue ventured out my mouth to collect the sauce trying to escape from my lips as I passed Liam the empty bowl and said, "More please."

Fist clenched he jumped in the air screaming the word, "Yes."

"I believe you need to call this recipe mouth gasm because it's that fucking delicious.'

Liam was jumping around in circles punching the air while saying the words, "Yes, yes, yes."

I laughed, "When you're done celebrating I'm keen to know how you went today and to get another bowl of those delicious noodles."

He turned and danced his way inside to fetch me a refill quickly returning with a glass of homemade lemon ice tea and a new serve of mouth gasm. He sat down on the wicker chair as he passed everything over to me.

"Thanks, how did you go today?" I asked while prepping my new fork for its virgin twirl.

"I found out the vaccine has been FDA approved and is due to be released within the next month. There's a massive marketing campaign planned for the launch so I would say it is definitely going to be released soon."

"Did you find out the name of the groups I was looking for?"

"Yes, I have all the details. An old buddy of mine knows the leader of two of the groups personally so I did exactly what you asked. If you are right then the wheels should be in motion. I guess we will see over the next week."

I paused for a moment looking at my noodles, the tea and then Liam. "I can't thank you enough for all your assistance. You have welcomed me into your home, assisted me in blind faith, cooked amazing food and been the best fast friend I've ever had."

Liam leaned across placing his hand on my knee, "You saved my life. If it wasn't for our friendship I probably would have killed myself by now or at the very least been back on my way to doing it slowly through alcohol. I've never felt more alive, more like me in my entire existence. When I show you who I am I get smiles, kindness and celebration from your reflection. You never questioned or judged me once for what happened in the past. All you did was hold me, cry with me, laugh with me. I love you Harper Perelle." He paused for a moment smiling at me thoughtfully, "I love you."

Liam's words touched my heart, "My noodles are getting cold. I've got no time for mushy moments." I said shifting my leg so his hand dropped off me while simultaneously poking out my tongue at him.

"Its okay Harper. I know you don't like expressing your feelings. I've been watching you too. Don't worry eventually when you get up from this swing chair I'm claiming my cuddle because believe it or not we just had a moment." He said sitting back with a satisfied smile on his face.

"I've got to say you're high maintenance, first with the whole cake demands which my thighs are not thanking you for and now this whole touchy feely thing. Liam, I have to say you are simply taking this too far," I said jokingly while shoving a mouthful of the noodles into my sink hole then exaggerating my chewing to gross him out.

"Keep going Harps and I'll squeeze the breath out of you while planting fast friend kisses all over your face."

"Its official get me the laptop I'm ordering you a male bride or a blow up doll, which ever I can get delivered before I have to leave this chair." I said laughing loudly.

With pursed lips and a large exhale Liam rose to his feet grabbed my bowl and glass of ice tea placing it down on the table behind him, "That's it Harps you asked for it." He grabbed the outside rim of the swing chair lifting it upside down to encourage my descent. When he realized I had positioned myself like a cartoon cat at a door with all limbs fastened to wedge me in he let go of the swing walked to the front and dove inside the opening with me.

I burst out laughing as he squirmed about wrapping his arms and legs around me. I was weakened by my incessant giggles at the experience of Liam's efforts. In the end I settled into his cuddle closing my eyes smiling. We lay there for a while enjoying the motion of the swing as I listened to him regain his breath.

"Admit that you like getting a cuddle." He said while resting his head on my shoulder.

"I'm getting you a blow up doll and a mail order groom." I responded while laughing.

"You are one stubborn creature. It's okay, I love you just the way you are." Liam gently kissed my shoulder and then shifted to get out of the chair. All of a sudden there was a loud cracking sound then BAM the chair, Liam and I went crashing to the ground. Lucky for both of us the cushions we were laying on absorbed most of the impact. We looked at each other in a moment of shock before bursting into a fit of laughter.

Once we ineloquently scrambled out of the chair I relocated to the lounge to greedily finish my second serving of noodles before I recommenced reading. Meanwhile Liam left to get what he needed from the hardware store to repair the chair. I was still smiling from ear to ear. I really was grateful for Liam's presence in my life. This whole experience was easier to manage with him keeping me grounded.

I'd taken a leave of absence from work and told my family I was vacationing overseas so they wouldn't worry about my lack of contact. I knew it wasn't in the interferons best interests to harm me but the protection didn't extend to the people who cared for me. The less they knew the better. I took a big gulp of the ice tea to wash the last of the delicious noodles down, nuzzled my back into the sofa and reopened the book.

*When the mud crusted on my skin I placed my clothes back on and began to run slowly down the way to warm my body. The lightening of the sky told of the sun awakening and stretching its arms out to soon brighten the world once more. There was something wonderful about being able to watch the transition from dark to light and visa versa. It felt like a privilege to be a witness to its cyclic evolutions.*

*Huck was happily keeping up on three legs. Occasionally he would trek ahead of me then circle back to travel by my side. It was strange to think I had only met him yesterday and now I couldn't imagine my life without him. We were already best buddies looking after each other along the way.*

*I stopped walking the moment I saw the luminescence of the sun quietly rise on the horizon. Looking at the beautiful colors reflecting on the underside of the clouds I wondered if Adeline returned to the room to check if I had left. I hoped she saw my message. There was so much more I wish I could have said. In the presence of the first light I swore I would one day return to her.*

*It took a greater portion of the day before Huck and I arrived at the bridge. The walk had taken its toll on my feet. They were beginning to blister from my sweaty soles sliding about in the oversized shoes. I found a spot under the bridge to shelter ourselves from the stifling build of the afternoon heat with the intention of remaining out of sight until nightfall. There was certainty where a bridge existed so did people. Adeline had warned me to keep myself unnoticed until I reached her instructed destination.*

*I awoke to the vibration of Huck's low growl on my arm. Dazed I rubbed the sleep out of my eyes before looking around to see what he was focused on. The sky was dark once more; we had slept through the worst of the afternoons swelter. I clasped Huck's nose gently shut as I saw two pairs of feet walking to toward the water. Every time he started to growl I tapped him lightly on his snout to discourage his continuance. I hoped if we kept still these people would leave without noticing us in the shadows.*

*They were in our full view, under the light of the*

*moon I watched as they turned to one another exchanging laughter while undressing. They threw their clothes to one side before running into the river hand in hand. The girl released a little squeal as he pulled her toward him. Their foreheads touched as he swirled her in circles. She placed her arms around his neck and they began to kiss. He then raised her above his head slowly letting the water drip from her body onto his face. During the course of bringing her back down she allowed his lips to glide up her abdomen until his mouth settled on her left breast. I noticed her face changed from smiles to an expression I had not seen before. Biting her bottom lip making little noises which seem to encourage Huck to restart his growling again.*

*The man returned her back to the water leaning forward so their mouths greeted. I had read of this in books but had never witnessed a real kiss before. My breath quickened watching intently as they moved like hungry animals consuming the contours of one anothers perimeters. Their hands seemed to have a mind of their own as they ran through each other's hair, slid down between their shoulder blades then disappeared under water. The noises they were making caused my body to respond with a confusing pleasurable ache as I continued to watch from the shadows.*

*The man flung his head back gasping while she kissed his neck as her arm jiggled the waters surface. His words eluded my comprehension but I could see the pained expression on his face as the jiggling quickened to a frenzied pace. Then all of a sudden she squealed as he scooped her into his arms carrying her across to the shallows. The man placed her down gently then hovered over her lips breathing heavy. Steadily running his hand along the length of her body he reclined back to be positioned on his knees. She squealed when he encouraged her legs to be apart. Using his hand to regain her focus by placing it on her stomach to still her body he then dropped his face into the darkness. The moon was shining on her body as a silhouette of shimmering glisten. She arched her back revealing ample bosom, which rose and softly fell slightly to the sides. Her hands caressed the mounds then with gentle strokes she touched the darkened ends while biting her lip as she had done before. The noises were louder this time with furrows creasing her brow. I could hear the word 'yes' between other ramblings.*

*The man pounced while supporting the center of her midriff as he moved back and forth grunting with fury. She joined in making strange noises. His became considerably louder when he shifted his pace of thrust; I leaned forward to try to see his face. With this Huck jumped out of my arm running toward them while barking.*

*"What the," said the man looking into the shadows trying to see Huck.*

*I quietly got up, placed my bag on my shoulder turned and ran to the other end of the bridge leaping straight up the right side and away from view. I heard the man yelling "Hey You," but the rest was muffled as my heart took possession of my ear's attention. In spite of my blisters burning my feet I kept pushing as hard as I could to maintain a speed to place as much distance between the bridge and me. There was no telling what that man would do if he caught me.*

*Huck came screaming past me then screeched to a stop in the distance. He turned released a bark while wagging his tail. I bent down picked him up and gave him a little squeeze then placed him on the ground again. He spun around in circles a couple of times looking rather pleased with himself then settled to walk beside me.*

*Reaching into my pocket my heart sunk as I felt the paper pulp. The map Adeline created had become a fused mess. It was with me when I ran into the water to get the fire ants off. I looked down at my arms now realizing I was still coated in mud. Huck's was almost all gone. He had rolled in the grass when it dried so there were only clouds of fine dust left when I patted him. Before I ventured too far away from the river I needed to have a wash. Just off the road there was a spot behind a shrub providing me a shield from passers view. I threw the rat in the air and watched Huck jump to catch it. Settling in the shadows I grabbed an apple for myself. We needed to wait for a while to make sure the others left the river.*

*A few hours had past before we cautiously made our way back to the river only returning under the bridge when I was certain I couldn't hear any voices or splashing about. I stripped off my clothes then walked straight into the black night waters. The air was still very warm so the coolness of the drifting currents was a welcome treat on my sweat clogged skin. Fastidiously I rubbed my body all over to remove the mud with earnest. The welts had almost all subsided; only three raised red lumps remained near the edge of my left ankle. Thankfully the sting had long left my body.*

*Once I was dressed again I pulled out the map in an attempt to carefully pry it open. The portions of the paper I was able to peel apart no longer held Adeline's writing. The ink bleed danced across the page leaving waves of blue. It was official with no map to guide me I was on my own.*

*Unaware of the time remaining until daybreak, I decided to make my way back in the same direction I had previously run. It felt right even though I knew I was completely lost. In my mind the image of the map was a broken picture. The river along with the bridge sat as the most prominent landmarks after this I was supposed to head toward a tree marked with red paint. The complexity was overlaid by my inability to recall which direction it was situated or whether the tree was indeed the next main marker to be called for attention.*

*Walking in the silence of the night feeling a little disheartened I compelled myself to march onward by thinking about Adeline. My body was tired, my mind was sad and steadily my feet were becoming increasingly sore from the shoes. I stopped to remove them; tying the laces together I placed them over my shoulder and recommenced down the path while trying where possible to ensure Huck and I remained out of sight.*

*After a few hours of travelling down a road that seemed endless I decided to find a place to lay down. When I had the map it felt like an adventure with purpose, now I was lost, scared and very much missing Adeline. Huck and I settled inbetween the roots at the base of an overgrown willow tree. He climbed on my chest licking my chin as I lay there feeling unhappy, I didn't know what I was going to do. I closed my eyes to welcome the draw of slumber.*

*Huck released a yelp as he flew in the air when I leapt to my feet. I remembered, I could see the map; it was there all there. I felt elated; we had travelled in the wrong direction. Huck and I needed to head back and cross over the bridge. The red tree was on the other side. Then the twisted road to the left would take us to the place Adeline told me would be safe. I felt as though I was bursting with energy. Picking up my bag I ran down the path toward the bridge, my lungs filled with air as I beamed a smile that could have lit up the night sky. Huck ran ahead doing little spins releasing a bark as he completed each twirl. I put my arms out and swung them mimicking the wings of an aeroplane feeling invigorated. We were going to be okay. I just knew it.*

*It only took us half the time to return to the base of the bridge. I was hobbling from the pain of the open blisters on my feet, which were coated in dirt and weeping tears. Dawn was looming near the line of the horizon. I mustered my will to push forward; we had already wasted so much time. There was a sense of urgency to get to this house. I knew there would be a hefty distance to travel however my need to arrive weighed far greater than the pain my body was experiencing so Huck and I trundled on.*

"Harps its not healthy for you to stay inside all the time."

I looked up from the book at Liam. "I didn't hear you come in. How long have you been home?"

"You never seem to hear me when you're reading that book." He said peering over my shoulder to look at the page.

"Nothing?" I asked

"Absolute nada. The pages are bald as a badger and I'm pretty sure I could have you certified for spending countless hours staring at blank pages and more so for thinking there is anything written there." He said folding his arms while raising his left eyebrow.

"Nice try Liam. Child psychology 101, you want me to feel the need to prove myself so I read it to you. It isn't going to happen. If you were meant to know what's contained on these pages you would be able to read them yourself. So you have no chance of me sating your curiosity."

"You are no fun Harper Perelle."

I laughed as I watched a grown man pout. "Trust me Liam, for the most part you really don't want to know the story. There are patches where it's really quite boring. I'm doing you a favor."

"Won't you tell me the tiniest tid bit?" He said persisting like a spoilt child.

I sat up, closed the book and placed it on the coffee table in front of me. "I've really got to try and complete reading the rest of the story before the end of the week if possible. There may be some things I need to learn in here which alter the plans for the full launch of phase one."

Liam rolled his eyes, "I know I've agreed not to ask questions but you have to understand none of what you have me doing makes sense and the curiosity is killing me."

I burst out laughing as I watched Liam jiggling up and down in protest to emphasize his frustration. It looked more like he needed to urinate. "I know. Once it's launched and things are beginning to unfold I'll start to provide you with some insights and maybe, <u>maybe</u>, place you in charge of operation spin top. The caveat is ensuring it's safe. I'm going to be an irritant to people who may wish to retaliate. If there is anyone to blame or get caught, it's mine to own. I won't do anything to place you at risk or have you associated with it."

Liam's eyes widened like a child who just realized he was getting his favorite toy for Christmas. "What's operation spin top?"

"Liam, please. Really? You will be told at the right time if it's clear to assign you to the task. In the meantime be happy I don't keep you like a mushroom." I said smiling.

"Mushroom?"

"In the dark and fed shit." I laughed; it was a saying I had heard years ago and still found it amusing.

"Well I feel like I am a mushroom."

"Oh, come on Liam. You are kept in the dark but I'm not feeding you shit. Everything I have told you is based on my truth. What can I do to make you feel better and get the subject dropped?"

I watched his expression transition to delight. We both said it at the exact same time, "Cake."

I stood up nodding my head, "You're so predictable."

Liam was sporting a cheeky smile, "Am I? So that's yes to cake? You have to, I'm feeling like a mushrooooom."

My eyes widened as my own smile on my face broadened while I reactively punched him in the arm, "I've been had! You set that whole thing up knowing I wouldn't tell you anything so you could guilt me into eating cake with you."

"I did." He said, chest out happily rising up and down on his toes with his hands clasped behind his back beaming with pride.

"Well played, you cheeky shit. Looks like I'm the only mushroom around here except you're feeding me cake." I said shaking me head.

"Can we still have some?"

"Yeeessss, It would be remiss of me not to reward that kind of thinking. I'm seriously impressed. It also highlights a weakness in my predictability not to mention a reminder not to trust <u>anyone</u>."

"Thank yoooou." He said now with his hands now in front of him swinging from side to side.

"Hey, didn't my punch hurt?" I said looking at his arm. "I connected harder than intended."

Liam instantly bent forward grabbing his arm, "Oh, God yes. I was trying to be all macho about it but fuck me, ouchie."

I burst out laughing and so did he. Liam was such a funny banana.

I followed him into the kitchen, "Really? The extent of your cheek is reaching beyond my expectations."

I sat down at the table where the sweets were already presented.

Liam had a look of delight as he picked up his fork to take his first bite of the triple layer chocolate mousse cake. I grabbed my fork and watched it glide effortlessly through my decadent slice of sin. When I placed it in my mouth my eyes automatically closed, feeling the need to pay homage to the textured multitude of chocolate flavors dressing my tongue.

In silence the two of us consumed our generous portions far quicker than we should have. Our eyes didn't deviate from the visual disappearing delight. It was as though any attention swayed from the consumption of this indulgence would be insulting to the experience. We took our final mouthful at the same time then rested our forks on the table coordinated like synchronized swimmers at the Olympic games. We both returned one another's stare as our tongues searched our lips for any escaping morsels. Once satisfied there was nothing remaining, a half smile mirrored on his face. We both grabbed our respective plates mercilessly licking the base clean. I dropped my plate to the table and jumped in the air with my hands raised.

"Yes, I win." We both cracked up laughing, as the manic sugar high was set to hit us hard.

Liam's expression changed to a look of concern as he whispered, "Shhh, Harps did you hear that?"

I looked at Liam nodding my head, grabbed the fork off the table placing it in the wedge of my tied up hair. I put my finger on my mouth signaling Liam to keep quite before gestured for him to stay in the kitchen and listen."

I walked into the lounge room to where I noticed the

front door was wide open and two men were near the sofa frantically tossing stuff about searching the place.

"What are you looking for perhaps I can help?" I said stepping forward.

The men stood upright with one fumbling to pull his knife out from his back pocket.

"Looks sharp, careful you might hurt yourself." I said smiling at him as I stared into his eyes.

The other fellow stepped forward, "Where is it?"

"Where's what?" I replied trying to keep myself as calm as possible.

"The book, give us the book."

"It's on the table." Yelled Liam. He entered the room walking cautiously sideways like a crab intermittently peering from behind the frying pan he was using as a shield for his face.

I smiled with a sarcastic tone, "Yep, there it is right in front of you on the table. That's what you're looking for right? A book." I shrugged my shoulders, "That's a book."

The fellow with the knife waved it in a swirl pointing it at me, "I've already checked. It's blank. Give us the book or so help me I'll cut you."

Liam, blurted out, "Its not blank you just can't see the words."

I burst out laughing as he said it. The two men looked at each other and then started yelling over the top of one another, "Give us the book" "I'll stab you." Give us the book NOW." "I'm going to stick you hard." "Where's the book?"

"OKAY, okay relax."

"Harper NO!" Yelled Liam.

"I have to Quagmire, I don't want to get stabbed. It's

hidden under the sofa. Shift it across and you will see it."

Liam stepped toward me saying through gritted teeth, "Damn it Harper, what the fuck are you doing?"

"STAY WHERE YOU ARE." Growled the man with the knife in his now adrenaline ridden shaky hand.

The other perpetrator grunted as he moved the sofa to reveal the book. He picked it up, flicked the pages and smiled. "There was that so hard?"

They both backed out the door, "Don't try and call the cops we know where you live."

I waited until they cleared the drive and could hear the car screeching as it made its overly dramatic exit before I stepped forward slamming the door shut then switched the latch to lock it. I turned to see Liam bent over holding his chest.

"Are you okay? You did really well. Even I almost believed you." I said laughing.

"Jesus Harper, I was freaked out."

"Really? I couldn't tell you looked so macho doing that sideways crab crawl thingy. What the fuck were you thinking? The mere sight of that alone only strengthened their confidence." I had tears forming in my eyes from trying to hold back the laughter. It was as I had expected. The interferons didn't have any idea of what they were looking for aside from it being a book. If they did know then they certainly didn't convey it to these amateurs. They weren't even wearing masks. 'Stupid dumbasses.' The best part was these guys just made off with a bastardized hand written series of notes plagiarized from, The adventures of Huckleberry Finn, The Scarlet Pimpernel, Ghost Busters, Treasure Island and The Hardy Boy Adventures. I would pay to see the expression on the interferons faces when they finally realize. It was my subtle way of saying 'Fuck you,' to these self serving ass holes and it didn't hurt to have the idea amuse me in the process.

I walked across to console Liam by giving him a manly firm pat on the back. "Deep breaths you will be fine in a minute. Guess this will encourage you to remember to lock the door. I told you it wasn't safe. I'm also going to need to be more diligent about keeping the book with me at all times."

Liam took a couple of steps backward to flop into his armchair while I went to the kitchen to get him a glass of water.

Upon my return he was sitting there slumped in silence staring into space, "Here you go."

He took a sip then robotically passed it back to me. He was clearly in shock.

"Liam I think it's in our best interest to get out of here for a few days. Do you have your emergency bag packed?"

He nodded his head without diverting his gaze. "It's real isn't it? There was a part of me, which secretly thought you might be eccentric or a little loopy. When you made me practice this routine I was bemused, going along with it because I thought it was a bit of fun, but its real. It's real Harper. It's all real, the book, everything, it's fucking real."

"Shhhhhh," I said placing my hand on his jiggling knee. "I'll understand if you would like me to leave Liam. I don't want to bring stress or complications into your life. Regardless it is best if you get away for a few days, lay low while things settle. I can make sure they see me leave on my own in the opposite direction."

Liam shifted his eyes to look into mine, "Are you

kidding? I'm just trying to think of what color cape I should buy to wear that doesn't clash with my fair complexion."

I burst out laughing. "I wasn't expecting that. You are full of surprises." I said slapping his leg.

"Ouch," He leaned over rubbing where I had hit him while he laughed.

"Yep real super hero material. Watch out world here comes crustacean man or even better crab man. Everyone's scared of a highly contagious sexually transmitted disease," winking at him as I stood up to head to my bedroom. "Grab your bag we have to get going."

"Crab man. Funny Harps, really funny."

Liam met me at the front door with his bag in hand. "Where are we going?"

"You will see. It's a blast from my past. I'm sure it will prove to be entertaining mostly at my expense. It will give us both an opportunity to relax while we wait for the FDA announcement on the release."

Liam locked the door then tossed the keys to me. Instinctively I caught them. "Guess I'm driving."

"It's probably best given my license is cancelled due to drink driving." He said frowning.

I threw my bag in the back and jumped into the driver's seat. When Liam shut the passenger door I commenced with reversing out the drive.

"What's the scowl for?" I asked glancing at his furrows.

"I thought we agreed my fake name was going to be Ronaldo."

I started laughing, "I'd forgotten all about calling you Ronaldo. Nah, you definitely looked more like a creeping crab walking Quagmire than a Ronaldo."

"But I don't want to be a Quagmire. Quagmire's ugly." He said in a half feigned whiney voice.

Bursting into laughter at the visualization of Liam cartoon versioned into Quagmire I agreed, "Okay, okay next time I'II call you Ronaldo." I wiped my eyes from the forming tears trying to compose myself in preparation for the drive. "So have you decided what color cape you are going to wear?"

His face lit up, "Can we be Batman and Robin?"

"I'm not too keen on the whole sporting jocks on the outside of my spandex but sure why not I'II give anything a try thrice. You can be Batman and I'II be Robin." I said with a serious tone.

"Really? Why are you Robin? Is it because it's a girls name?"

"Fuck no, it's because the villains always try to kill Batman first. If they are after you then it gives me a chance to escape." I said releasing a big loud laugh and more tears of joy.

Liam's eye's widened, "I'm Robin. I want to be Robin. You're Batman, I'm Robin okay?"

We both laughed as we drove down the road toward the highway.

# Stimuli

Seven long hours later we arrived in San Francisco and more importantly at the door of a couple of college buddies of mine. I woke Liam up from his drooling slumber with a nudge as I jumped out of the car. We walked across the road together climbing up the steep stairs to the front door.

"Are you going to tell me who this is? You haven't brought me home to meet your mother unannounced have you?"

"Ha, you wish. Why should I tell you when it would spoil the fun. You will get a kick out of this I promise." I said with a wink. As I turned to face the door I pressed the doorbell multiple times then proceeded to yell at the top of my lungs "PEPPY THREADBOW, SAM ESPLANADE, I KNOW YOU'RE IN THERE. YOU CAN'T HIDE FOREVER. YOU BOTH LIED! THEM CRAB CRITTERS DON'T COME FROM NO TOILET SEAT. OPEN THIS DOOR NOW." I pressed the doorbell consecutive times before continuing my rant, "AND DON"T THINK YOU CAN FOOL ME ANY MORE ABOUT BEING TEN INCHES NEITHER. I BOUGHT MYSELF A RULER!"

Liam laughed nervously while he looked around at the neighboring houses switching on their lights to see what was going on.

The door was opened just enough so Sam could sheepishly poke his head out to see who the crazy person was causing the commotion. All of sudden it was flung wide open as he leapt on me, "Oh my God, Fluffy fucking Tallintyre, PEPPY COME DOWN HERE YOU'RE NOT GOING TO BELIEVE IT. IT'S FUCKING FLUFFY." I laughed as he squeezed the breathe out of me. "Quick lets get inside before the neighbors report us again."

We walked into the hall as Sam swiftly shut the door behind us.

"Sam this is Liam a friend of mine. Liam this is Sam." They both shook hands exchanging polite greetings.

"We decided to go on a bit of a road trip and seven hours later happened at your doorstep. Do you still have the basement hangout set up?"

"Of course, you two are welcome to stay for as long as you like. I still have your key hanging on the board."

"Cool, Liam will need a room upstairs with you guys. The hangout is all mine baby."

"Oh, so when you said friends you actually meant 'friends.' Righto." Said Sam scratching his head.

I looked at both of them with a cheeky smile, "Peppy's still a slack ass. I'm going in." Quick as a whip I ran up to the top of the stairs straight into Peppy's room unannounced leaping onto his bed landing not so gracefully beside him.

He raised his head in shock glaring at me as I smiled. "What the? Fluffy, Fluffy Oh my God, FLUFFY!" He said with a big smile as he wrapped his arms around me for a cuddle.

"Hey you," I said as I returned his embrace. "Come get up we have some catching up to do."

I slid off his bed turned to look at the whopping big smile on his face.

I nodded my head, "I've missed you too." I walked out the door. Feigning an angry tone I yelled, "GET UP lazy ass," laughing to myself as I made my way back down the stairs. I wandered into the kitchen where I could hear Sam and Liam tinkering about. When I saw what they were doing I shook my head and thought 'God help me.'

They were both busy setting up the tequila shots, four rows of ten to be precise. I looked across at Liam. "Are you sure?"

"Yessss. This is for fun. It's different."

I nodded my head. I had to trust he knew himself well enough to know whether it was okay to consume alcohol given his past.

Sam stopped pouring to look up at me, "Did Peppy freak?"

"He was in shock and then he reverted to happy puppy just like old times." I said smiling.

Liam stepped across to position himself closer to me, "Do I get to know the history behind Fluffy Tallintyre?"

"It's the combination of the name of the first pet I ever had and the first street I ever lived in. Fluffy was my Pomeranian dog and I lived on Tallintyre Road. When combined they make up my porn star name. This is Sam Esplanade and you will get to meet Peppy Threadbow any minute."

Liam instantly placed his hands on his face and said, "No, no, no, no, no, no, no"

This naturally got Sam and my attention as I said,

"Oh fuck yes, spill it. You have to tell us, its part of the rules of entry to our inner sanctum. Spill it."

"I can't. I just can't." He said peering between fingers. I saw his face was flushed red.

I flipped my head up toward the ceiling releasing a laugh then yelled, "PEPPY, GET DOWN HERE YOU WON'T WANT TO MISS THIS!"

I could hear Peppy's footsteps coming down the stairs.

"Liam, this is Peppy. Peps focus, we are about to hear what I am suspecting might be the best porn star name ever accidentally made."

"Cool, spill it." Said Peppy still half asleep leaning on the fridge door.

"No, really it's awful." Insisted Liam.

"You can do it Liam. It will liberate you and bring us endless joy. Come on Liam, don't back out now."

The three of us started chanting as we circled him, "Say it, Say it, Say it, Say it, Say it, Say it."

Fists clenched, eyes shut tight he blurted, "PRECIOUS CLINT," then hid his face behind his hands again.

The three of us for the briefest moment paused to look at each other almost as a silent validation to ensure we all heard what we thought we heard, then quickly transitioned to screams of insurmountable joy. We laughed so hard we were falling over ourselves. Liam also laughed but I could see through the squints of my eyes he was feeling uncomfortable.

Between chuckles I tapped Sam and Peppy on the shoulder to gain their attention, "Guys, guys, come on we need to be respectful about this."

Instantly Peppy stood up wiping his tears from his eyes, "No worries man, honestly I think your name's really Preciousssss." We all cracked up again.

Sam stepped forward "Come on let's compose ourselves and make a toast in honor of being in the presence a Precious CLiiiinnnt." There were waves of laughter bouncing off the acoustic walls of the kitchen while the three of us tag teamed with an endless stream of one liners.

The laughter was contagious, Liam had tears streaming down his face as he piped up, "It could have been worse I originally wanted to call my rabbit Chubby."

That was it, we were out of control. Sam was on his back on the floor holding his stomach with his legs flapping in the air. Peppy was facing the fridge door slapping the side as he released his loud laughter. Leaning over the island bench Liam had his fist clenched as he squealed the words, "I can't breathe," over and over. Meanwhile my laugh had converted to some hybrid cross between a hyena and a dog that swallowed a whistle. The mere sight of each other spurred the laughter to continue for the better part of an hour.

We finally managed to settle down, gathering our drinks, the salt and lemon wedges we followed Sam to my old downstairs haunt. He switched the light on pointing to the pool table where we placed the items.

I twirled around with a smile on my face as I surveyed the room. "It's like a shrine. You haven't changed a thing. Although it's not surprising, you are both lazy." I nudged Peppy playfully out of the way to get closer to my study wall. Precious followed closely behind.

"What the fuck?" Said Precious in disbelief of what he was seeing.

"It's my wall map of cognitive extremes. To the left you can see all the examples of emotionally moving humanitarian activities, people and experiences. To the right genocide, detailed analysis of every permutation of serial killer known. The center is my social media observations drawing on both parallels of children receiving media coverage for acts of cruelty to kindness, full profile breakdowns from my perspective and associated predictions about their futures.

Peppy laughed as he placed his hand on Liam's right shoulder, "Guess you have a lot to learn about our Fluffy, Precious. She's no wallflower."

Sam placed his hand on Liam's left shoulder and leant in, "Two of the key things to remember, don't underestimate Fluffy and never sneak up on her."

I spun around to look at all three of them, "Knock it off guys. Ignore them Precious, I don't know what they are talking about. Look at me, I'm adorable." I said momentarily pausing to flutter my eyelashes. "Now outa my way it's time for us to get our drink on."

Sam selected Bay City Rollers on our old style vinyl turntable jukebox sitting in the corner. Precious couldn't believe his ears as the tunes started to crackle in the air. We all grabbed a shot each, prepped ourselves for the lip, sip, suck, raised our glasses toward the ceiling and sent the first of them down the hatch. I picked up the next one to repeat the same.

"Really?" Questioned Peppy.

"I do believe gentleman where we left it I was the next leader."

"Oh, fuck." Said Sam looking at Peppy nodding his head to confirm.

"What, what, what…" asked Precious glancing at all of us.

"It all begins with the ten shots then it's free reign to

drink whatever you want when you feel like it. However the drinking rule of the house is follow the leader. It means you need to drink the shots at the same pace as the one who's charged with leading. This way we all start from the same place. It's Fluffy's turn to lead and she always starts big. Get ready to drink my friend."

Liam scrunched his face as he looked at me, "Who are you?"

Peppy chimed in before I could respond, "She's the one if you are able to follow will lead you down the rabbit warren into the depths of the real wonderland. Imagine what you think you know and recognize Fluffy will show you why you don't know anything."

Sam stepped closer to Liam, "Precious, she's the kindest person you will ever meet and the most dangerous you will ever know."

"Think back to the antics of the Mad Hatter and recognize he's sane in comparison," said Peppy still persisting with his Alice in Wonderland theme.

"Honestly Precious if you can picture a fusion between Hannibal lector and Mary Poppins you might start to appreciate ..."

"Quit the stalling guys. They are having a lend of you with the exception of me liking to start big. I'm calling it, ten down. Shut up and get ready to drink you pack of pussies." I raised my glass downing my second shot reached for the next and the next machining through the remaining eight shots. Sporting a smile of satisfaction my last shot glided effortlessly down my gullet. I placed the final empty glass on the pool table with the others then watched the crew.

Peppy being a naturally competitive beast came a close second, Precious came in third and of course Sam was last. There was one thing about Sam, he may have been a weak drinker but Mr. Esplanade knew how to put his major in Chemistry to good use. No one could flip the switch on a blender quicker to make a hungry hoard of party goers the most delicious psychedelic mescaline cactus shake they had ever tasted.

We all waited for Sam to finish the last of his shots.

"Well done." I said as he placed it on the table.

Peppy, passed around the beers while I fetched the bottle of vodka I knew would be stashed in the back of the freezer. They spread themselves across the mismatched college student budget sofas while I jumped into Ol' Yella, my garishly bright yellow fluorescent beanbag.

"So you all met at College?" Asked Precious.

"Yep. That sums it up." I said unceremoniously taking my first swig directly from the Vodka bottle.

Precious readjusted his seating position, "Hold on. There's a story here I just know it. What is it?"

I jumped in before the others started another of their tangents, "Once upon a time I was heading to my next lecture. When I turned the corner of the college corridor Peppy and I almost collided. We looked into each other's eyes, politely smiled and went our separate ways. The next day the same thing happened, then the following day again. On the forth day I entered the stairwell to head to the floor below. Part way down I heard the door open behind me. I looked up and there was Peppy. I burst out laughing calling out to confess I wasn't sure who was stalking whom but I was certain someone was. He released a big laugh walked to where I was standing, held out his hand to introduce himself. A week or so later I was walking to college and noticed Peppy was too except he was on the other side of the road. He came across joining me so we walked the remainder of the way together. In those days Peppy was the front man for an up and coming Hip Hop band. As part of the general banter he asked me what type of music I like to listen to. My response was I liked it all. Without a skip in his beat the evil minx jumped in front of me and started walking backwards so we were facing each other. He had that same contagious wide smile on his cheeky face he has right now."

Liam looked at Peppy then back at me.

"Anyway, he asked me to confirm I liked <u>all</u> music. I of course responded with a 'yes' totally suspicious and on guard knowing he was up to something. That's when he asked the question, which made me realize he and I would be destined to be friends for life. Peppy asked whether I liked yodeling. My immediate reaction was to burst out laughing, but in the back of my mind I was thinking you cheeky mother fucker. Defiantly I responded 'yes' to his question. He persisted by then asking what was my favorite yodel. I sang 'I did your old man last night and your olda lady tooooo.' Neither of us from that point on looked back. We saw the potential in each other quickly becoming partners in crime mercilessly taunting, teasing and harassing the shit out of each other while also uniting our powers of shining wit to afflict the unsuspecting with the same. No-one was safe in our presence. Then one day Peppy announced he wanted me to meet his best mate Sam. We caught up, got along and eventually formed what we called the breakfast club."

"Ha. Just a second." Called out Sam as he placed his half drunk beer on the table and leaned forward, "Imagine your best buddy keeps talking about this person and then says you have to meet her. I mean I've never seen Peppy talk about someone like he did about Fluffy. I was curious so I agreed to join them for dinner. In comes Fluffy who immediately engages the waiter and openly flirts with him. This dude never had a chance; he was complete putty to her enigmatic hands. Once we all completed the usual obligatory introductions we spent the first part of the night talking about business ventures, aspirations it was all rather vanilla but interesting conversation. Then as the meals arrive Fluffy announces the serious portion of the evening conversation had concluded. Peppy and I looked at each other shrugged our shoulders in agreement no more business banter was to take place. Just as I was about to envelope the first mouthful of my steak Fluffy asked what my take on genital herpes was. I kid you not I momentarily froze to process the fact that I was even asked the question, then burst out laughing. I looked at Peppy and smiled to confirm I get it now. The three of us have been thick as thieves ever since."

Peppy and I looked at each other chuckling, "Holy shit I forgot about that. Ha! I did too. The expression on your face was a classic."

The remainder of the night and most of the early hours of the morning was spent recalling our colorful college years together. It was an evening fused with countless wonderful memories and much laughter. Precious was completely engrossed in the banter. I could feel his starved soul being replenished by the laughter provided from the tales of three.

* * *

I returned from my run to see the three of them were still

sprawled all over the sofas. The room held a cocktail of aromatic fumes. I detected stale breath, essence of booze with an overpowering beer based flatulence floating so thick it was ready to form yeast clouds above their heads. I covered my nose braving the room to open the windows and switched on the ceiling fan for effect.

The rickety noise of the whirling fan made Sam stir. He raised his head with one eye opened and the other squinted tight. "What time is it?"

"Morning Princess, it's eleven am."

"Did you go for a run?"

"Yep, I wanted to sweat all this alcohol out of my system."

Peppy gasped as his body pulsed with a jolt then he quickly sat up. Dazed he looked around the room, then realized where he was. "Hey Fluff."

"Morning."

Sam leant across nudging Liam, "Precious, Wake up. It's your turn to make breakfast."

Peppy and I laughed.

Precious kept his eyes closed but responded with a smile.

"He's alive," I said in an exaggerated tone looking up at the ceiling with my hands reaching out my contorted fingers.

"Mary Shelley's Frankenstein" Yelled Peppy.

"Correct."

Precious sat up rubbed the back of his head and mumbled, "Where's the kitchen. I'm ready."

"It's okay Precious, the boys are taking you out for breakfast." I said.

"We are?" Responded Sam.

"Yes you Mr. Tight ass and Mr. Slack ass can take

Precious out for a late breakfast. Does Dwayne still run that groovy café out on the main drag?"

Peppy was rubbing his eyes with vigor, "He owns it now."

"Awesome. Take Precious there and make sure you introduce him." I said with a twinkle in my eye.

"Okay, you aren't joining us?" Asked Sam a little suspicious.

"Nope, I have some business to take care of. You guys should hang for the day and seriously I meant it when I said make sure Dwayne meets our Precious." I said with a chuckle. "Now get up and get out of here this place reeks of butt hole stank thanks to you three. It's time to get up and go cause I can tell by the smell you are already off."

Peppy slapped Precious on the leg. "Come with me I'll show you where you can shower."

They all meandered out of the room looking a little head sore and sorry for themselves.

Once the boys were showered they left without too much of a fuss to spend the day together. I made myself a coffee settling on top of the fold out sunbed in the small rear courtyard. It was a mild day, perhaps leaning more to the side of chilly. The cool breeze floating over the fence line justified my reason to be snuggled under the faux fur blanket I had myself wrapped in. The sky was a cloudless deep blue with a beaming sun pulsing its rays to shine. I took one big gulp of my coffee and opened the book to read.

*The day had passed by quickly as did three quarters of the night. I was thirsty, hungry and very tired. Huck was walking beside me with his tail partially drooping. We needed to rest before we both died of exhaustion. The moon wasn't as prominent in the sky so our visibility made it too hard to look* for the tree with the red mark. I didn't want to even think about the possibility of us accidentally passing it by.

In the distance there was a silhouette of what looked like a dilapidated barn. I climbed over the fence to get a closer look. Peering through some rotted palings I could see it was mostly an empty shell. There were portions of the roof absent; ample knotholes and whole sections of the main walls were missing. The floor was hardened dirt with the exception of some refuse staked in a corner. The only items I could recognize in the pile of dark mass was the outline of a broken ladder and a wheel. On the outside I walked the perimeter until I arrived at the section, which had the largest opening. I placed Huck inside before climbing through myself. This would be our home for the night. Laying down I bent my arm positioning it under my head to use as a pillow, closed my eyes almost instantly feeling my body succumb to sinking into welcomed slumber.

I heard the croaking of a rooster in the distance. Huck had already been up for hours catching his breakfast, lunch and dinner all in one. He must have caught over a dozen of them or at least that's the amount of distinct squeals I heard before deaths invited silence cloaked their little bodies in stillness. It was the same noise the rats I killed made prior to perfecting my art of the snatch, twist and pull to snap their necks before they could release a sound.

My whole body was aching from cause. The skin on my face was pulsing from the sun's heat blistering kisses, the soft soles of my feet were raw from traveling barefoot, little scabs had formed all over my body where I had been unconsciously scratching the fire ant welts and worst of all the muscles in my legs felt like they quit working. I lay there trying to jiggle them up and down slightly to wake them up. The light in the sky was shifting quickly so I knew it was a matter of a short while before the day was upon me.

*Huck pounced on my chest manically licking my face. I instantly stood up from the shock of the unexpected intrusion. I released a surprisingly loud laugh as I saw his little eye's looking up at me licking his lips. He was wagging his tail so vigorously his whole body was following its lead. There were little specks of blood on the underside of his coat, some on his pores; this and the scattering of a few tails, feet and a partial snout were the only evidence of the murderous feast.*

*I tucked Huck under my arm, grabbed my bag and headed back to the main road. At first I was a little disorientated. It was dark when I arrived so the only landmark was the barn we had slept in. Closing my eyes I attempted to replay which direction we had come from in my mind.*

*"Beep, beep, beep."*

*Huck started to wriggle in my arm wanting to be freed. I released my grip to allow him to jump to the ground and then looked at the car now stationary in front of me.*

*"You lost boy?" Asked the man.*

*I shook my head to say no in the hope that he would go away.*

*"You look like yer lost." He insisted with a smile.*

*Shoving my hands deep into my pockets with my shoulders hunched I looked down at the ground as I shook my head again.*

*"Well, if yer not lost than why yer walkin in the wrong direction? The tree marked in red is half a mile or so more down dat way."*

*I looked up with a puzzled expression on my face as I took a better look at the man in the car who was now leaning across to unlatch the passenger side door. Huck turned, barked once at me before jumping into the automobile greeting the man with licks to his face. I watched as he laughed and patted him. His voice was familiar but I didn't recognize his face.*

*"We were expectin yer over a day ago. Adeline said you would be on yer way. Thought yer might be dead. Are yer comin or walkin boy?"*

*My eyes widened at hearing her name. I stepped forward to enter the car, paused again to look at his face and then smiled.*

*"Ah, recognize me now don't cha boy?" He said beaming with a smile that gave a sense of overwhelming relief. "I look a little different with some meat on me bones."*

*My eyes sparkled with a reciprocal smile as I nodded my head.*

*When I sat in the seat Huck jumped into my lap. I shut the door and turned as I felt his hand on my shoulder. He squeezed as he looked into my eyes.*

*"I'm sorry boy. Fer what happin. They said yer died told us yer knifed yer own neck to kill yerself. We would a come fer ya if we knew them cock suckers lied." He said through gritted teeth.*

*I nodded my head as I looked at my hands. I wanted to forget the past, knowing I never would but my wish existed none the less.*

*"Let's get yer home and shovel some food in yer. You're skinny boy and yer muts fat." He said releasing a laugh.*

*Huck nestled into a plump ball in my lap. I closed my eyes to enjoy the breeze. The last time I was in an automobile I was being delivered into the clutches of Greyhaven.*

*"Beep, Beep, Beep, Open yer eyes were here boy."*

*We steadily turned into a driveway approaching a lovely house on an expanse of mostly naked land. The porch wrapped around the body of the building. A man with a mid length white wiry beard, which framed his face to extenuate his protruding cheeks, wide nose and overly wrinkly brow stepped out. He was smoking a pipe in one hand while waving to acknowledge our arrival with the other.*

*Huck jumped out of the vehicle before it stopped. He barked and twirled in circles all the way to the stranger on the porch. I watched as the man bent down picking Huck up to let him lick his face while he squinted his eyes and laughed. He then held him out in front of him twisting left and right looking at Huck's body. Before the vehicle was at a stop the man had disappeared inside with him.*

*"Its okay boy. He'll be fixin yer mut's leg."*

*I jumped out of the car, ignoring the sting in my feet I ran straight inside to find them. The man was hunched over Huck who was on the kitchen table. He was fumbling about attempting to untie the knots in the piece of material, which was now tightly fused with mud and sticks. I stepped in placing my hands forward. The man looked at me with his piercing blue eyes, nodded his head and stepped out of the way. It took me a couple of minutes of picking at it with no success.*

*When the front door opened the man called out, "Cletus, get me the knife." The man then placed his right hand on mine, "It's easier if we cut it off."*

*I nodded my head and stepped back.*

*"Yer both met." Asked Cletus as he passed his personal knife to the man.*

*"No, not yet. I was going to fix the dog's leg first. York, look at me."*

*I looked at the man who knew my name and then across at Cletus whose face was still dressed with a big smile.*

*"I'm Vance Sinclair, Adeline's my daughter." He nodded his head to reassure me as he watched me.*

I looked around the room searching for evidence of Adeline, then back at Vance.

"She's not here. We have been looking for her for the last couple of days and for you since yesterday. The last time I saw my daughter she was going in to quit her job when she was certain you had escaped. We haven't seen her since. I'm not going to lie to you child I have a bad feeling something awful has happened to my girl. I know what they did to you. I know what they did to Cletus." He paused dropped his head to clear his throat before looking at me again. "Let me fix this dog's leg. Cletus get some food for York's belly."

Vance cut off the strip and started cleaning the wound using a fresh cloth dunked in a bowl of warm water. I watched the goop slowly ooze out the bottom of the wound.

"Tree sap, very clever York. You saved this dog's leg from having rot set in."

I thought back to the man at the river, his breath on my neck as he pressed against my body.

"I know my Adeline taught you to write and read. There's a pencil and some paper over there on the side table. Write down your questions while you eat. I'll look at them when I'm done helping your dog."

Cletus was still in the kitchen rummaging around. I fetched the paper and pencil. The first thing I wrote was 'Huck' the second was 'thank you.' Vance titled his head to the side, "Huck. Well hello fella." Huck lifted his head up from the table and wagged his tail in response to Vance's hand patting him. "You are welcome York." He said refocused on cleaning Huck's leg.

When Cletus placed the food on the table I pointed to the third thing I had now written. He looked at the paper and then at me, "Shit boy I can't read none." I turned to Vance holding out the paper so he could read it out.

Vance read it to himself first and then out load for Cletus to hear, "I'm sorry you got punished for trying to help me escape. Thank you for trying, thank you."

Cletus tapped two fingers on the table then looked at me, "You're welcome boy. I'd come git yer but they said you kill yerself after the electric shock. I saw them git yer ready. They did me, you were next. I saw yer all bloodied and such."

I nodded my head.

"Sit, eat." Said Cletus.

My stomach rumbled as I looked at the steam rising from the bowl of thick vegetable soup on the table. I grabbed one of the two crusty rough torn pieces of bread dabbed it in the swab of butter sitting on the side of the plate and threw it in my mouth. I repeated the same as Cletus let out a laugh.

"Slow down boy. Plenty more to be had. Sit."

I pulled out the chair sitting down while shoveling spoonfuls of the soup in. My stomach extended as I transferred the contents from the bowl to me. There was an ache growing from the swill inside but I couldn't stop myself. My head remained down focused on my meal until it was all gone.

Vance placed Huck on the ground giving him a final pat before he straightened up. His eyes glistened as his cheeks rose to the command of his smile. "He will be as good as new." He walked across to where I was sitting. "Eat slow, your stomach isn't used to good food so it might hurt to eat too much too quickly. Cletus was throwing up for days until he learnt to slow down."

Cletus patted his stomach, "Yep."

"Cletus, round up the men. Tonight we make plans. If she's not back we're going in guns a blazing."

Cletus punched the air as he did a little jump, "I'll get

*em' so we can get em,'" with this he walked out the door slamming it behind him.*

*I wrote down the word, Cletoos.*

*"No, here." Vance crossed out Cletoos replacing it with Cletus, then he added Vance, tapping on the word then pointing to himself.*

*I raised my finger to point at the word Cletus and then to Vance.*

*"Ah, no he's not my son. Adeline and he grew up together. He came from a very poor roustabout family. Cletus took a shine to Adeline and would walk her to and from school every day. He would do anything for Adeline including protecting her from all the boys who wanted to court her. He may be uneducated but he has a heart of gold. I'd be proud to call him son."*

*I nodded my head.*

*"You need to understand some things York. Cletus was like you when he was little. His folks put him in Greyhaven and no-one knew. It was years before we found out what had happened. His folks had been long gone, moved from one town to the next, always leaving when they raised trouble from their drinking, gambling, cheating and lies. I went into Greyhaven and said I was his father to get him out of that place. Cletus was skinnier than you are now and wild like a feral cat cornered. He didn't look right in the head and didn't behave like it. The father in me felt compassion for him but feared for my daughter. I almost left him there but knew my Adeline would never forgive me. I'm not ashamed to say I kept him restrained all the way home. He kicked, spat and screamed foul God cursing words while lunging to bite. When I drove over the bridge I looked at the river waters and wondered would it be a kindness to drown the poor child. Still believing in the idea of miracles*

*I continued home. Adeline was pretty as a picture pacing the porch dressed in her Sunday best waiting for us to arrive. The moment he saw her, his body stilled. She called out his name and ran toward the vehicle. I leapt out of my seat catching her by the waist before she got to his door. I told her he wasn't the same boy she once knew that he was wild and may hurt her. Adeline walked up to him slowly, they stared in each other's eyes, she nodded her head and we both helped him out of the car. When I stepped forward slowly he flinched. Adeline reassured him it was okay to let me get closer. I undid all the straps on the leather restraints watching closely as Cletus now free lifted his arms open inviting Adeline into his embrace. Those two hugged each other so tight crying. It's not a man's place to show emotion but I was broken with tears streaming down my face while I listened to them both howl their pain into the skies. Cletus wasn't wild he was terrified of men. He never spoke about it nor did he need to. It took him years before he could look me in the eye and smile let alone stay in a room alone with me. He lives in the old converted barn out the back. I pay him to do the chores I'm too old to do and I would trust him with my life."*

I was staring at Huck's chest rise and fall as he slept near my feet. I hated the idea of someone else experiencing what I had been through.

"There's more I feel you need to know York. Adeline, she insisted on getting a job at Greyhaven. I was against it and so was Cletus but she said she had to. It was like she was looking to correct the wrongs being done. She insisted it was her destiny that she had to be there. I never understood it but Adeline was her own person just like her mother, God rest her soul. One day my Adeline rushed through those doors announcing she had found 'him'. I've never seen the *light in her eyes shine so bright and her heart so sad. It was you who she said she had found York. We tried to pull the same trick where I went in saying I was your father but they knew he was in jail for bootlegging. One of them recognized me as Adeline's father so they placed her on shifts in other sections of Greyhaven where she wasn't able to see you. Cletus watched Adeline grow sick with worry so he insisted on helping. They fought for days with Cletus eventually winning. The next day he admitted himself into Greyhaven so he could be there with you. After all he had been through he still chose to go in there to assist Adeline and protect you York. In the meantime I helped Adeline search for your mother. It took months but we finally tracked her down. Adeline told her it was important to get you out. Everything was set to have you freed but your mom arrived a day earlier than agreed so Adeline wasn't there. Those attendants told your mom you were dead so she would leave and never come back. That's when Cletus tried to help you escape. The last you were seen was at the electric shock treatment room. Everyone was told you were dead, that you killed yourself. Adeline brought flowers to the place where they said you were buried in the garden between the three big oak trees. She visited you every day and cried herself to sleep every night."*

*Vance leaned down to get me to look into his eyes. "I don't know what it was that she saw in you York but you are as important to her as her own blood. She loves you as she loves herself. When the staff told Adeline you were dead the light in her eyes went out. Not even Cletus could make her smile."*

*I nodded my head as the tears were forming in my eyes. I felt exactly the same way. The whole time in the black hole all I could bring myself to think of was seeing her one more time.*

*"Adeline stumbled upon you when she did by the fate of God. Those men who retrieved you from the gallows weren't*

*going to take you back to the others. They were set to kill you because they already told everyone you were dead. Adeline didn't even recognize you at first. The way she described what you looked like they must have retrieved you from hell boy. The men didn't resist because the screams would have brought more attention so they let her take you. Adeline cleaned you up then hid you away so she could nurse you back to health. She told those men Eugene and Leroy that you had escaped. They were out every day after their shift was complete secretly looking for you for months. We left enough trails of scent to keep them interested so they didn't think to look inside Greyhaven. Then a few days ago Adeline came home telling me she had to get you out. You had to escape and she needed to quit. I never received an explanation on why the sudden urgency but I knew by the look in her eyes it wasn't good. We all immediately put a plan together to get you here. Adeline gave you the instructions to ensure you were able to arrive here undetected by foot. Once she was able to confirm you had started to make your way she went in the next day to quit and"* Vance paused to take the tear rolling down my cheek onto his thumb. *"Adeline is going to be fine. If she is in there we will find her."* He placed his hand on my right shoulder and squeezed.

*"Come with me, I'll show you where you can lay to rest for a while. When Cletus returns with the others I'll wake you. We need to know everything about the place so we can get in and out as quickly and quietly as we can. If either of them two have done anything to my Adeline. I will see them hang."*

Vance pointed to some clothes folded on the corner of the bed. *"Adeline had these all ready for when you arrived. Get changed so we can wash what you are wearing. I will wake you later, try getting some rest. I'm going to need your help."*

I nodded my head and began unbuttoning my shirt

*when Vance left the room. I was right Adeline was an angel.
All of this effort she went to was for me. My mind was
weary and my stomach achingly full. The sight of a proper
bed seemed like a fantastical dream. There was so much of
what I now understood, which caused me to stir emotionally.
I loved Adeline but I never dared to wish for her to love
me too. I thought she took pity on me like an injured fawn
found helpless in the woods. Overwhelmed I closed my
eyes drifting off to sleep reflecting on the two people I had
watched dancing in the river.*

"What has you so engrossed you can't hear us
calling you?" Asked Peppy who was walking out to the
courtyard.

"I wasn't expecting you guys to be back until later
tonight." I said repositioning myself to sit up.

Peppy leaned in giving me a kiss on the cheek then
sat at the edge of the sun bed beside me. "You didn't
answer the question. What are you reading?"

"It's a meditation book. You stare at the blank pages
and meditate until you can see the mantra you need to
focus on. Every day a new blank page, every day a new
mantra."

"Sounds cool can I have a go?"

"Sure." I passed the book to him.

Peppy stared at the blank page for a minute at the
most which was longer than I was expecting before he
said, "Nah, I got nothing."

Liam waved from the back door, "Harper come in we
organized lunch."

Simultaneously Peppy and Sam yelled, "It's FLUFFY"

Liam laughed, "Oh yes I forgot. Fluffy, Oh Fluffy my
dear, come hither."

Peppy and I joined Sam and Liam at the table. "So

Precious tell me. How was your breakfast? Did you get to meet Dwayne? Was he to your liking? When is the big date night?"

"Breakfast was divine. Dwayne is a total honey. He isn't to my liking because he already advanced to my total loving. Date night well that would be TONIGHT!" He said with both hands flung in the air.

I picked up my veggie wrap and took a bite.

"Fluffy has this uncanny ability of being able to match people up. Anyone who has been guided by her swears she was cupid in another life." Said Sam.

Precious looked at both of them, "Did she ever try to set you two up with anyone?"

"Sure but only for her own entertainment." Said Peppy. "Fluffy has a very perverse, sick sense of humor and is pretty indiscriminate when it comes to whom she subjects to it. Sam and I are her favorite targets. Guess that's a sign of her love."

I chuckled as some old memories came flooding in of my antics. "Yep, there was this one time at band camp …"

"American Pie," Blurted Peppy before taking an oversized bite of his wrap.

"Damn strudel." I said in reply.

"That's the second time I've seen you two do that movie quote thing." Said Precious.

Sam laughed, "There are a lot of things these two will do. They have their own language, in jokes and really quirky stuff only they will do together. You get used to it after a while."

"If you paid any attention to the clothes Dwayne wore today you should be aware he likes royal blue and vibrant purple. If you want to get laid tonight wear a tasteful blue shirt and give him a single stem of the nicest purple flower you can find. Don't try to impress with a big bunch. Simplistic offering alludes to the complexity within. It will intrigue him to want to know more about you as a person. Make sure you give him three interesting compliments within the first hour and one every hour there after."

"She's the master when it comes to this psych shit so trust her," confirmed Sam.

Liam looked at Sam, Peppy and then at me, "If she's the master then why is she single?"

"Fluffy has a standard no one can meet. Trust me she is single because she wants to be," Said Sam.

Peppy jumped in, "Fluffy never dates, she tends to be more of a binger of fornicating fine flesh. She hunts and sexually feeds off the unsuspecting until she feels sated or gets bored."

"Thanks, Sam, Peppy. You both make me sound soooo impossible and heartless, however do I manage to keep you two as friends?" I turned to Liam, "For the record I'll never be sated until I meet my one true match."

Peppy and Sam concurrently responded, "We know."

"Did I just raise a touchy subject?" Asked Precious coyly.

"Ha. No. There is a definite delineation when it comes to our perceived concepts of love, what it means for each of us. My beliefs are considered by most as too high a standard when for me it's not the case. Love and be loved is the universal rule. I will honor the one I fall in love with. It just happens I have never fallen in love with anyone thus far. It isn't a priority or a desire in my life. In saying this I openly admit I want to fall in love, to be in the right relationship. I'm just not willing to settle down for the sake of companionship with some random person I like. My allocation of total devotion into lovers union will only be with the one my soul's light shines for and my heart calls home. It's who I am. It's always who I've been."

Precious leaned forward, "What if it's one in a trillion chance or worse you never meet them?"

"A chance for true love, the kind of love I want to give and receive, is a chance I will wait for."

Liam thought about what I had said for a moment, "Don't you feel sad, you might never experience the love you want to have?"

I smiled, "I feel sad knowing a single female is known as a withered spinster when a man gets labeled a sexy bachelor. Just as a side note this needs to change, remind me later to mark it in my lifetime achievements things to do list."

The boys laughed while Liam still seemed to express dismay.

"Precious, being alone is not a negative experience or an unhappy one. I would much rather spend time with me than be surrounded by people who make me feel lonely. There are very few people I allow into my life or social space."

"OOooooh yes." Said Peppy. "She is totally clandestine. You are the only person since the three of us have been friends who she has introduced. One person in ten years, now that's Precious."

We all laughed.

I winked at Liam who was obviously taken back by how special it was to be here with the crew. "Peppy, Peppy, Peppy, your down side is you are too arrogant to see the alternate possibility which is also the real truth."

A smile spread across his face with his hands at the ready, "Go ahead Fluffy, enlighten me."

"I thought it would be obvious by now. Isn't it clear after ten years I've been too embarrassed to introduce people to you guys?" I swiftly shifted from my chair running out the room with Peppy in hot pursuit to playfully attack.

Sam looked at Precious, "That's another one of their things."

# Forlorn

The boys did an exceptional job of getting Liam ready for his hot date with Dwayne. He walked out the door looking five years younger and a million bucks. Peppy and Sam organized dates so the six of them could start the evening together. The game plan allowed Precious time to become comfortable with Dwayne taking the pressure off him from being the initial primary focus. Once dinner was complete the aim was for all of the couples to go their separate ways. The separation would only occur when Precious gave Sam and Peppy the agreed signal. Of course it all sounds fantastic in theory but the reality was vulnerable Precious was left in the hands of two seasoned jesters of the court. He would soon learn it is far wiser to attend the date on his own than to be subjected to the continual taunts from these jokesters tag teaming at his expense. All in all they would have a great laugh and a fantastic story to tell when they eventually came home. I looked forward to hearing their antics upon their return. My hopes were they would all stay out for the entire night. I really needed to complete reading the book.

I got myself into a comfy position in my trusty old beanbag ready to settle in to read when my wall map of cognitive extremes caught my eye. In light of all the new information I had obtained it would be interesting to review my thoughts on the predictions I made about the children. There was something I felt drawn to learning from my past assessment. The priority for now had to be the book.

*I awoke to the sound of voices talking over one another. My eyelids were heavy and I was feeling a little disorientated. I sat up and rubbed them to encourage the ease of opening. I felt like a steam train had hit me. My head was throbbing and my stomach was not at rest. I could tell it was in protest of the food I had consumed by all the noise it was making.*

*Vance approached the entrance to the doorway, "I was just about to wake you. Come the men have been talking and we're ready to ask you some questions. We need your help."*

*I nodded my head then raised my hand to hold it still as I felt a sharp pain surge from the back of my neck through to my eyes.*

*"You got yourself a thumper. Wait here I will get you something for it."*

*I sat still with my eyes closed trying to ignore the fact that my need to release the contents of my stomach was growing. The room seemed to sway. I barely heard the footsteps returning over the sound of the throbbing of my pulse on the side of my head. It was unbearable. Just as Vance entered the room I leaned forward to discharge the vomit burning its way up my throat and out my mouth earnestly. I screwed my face up when the taste of bitters coated my tongue.*

"*Come with me.*"

*I followed Vance to the bathroom where he pulled my hair back to wash my face. The cool of the water brought some ease to my burning skull. All I saw were flashes of white spots as the pounding in my head persisted.*

"*Ok, York drink this and then back to bed. You're burning up.*"

*I had no desire to argue. I drank the water, took the medicine then followed him back to the bedroom. Crawling under the covers of the bed with my eyes already closed I could feel him gently tucking me in. Vance cleaned up my mess and quietly closed the door behind him. The voices were still present but muffled through the door. I knew I had to get out there; they needed me to help them. Adeline needed me to help her.*

*Unaware of the length of time, which had passed I woke to feeling better. The sting in my mind had subsided quite considerably as did the pains of my body which were now also settled to a light ache. Cautiously I rose out of bed and headed into the main room to see where the others were. Looking around I saw the evidence of people having been present but no-one was in the room. I felt as though I had let them down, they needed me and I wasn't able to help.*

*My head turned as I heard Huck scratching at the door while releasing a series of high pitched barks. Instantly I smiled walking over to let him in. Just as I reached for the handle the door opened. Cletus entered and unexpectedly embraced me.*

"*I've been checkin yer. I waz worried the fever waz takin yer like it tried to take me when I waz ...*"

*I could feel his body shaking as he cried. Vance was right about Cletus, he did have a heart of gold and Huck seemed to really like him.*

"We're all outside smoking and drinkin bootleg shine waiting for yer to wake." Cletus turned to head outside. Huck and I followed him.

Vance was the first person I saw sitting on the sawn off edge of an old tree stump. He nodded his head as he took another puff of his pipe. Scanning around the perimeter of the fire there were the silhouettes of nine men whose faces were revealed intermittently when the flames flickering light danced to the rhythm paced by the cool evening breeze. Huck leaped into Cletus's lap as he sat down. I smiled and took a seat next to them.

"You must be feeling better York." Said Vance.

I nodded my head as I placed the palms of my hands out to greet the heat from the fire.

"My Adeline is not back. Alfred works in the kitchen and he says he hasn't seen her. One of the other nurses told him today she quit the job." He said while everyone else remained silent.

I stared deep into the hollow of the tree stump on fire exuding its luminescent brilliance. The inviting saturation of orange embers seemingly harmless, until lured close enough to be effected by its hunger for consumption. It held striking parallels to Greyhaven. The awe of its architectural splendor was short lived when in the clutches of the horrors its walls contained. These men could never have enough time to prepare their mental acuity for what they were volunteering themselves to witness.

"York, we are planning on going in tonight and we need your help to show us how to get in without being seen. Now I'm not asking you to come with us. You have been through enough. What we need is a map. Tell us everything you can think of. Can you draw us what it looks like on the inside?"

My eyes widened as I sat upright, nodding my head.

"Good, go get the pencil and paper. Draw it as best you can, the sun only just set so we have some time but not too long."

I leapt up and ran inside to draw the map on one page, posing a series of questions on the other as ideas flooded my mind. It took me a little over an hour to complete the finer details of the plot. There were aspects missing, I knew where some places were visually but not in relation to the layout of the drawing.

Outside the men were talking through the approach they were planning to take. I handed the map across to Vance who leaned forward to look under the light provided by the fire. "This is good York. Here is where we enter men. The orchard side has a hole in the wall." They all shifted to look at the map.

Crouching down I tapped on the paper to get Vance to turn it over. Listen up men,

"When you enter the hole the corridor to the right takes you past a series of doors. It's the section where they conduct experiments on people and animals. If you go straight it takes you to a hard left, halfway down there is a corridor to your right if you follow this you enter the front section of the building. Somewhere in the building is a stairwell that takes you underneath the building. It's filled with small-enclosed rooms. That's where they took York when they announced he was dead. It's where he thinks those men might have Adeline, he knows there were others down there when he was left there to die. These two are the same men York has seen throw patients off the roof."

"Let's teach them men the lessons of God." Rumbled one man.

"I know who they are York, Eugene Styple and his shadow Leroy Muddler." Said Vance.

I looked at all the eyes reflecting in the firelight nodding *my head to acknowledge them.*

*"These men can wait, first we find Adeline, make sure she's safe and then we will teach them all a lesson they won't soon forget."*

*"Yeeeessssss." Hissed Cletus.*

*"Right men, let's go."*

*They all rose to their feet and headed off into the darkness back toward the house where the automobiles were parked. Piling into two of the five vehicles they without a glance drove off while I was left sitting by the fire with Huck who was now laying at my feet hypnotically glaring into the roaring flames.*

"Hey Fluffy, are you still working on that mantra thing?"

I looked up to see Peppy at the bottom of the stairs smiling.

"Hey, I thought you were out to dinner with the others. What happened?"

"I forgot my wallet."

I laughed, "You came back to check up on me."

"Maybe, that too." He said smiling. "Come out with us."

"Honestly Pep, I have so much I need to do. Last night was a welcome distraction but buddy I'm here trying to find a solution to conquer the evils to restore balance and all things willing world peace. I need to focus."

"Ha! Sounds like a good reason but I still want you to come out. It's playtime. I haven't seen you for the longest time. Can't world peace wait a few more days?"

I shook my head as I smiled looking at the book, "It really can't."

Peppy changed his tone to one of concern, "Is everything okay?"

"Sure." Peppy knew my response meant, no I'm not but I won't talk about it and I'II be okay.

He walked across leaned down and gave me a cuddle. "I'm here when you need to share the burden."

I hugged him back, "I know you are." I squeezed him tight, "Thank you." I whispered.

Peppy went back up the stairs without imparting another glance or word. I listened to him fumble around chuckling to myself. In all these years passed nothing had changed; he was always losing his keys, wallet and shoes. Thank the stars his head was screwed on. When the front door clicked shut I resumed my reading.

*It was only a few hours before first light was due when the men returned. The moment I heard the engines I ran outside to greet them as they came up the drive. My heart was palpitating while my eyes madly searched for Adeline among the sea of sullen eyes. Cletus shook his head and looked down. Instantly I closed my eyes and lifted my head to the sky as my heart sunk.*

*Cletus alighted from the vehicle before it stopped. "We can't find Adeline. The place is too big, we can't find her."*

*The angst in his voice was wrenching my heart. I rolled my eyes as I nodded my head. Then it struck me. I ran inside to grab a piece of paper and wrote on it while running straight out again to pass it to Vance.*

*He glared at it, paused then said, "That's clever boy, real smart thinking." He turned his head and waved his hand in the air with a smile. "Men we're going back, I'll explain on the way." The cars turned and headed out the drive. Cletus ran to catch up and dove inside. I watched them turn the corner remaining outside until I could no longer hear the churn of their engines.*

*This time when they returned all of them had smiles on their tired faces. I looked at Cletus who nodded his head, "We did it. Good boy."*

*I felt relieved.*

*With the vehicles parked Vance came toward the porch with a spring in his step. He called out, "Gentlemen, now we wait. Get some rest and be back here just after noon." The men went around shaking each others hands, got into their vehicles and left. Cletus, Vance and I went inside.*

*"Cletus, go get yourself some rest. York you too. I know I said you didn't have to go back there but it's a big place and we need as many people we can trust to come and help search. The men are going to bring their eldest boys now that it's going to be safe to search. Well done York, I'm proud of you son." With this Vance gave me a wink and headed in the direction of his room.*

*I nodded my head and picked up Huck to take him to my room.*

*Cletus waved to me then proceeded to walk out the back door. Huck wriggled then leapt out of my hands running after him managing to exit just before the door closed. I was too excited to sleep. My mind was reeling at the thought of seeing Adeline again. I wanted to hold her, finally tell her I loved her that my heart has never stopped aching from missing her since the day she told me I had to leave.*

*Vance's voice startled me, "York, get to bed."*

*I unexpectedly released a yawn then walked to my room to try and sleep. We were all going to need our strength.*

*Wild winds made the house creak as it rushed through the small cracks of broken seals. I got out of bed just as there was a knock on the door. I could hear Vance shuffling about in the background so I opened the door. Most of the men were present while two more vehicles were approaching. I stepped back to let them in as Vance entered the room.*

*"How many men do we have now?"*

*The short man with the stout build stepped forward,*

"We have twenty three with two more to meet us there so twenty five in total. If she's in there we will find her Vance."

"Much obliged to you all. Cletus, York and myself bring the count to twenty-eight. Let's all make our way over there and wait for the signal."

I went outside and knocked on Cletus's door to wake him while Vance got the vehicle ready. Huck came running out the door and onto the nearest tree to pee. I watched as he sniffed around, kicked some dirt with his one good hind leg and then bounced back toward us.

Cletus was still dazed rubbing his eyes when I swooped down picked up Huck and ran inside. I searched each of the rooms until I found Adeline's. I took one of her scarves that was draped on the edge of the bedpost smelled it and smiled.

*Beep, Beep.*

When I got to the vehicle Cletus had already positioned him self in the back seat.

"You are going to have to leave the dog here. Lock him in the house so he doesn't try to follow."

I shook my head, raised Adeline's scarf to my nose and inhaled it. Then placed it to Huck's snout.

"Okay York. I'll try anything to find my girl. Get in, Huck too."

We were the last to arrive. All the vehicles had been positioned out of view. The men huddled quietly looking across at the south side of the Greyhaven wall. My hand was gently clasped across Huck's snout to ensure he didn't start barking. It was important to be quiet until we knew it was safe to enter the grounds.

Fifteen minutes had passed it was heading towards one in the afternoon when the white sheet appeared to float in the breeze from the rooftop. In response a man behind me masked his call out as a bird. This triggered the person *on the rooftop to retract the sheet, he waved his arm then disappeared.*

*In a flash the men spread out to jump the fence before casually walking across the manicured lawns at a tempered pace to the front steps. The first two entered while the rest of us remained behind. It was a matter of moments before one returned with a smile and open arms calling out, "Welcome to Greyhaven, where everyone is medicated to sleep."*

*The others laughed running up the stairs to enter the main doors.*

*Vance patted me on the back, "Let's find Adeline."*

*Cletus was waiting at the top of the stairs. "I'm gonna get me them two and make em' tell me where Adeline is at."*

*Vance paused took a breath and nodded. "Gideon, Hugh go find a couple of wheel chairs to transport some men. Cletus and York will point them out."*

*Cletus and I immediately went from room to room looking for Eugene and Leroy. It was a certainty where there was one the other would be close by. The place was a buzz with men searching for Adeline. Huck was getting restless under my arm so I placed him down holding Adeline's scarf in position so he could smell it. At first he jumped around between the feet of the men, then he seemed to sniff the ground and off he ran out the front door twirling in circles and barking.*

*"Leave him be boy, we got work to do." Said Cletus*

*I nodded and resumed my search for the dastardly two Eugene and Leroy.*

*Midway down a length of hall Cletus suddenly looked down at the extension of a leg jutting out from a room. It was an unconscious lean fellow with a thick bristled white beard laying on his side.*

*"Git me another one of them wheelie chairs. The doctor*

*is in the house." Cletus yelled as he arched his neck back to release a howl. "I'm gonna show him some electrics." He said before laying his boot full pelt fair in the middle of his guts. A couple of the men collected him into a wheelchair and took him to the room Cletus directed them to.*

*Cautiously I walked ahead into the large elongated room where the shared sleeping quarters are. Cletus followed me in then proceeded to walk ahead. Pulling out his knife from his pocket he began cutting the leather restraints attached to the sides of the beds grunting as he yanked to break them. I tapped him on the shoulder when I heard the water running in the wet room.*

*"Wait here boy," He said as he ran into the room screaming with his knife raised in the air.*

*"York, get them boys to bring the wheelie chairs."*

*I ran out the door to find them. When I returned Cletus was already dragging Leroy's naked body across the floor. The boys grabbed his feet helping to lift him onto the second last bed then followed Cletus to fetch Eugene. By the time they returned I had strapped Leroy into the bed extra tight. Cletus saw my handiwork and smiled, nodding his head as he dropped Eugene's body down hard on the bed I had once occupied. I set to work tightening the straps.*

*"Thanks boys, Go join yer Pa and keep searchin for Adeline. York and I will do what needs to be done here."*

*The two of them jumped into the wheel chairs racing each other out the door.*

*"I need to sharpen my knife so it cuts nice and deep." Said Cletus running his finger along the edge of the blade.*

*I reached into my pocket to retrieve the two tools I stole passing them across to Cletus. He grabbed the handles, inspected them closely then looked at me. "This is a scalpel, them's doctors use to cut us. Where did you git it?"*

*I lent forward to pull on the straps to ensure the two attendants were locked in position. As I stood up I grabbed Cletus by his shirt to gesture for him to follow. I ran out the front door, down the side and to the back where the orchard was visible. We walk to the other end of the back wall and straight inside the hole I used to escape. I listened intently for sounds of life before I opened the door to enter the laboratory of horrors.*

*Cletus immediately placed his hand across his nose as I flung the door open. While I ventured in he turned away releasing projectile vomit, which slid across the corridor floor. The color of his complexion seemed to alter instantly to a pale sickly green. I tapped him on the shoulder to encourage him to look at me. I held my hand up to suggest he remain outside then I reentered the room. Switching on the light I shifted to the center where there was vacancy allowing me to freely spin around. What I had witnessed the first time I graced this room with my presence wasn't even an inkling of how much senseless malice these wall contained. There was a room off to the side sealed by a heavy door. Through the tiny viewing window I bore witness to countless blue hued bodies hanging from large hooks through their necks while others had it protruding from their vacant torsos. I didn't try to open the door. There was nothing to be gained by standing present to such an abomination.*

*I searched the benches and drawers for more implements. Once Cletus regained his composure he joined me. There were no words parted from his lips as he walked the circumference starring into the rows and rows of jars containing liquid suspended human anatomy. I could tell by the expression on his face this insight only set to fuel his contempt for Greyhaven and the people contained within. The cages at the back were replenished with livestock no doubt for their insensitive experimental endeavors. I located the tools under a retractable drawer on a transportable trolley. Once I showed Cletus where they were I shifted my focus to release the innocent from their prisons. Unfolding a large lab coat I spread it out and started piling the animals onto it. Cletus came across with another one following suit to assist. We gathered the wriggling bundles and took them to the hole in the wall where we both shook them off the coats.*

*Cletus went back into the room to get the trolley while I continued down the hallway. My walk transitioned to a quickened pace eventuating into a frantic speed as I realized there might be a chance Adeline left a message on the wall. When I got to the room the door was already ajar. I held my breath as I pushed it slightly wider so I was free to enter. I searched everywhere but it was gone. Nothing remained of my writings. The furniture had been removed, all the walls were painted and the floors scrubbed clean. My stomach sunk, they knew.*

*Upon my return Cletus was waiting for me at the hole. We headed out and back toward the front entrance with him carrying the drawer of tools under his arm. I spied from my peripheral vision Huck sitting across the way in the shade near a lovely garden bed in bloom. His head was down on his feet resting with his tail wagging as he watched us.*

*"Leave him be" said Cletus preemptively as he saw me flinch.*

*Keeping my pace aligned I wondered if the painted room had anything to do with Adeline being missing. I felt unwell holding the thought, which gave rise to the belief that the answer was yes. The sense of urgency to the situation was heightened by my new insight.*

*The two men were still unconscious strapped to the beds. Cletus clanged about sifting through the drawer until he settled to hold up a sharp looking object, which was curled like a half moon. He lifted Eugene's penis, shifting it to one side.*

*"Do you see them boy? Them's what hold the seed fer yer children. Mine were cut. Yers been took too."*

*I looked at Cletus a little puzzled. Reading the expression on my face he placed the tool on Eugene's rotund belly and dropped his own trousers to show me. "See thems missin. They took em, call it sterilization. Tore em clear off." He pulled his draws up again and then with a raised voice said as he tapped the side of his head, "We may be mad but what they dun to yer, what they dun to me, ther sick in the head takin to castrate a man's seed."*

*I slowly reached down my pants and felt around. As my fingers explored the jagged edge of a rough cut thick scar, flashbacks of my first night in the bed came flooding back of the nurse jabbing me with the sleeping needle, the surge of pain, days later waking to blood in my bed. There was an anger bubbling through my veins I had never felt rise with such fury as I continued to trace my finger along the fat raised scar line.*

*Cletus picked up one of Eugene's sacks and was about to cut into it when I placed my hands out to stop him.*

*"What boy, they took mine I takin theirs. Get goin if yer don't want to see."*

*I kept my left hand up to signal he wait as I reached into the left side pocket of my trousers to retrieved a small bottle I had taken from the room of horrors. Placing it under Eugene's nose I lifted the cork stop allowing the waft of pungent fumes to travel straight up his nostrils.*

*"Them smellin salts boy. God Dam Yesss." He said punching the air. "You good and angry?"*

*I nodded my head with a partial slow blink as I raised*

*my eyes to invite him to look straight into my gaze. He quietly returned my stare and then nodded his head. What I felt was beyond rage. My mind had ventured to a point of no return. It was a space where even my silence was silenced by the limitless sadistic urge for retribution compelling me with ideas on how to relentlessly torture these two putrid spawns of demons rejected seed.*

*Eugene wasn't responding to the salts so I closed off his airways until his body was turning purple for breath. When I released him Cletus held the salts to his mouth watching him gasp greedily at the air while I unleashed a series of mercilessly hard slaps to his face. It was a trick I had watched my mother do to my father when he had sampled too much of his own moonshine and was set to be late for a days honest labor.*

*Eugene started to cough as his eyelids fluttered open. I snatched the bottle from Cletus swiveling around to repeat the process on Leroy. It didn't take long before both of them were aware of their environment and began fighting against the straps cussing in threatening tones. Cletus positioned the moon shaped knife to Eugene's throat.*

*"Where's Adeline?"*

*"She quit her job. She's gone. We haven't seen her since she left." He said with his eyes shut tight holding a pensive expression.*

*"I'll ask yer again and then I start cuttin."*

*"Where's Adeline? Did yer put her in the dungeon like yer did the boy? Tell me." Said Cletus raising his voice as he shook Eugene's torso.*

*"She quit. He told you, she quit. You lunatics." Hissed Leroy.*

*Without warning I snatched the tool out of Cletus's hand lifted Leroy's penis cutting the length completely off. I held it up to show Eugene letting the blood drip on his face then turned to shove it deep into Leroy's screaming mouth. Without hesitation I grabbed Eugene's penis pulling it taught in the air holding the knife against his delicate stretched skin. Leroy in the background was choking from the blood oozing down his throat then fell silent as he fainted.*

*Cletus pushed the edge of the scalpel into the underside of Eugene's right eye. "I reckon I can pop one out leave the other so you can watch what the boy does to yer."*

*Eugene defiantly lifted his head slightly to let the scalpel sink superficially into his flesh then spat in Cletus's face. Blinded by rage I released his penis to remove the scalpel from Cletus's hand while he was reactively wiping off the dripping phlegm. I fumbled about to locate the thick leather strap from my side of the bed and placed it across the brow of Eugene's head. Cletus retrieved the strap on his end buckling him ruthlessly tight.*

*Through gritted teeth Cletus asked, "Watch yer planning boy? Popin his eye?"*

*I looked directly into Eugene's gaze and gave him a slight smile as I lifted Eugene's left eyelid removing it with one strike of the blade. The veins on the side of his neck grew from the build of screams he released as I tossed his eyelid into his gaping mouth and proceeded to do the same with his right lid. Now he was set never to squint or miss a thing.*

*In shock Cletus turned away at the site of Eugene's exposed eyeballs to throw up while Eugene filled the room with a cacophony of choking sounds stimulated by his eyelids being lodged in his throat.*

*There was one thing I was certain of Adeline was dead and these were the men who killed her. No person in their right mind would react the way Eugene did unless he was looking to provoke anger to receive a swift death. He can't confess to killing her in fear of the punishment, so he remains falsely defiant with the hopes of one of two outcomes, he is believed and set free or he is killed swiftly. Neither of which would be granted this day to these men.*

"Are you still up reading?"

My body jolted out of a half daze as I looked up to see Liam standing over me. "Yeah, I was engrossed and lost track of time. Why are you home? What's the time?"

"Its just after three am. I had a nice night but it didn't feel right to sleep with him on the first date. Were not in high school, its not prom. I just want to wait, get to know him before I blow him." He said with a mock curtsey.

"Okay sounds fair. Now tell me the real reason." I said while surveying his body language.

Liam put his knees together and did a mini sway, "I really, really, really, like him."

I smiled, "Good reason. When is your next date?"

"We agreed to meet at his café for breakfast. He kept mentioning you all night. You should join us."

"He only spoke about me because I'm the common denominator. Try to focus on getting to know one another rather than talk about me." I said stretching my arms out now feeling drowsy.

"Did you know he used to have a mad crush on you?"

"Yep. Do you realize you are sounding like a gossiping gerty?" I said with a smile.

"I just found it fascinating." He insisted.

"Meh, it doesn't have the same appeal for me."

"Is everything alright?" Asked Liam now crouching down in front of me.

"Yes, I'm just trying to process a lot of things at the moment. You caught me off guard while I was in the midst of a crucial section in the story. I don't mean to be dismissive of the topic and at the same time I do. It's no disrespect to Dwayne or any of the others I know he would have told you some of the stories. You listen no doubt glorifying this drove of admirers and possibly romanticize the ideals of having the capacity to evoke such a response in people. As the recipient of this devotion, for want of a better word, I can tell you it's no picnic having people desire me when simply put, I don't want them. I have unintentionally broken more hearts than any one person should have the right to do and I'm not even trying."

"Maybe you should give love a chance. You can fall in love with someone over time. There are a lot of nice people out there." Said Liam.

"No Precious <u>you</u> can, the rest of the world seems to. It's not who I am. I'll accept nothing less than extraordinary. Love and be loved is my universal rule of truth. It's not something I can force or alter over time. It exists or it doesn't for me. Just understand the love I seek is the one true companion to my soul. Whose very breath when they inhale nourishes my life in unison. I will accept love into my heart when I meet the one who evokes a deep insatiable fierce passion for me to be with them and cause me to feel any absence of them to be unbearable. I'm talking about an imprint ingrained into the fabric of our mutual core that's forged in total unconditional acceptance and love. When he or she crosses my path I will fall deeply and irrevocably in love and enjoy my entitlements of giving and receiving all the pleasures thereafter."

Liam placed his hand on my knee, "Do you actually think such a person exists?"

"I'll spend what lifetimes I have searching to find

my one. I know how to love and I know how I want to be loved. I would never settle for less. To do so would be a dishonor to my soul and overall happiness." I shrugged my shoulders as I released the breath I had been unconsciously holding.

"Well, for what it's worth I think I just fell a little bit in love with you too. The way you describe love, it's what we all want."

"Ha! Of course you did. Seriously get in the queue." I said playfully giving him a nudge. "Trust me Precious it is a rare breed in deed who have the capacity to love as love is set to be. All others are learning, growing, developing the tools to graduate toward what I described. Consider me to be the exception to the rule. I only want my utopian love or nothing at all. Now get to bed, you have only have a few hours before you need to get up again to meet Dwayne for breakfast."

He smiled, "I do." Liam rose to his feet and gave me a little wave as he walked toward the staircase.

"What are you looking at?" I asked noticing his jerk to a standstill.

"Did you make changes to your cognitive reasoning board at all?"

I sat up, "No why? Tell me what you see."

"The third child you have in the list of predictions is Vernon Wreath's brother. It's his twin brother to be precise. I didn't notice it the other day."

I jumped to my feet rushing across to the board, "What do you mean this child's last name is MacRowny."

"Vernon has no other siblings except for his twin brother Tyson MacRowny. Tyson was the boy who got caught by witnesses after they watched him swing that little kid in circles and then released him so he flew in front of an oncoming train. Vernon and he were split when the parents filed for divorce. Once Tyson was found guilty he went into a juvenile detention center then post serving his sentence he was flung into the system living in government run institutions and foster homes. Meanwhile Vernon was forced to live with his alcoholic father whom he despised. When Vernon was of age he changed his surname to his mothers maiden name Wreath."

I looked at Liam.

"I was obsessed remember. I researched you and of course I researched everything to do with him."

I slapped my hand on my forehead wondering how did I not pick this up before. "Do you still have all the information you collected, on us?"

"Sure, it's at home. I was going to have a bonfire one day when I felt ready to let it all go."

"Great, I'm going to need to read it. I can't believe I missed this. Seriously I could kick myself."

"I don't understand how you could expect yourself to know he had a twin if the names were different and you haven't researched his past?"

"No, that I understand. I'm talking about overlooking the fact that you did research. You told me from the start you hired an investigator I should have asked to see what you had on me in the first place so I could be aware of what information was readily available to anyone who might be interested in knowing more about me. The insight into Vernon's past is also becoming of more prominent importance. It was all there and I didn't pick up on it. Anyway, it's just another subtle reminder from the universe highlighting why I can never assume I have covered all my bases. Damn."

"I'd better head off to bed."

I patted Liam on the back, "Good night Precious." I could see his shoulders were slumped as he walked away. The association to all of this held heinous memories for him. I needed to be more considerate of this in the future.

"Night Fluffy."

I sat in my beanbag with my arms behind my head leaning back staring at the board while I thought about the interconnections I was discovering everywhere. Zivah had mentioned I carried the knowledge of the river within me. If this is true I had to find a way to locate where the information is stored in my mind. This piece meal insight into my position on the game board of life was far too precarious. I need to shift to a level of accurate certainty regarding my interpretations and conclusions. If I am to believe my charge then the quality of all our lives depended on it. What a strange life I lead I thought to myself as exhaustion crept in to force me to yawn encouraging my tired eyes to close.

# Retribution

I woke to be greeted with a stiff neck and my face stuck to the side of the beanbag caused by the onset of night sweats. A fury of dreams rushed through the few hours I managed to escape into slumber. I had tried not to drift off with thoughts of York's actions however this did little to save me from reliving the scenes. I became a part of it all, line by line right beside him. I felt the insurgence of his rage at the realization of what they took from him. There was a sense of humiliation and shame associated to his awareness of being castrated. This clearly provided access for him to leverage a darker side of his persona. It was as though his emotional dam was a spiral of white rapids and this one additional piece of knowledge sent his waters to overflow swaying toward ruthless retribution. The flashes of images being presented to me were grueling acts of cruelty with which he executed with ease. It was one thing reading the words and very much another standing beside him feeling the extension of his hand. I knew by the emotions we were exchanging that this beast lived inside of him. It was not born of circumstance; this monster coursed through his veins as a part of his life force. The experiences fueled the contempt he held internally until it crossed the threshold of tolerance, enabling him to unleash this part of his psych to prominence. York was flourishing as a true aspect of his personality, a natural born killer.

I went upstairs to the kitchen to make myself a coffee before I continued reading. The clock struck six am just as I switched on the light. In the background Liam's snoring was echoing from his sleeping quarters. It was still black outside but there were birds breaking out in song so I knew dawn would be kissing the horizon with the warmth of its first light in due course. I smiled as the quote by Rabindranath Tagore came to mind, *'Faith is the bird that feels the light and sings when the dawn is still dark.'*

I methodically made myself a cup of coffee as I considered the concept of the act of faith. There is so much of what had occurred to me that was surreal. It made me wonder how much was embellished by my hyper stimulated imagination versus actuality. I couldn't prove those episodes Liam had where different people presented their voice through him weren't associated to a variant of multiple personality disorder. At the same time the experience although foreign was coated with familiarity. My instincts held steadfast encouraging my need to believe they were spirits set to guide. The key delineation was I didn't hold faith to the experience I held faith within my reaction to it. I guess this was the underlying delta. The faith I had was in me for me.

In the back of my mind while reading York's story I held an image of myself trapped in the room of madness adorning a straightjacket while staring blankly out a window. The visual imagery made me wonder if the real me was locked in some institution drugged to the eyeballs and all of this was my escapism into a world of my own creation where it looks and feels so real that I am lost in this labyrinth forever. The idea fascinated me. This was all stemmed from the cross parallel analytical processing my mind was compelled to do. If I sat with a psychiatrist and told them word for word what has occurred they would most certainly suggested I was in a hyper delusional state with recommendations encouraging me towards medications and volunteering to be institutionalized. They would no doubt suggest the two men who came to rob me were just a coincidence. The fact that Liam saw some writing in the book and then it disappeared were shadows cast over the pages or some other anomaly. I've seen the dismissive attitude projected countless times before in psychiatric sessions I attended during my observation outplacement semester at college.

There was this one fellow the psychiatrist I was assigned to held in session who kept talking about how 'they' spy on him, take photos, he would always say 'they' are everywhere masked in ordinary faces and as hard as he tried he couldn't escape them. The psychiatrist had him on a cocktail of prescribed drugs in an attempt to temper his assumed paranoia, depression and suspected bipolar disorder. The psychiatrist didn't consider any of what she was being told as even remotely true. To her, anything this patient said was an embellishment of a partial truth entering his mind and being retrieved distorted in a coating of technicolored fantastical imagery formed into beliefs and statements.

In the debriefing sessions she held with me as part of my observation skills assessment I recall asking her, what if he is telling the truth and all those things raised by him are actually happening? She laughed and suggested I might need therapy too. Was it ironic, coincidence or fate that here I am years later in a position where I can look back at the things this man said and associate them to Interferons and their limitless access to involuntary watchers. The new question I have is why were they focused on him? I was now very present to my reality. All those who crossed my path may very well have done so for a purpose. There was a reason I met him and there was certainty in my core that there is a reason I am thinking about him right now. I have to find him. If only I could recall his name.

"Find whom?" Asked Liam who was standing at the entry to the kitchen unceremoniously scratching the crack of his ass.

I didn't realize I had been speaking aloud. "Morning, I dare you to smell your fingers." I said laughing.

Liam put his digits to his nose inhaling deep as he fluttered them about. "Morning now let's not change the subject. You need to find someone? Can I be of assistance?"

"I do need to locate someone and will ask when I can recall his name."

"Old flame?"

"God no." I said with a wink as I lifted the cup to my lips to take my first hit of caffeine.

Liam smiled as he stretched his arm out toward me, "I dare you to smell my fingers."

I rolled my eyes, "Precious, Precious, Precious, a couple of days with the boys and you're a changed man. Tsk. I'd love to BUTT it's a personal rule never to spoil my appetite before breakfast. Come see me in the afternoon and I might be ready to have a crack."

We both laughed.

"On a serious note, I'm going to need your house keys. I believe there might be some clues to my puzzle which reside in the information you gathered on Vernon and I."

"When are you going? I'll come with you." Said Precious stepping forward.

"No, you stay here and hang out with the boys. Get to know Dwayne, I honestly feel you are a match."

"Robin never deserts Batman."

I looked at Liam and smiled as I reached across touching the side of his face, "You dear, sweet man. Robin needs to get laid so he stops feeling compelled to jump in swinging chairs with Batman. Dwayne is a cheaper alternative to a male order groom and better than needing to clean up after the mess you have made of a blow up companion doll. Stay."

Liam leaned against my hand as he looked into my eyes and half smiled, "I can no longer imagine a day without you in it." He reached into his pocket passing me the keys.

"I know, this is another reason you really do need to find your place in the world in the absence of me. I'm not going to be around forever. That's why I brought you here. My crew is your crew now. If you give it a chance, rise above your fears you can experience the kind of love your heart seeks with Dwayne. He is your match in every way for this lifetime I know it. Grasp the opportunity with both hands and tug on it hard and fast." I did the hand motion and smiled. "Seriously Liam, this trip here was my only way I could think of to repay you for assisting me."

A tear fell from Liam's right eye, "Why do I feel like you are saying goodbye?"

I picked up his clean hand and kissed the inside of his

palm, "I'm not and I always am. I can't afford attachment or karmic binds in my life of any kind. This cycle of my flesh is not one of love. I'm destined to gather all the remaining pieces of the frayed ends to heal those who I can, learn what is required and then seal it all to closure so my final entry into my next life is one of strength."

Liam stepped in giving me a big bear hug, "You're so weird Fluffy. I love you."

I patted Liam on the back, "I know Precious, back at ya bud."

"Is it going to kill you to just say it?"

"Not at all. Now go get yourself ready for your hot breakfast date." I responded.

Liam released a big laugh as he stepped back. "One day you will admit you love me."

"HA! Don't hold your breath. Fluffy took nearly three years before she told me she loved me and even then I had to tickle it out of her!"

"Hey, morning Peppy, it's a true story told. In my defense I only caved under the duress of being mercilessly tickled."

"Really? Three years." Said Liam now sporting a big pouty lip.

"Get over it already," I said with a wink slapping him on the back as I passed by. "Oh, before I forget Pep you might know what this scent is. Precious trust me he's really good at this stuff. Pep, Precious has a scent on his hand can you tell me what aftershave you think it is please. It has undertones of musk and some floral bouquet I'm not familiar with."

Liam lifted his hand out waving his fingers while Peppy stepped in to smell them. I watched as he took a deep inhale of essence of ass. The expression on his face was priceless quickly converting from contemplation of scent detection to acknowledgement's cringe coupled with immediately recoiling from the vinegar stench. Instantly he punched Liam, who was laughing, in the arm and turned toward me.

"It's Odor De Precious Crack," I said in possibly the worst French accent ever attempted then made a run for it down the hall and out the front door barefoot screaming from laughter as I heard Peppy's thundering footsteps in hot pursuit yelling, "You're fucked Fluffy, come here."

Unfortunately for me my laughter betrayed my ability to make a clean get away. It didn't take too long before Peppy had me by the waist. He threw me on the grass sitting on top of me using his knees to pin my arms on either side. Between panting and still laughing I looked up into his eyes with the cheekiest grin I could muster and said, "Whatever do you plan to do with me now?"

Peppy glared fixated on my lips while trying to catch his breath. Swiftly he shifted to grab my hands placing them above my head using his right hand to hold them in position.

Defiant I didn't flinch; I bit my bottom lip using a sexy tone to say, "Ohhhh, Peppy."

He leaned down hovering inch close over my face while he stared into my eyes before whispering in my ear, "Pay backs going to be a bitch." He lifted his head, lightly flicked my nose then released me.

I laughed as he offered me a hand to get up. "Nah, I'm good." I said as I rose to my feet brushing the grass off. Peppy stepped forward to help remove the remaining blades off and took the opportunity to slap me super hard on the ass.

"Ooooo baby, was that payback?" I said wiggling my butt.

"No that was for pleasure." He said raising his left eyebrow while sporting a smirk.

"Well hello there sailor" I said laughing.

He shook his head while releasing a chuckle, "You're impossible and torturously cruel Fluffy, payback, there will be payback."

I placed a finger seductively at the edge of my mouth as I started to swing subtly from side to side, "Gosh I hope so."

"GRRRRRrrrrrrrr, come here." Peppy put his arm around me as we walked back to the house.

Liam was standing at the front door with Sam, both were grinning from ear to ear as we made the ascent up the steep stairs.

"I bet you needed a breath of fresh air Pep," said Sam with a smirk.

I called out, "Precious, you wasted an opportunity?"

"No way, I'm not risking getting punched again. I can't lift my arm besides it was too funny not to share."

Peppy and I laughed as Precious tried to demonstrate lifting his arm.

All three of them decided to head out for breakfast. I once again declined to attend. When they were gone I took the opportunity to pack my stuff, called a cab and left the boys a note on the coffee table downstairs letting them know I was off to walk the earth. I've never enjoyed the fuss people made with departures so I avoided them. The last time I wrote a note for Peppy and Sam I didn't return to visit for five years. At least when I did finally grace them with my presence this time round I left them Precious as a gift.

\* \* \*

Liam's house had an odd musty smell to it. We had only been gone a few days and already there was a thick film of dust coating the surface of his furniture. In the back room where the office was situated the window was partially ajar. Cautiously I searched the house to ensure I was on my own. The place was empty but someone had been here. I sensed a change, there was something different about the atmosphere.

I gathered the folders marked research into a couple of hessian carry bags I found in Liam's kitchen. Shutting the window I took a quick glance around the room to see if there was anything else I might need to take with me. Just before I left I placed the keys as agreed under a layer of dirt in his potted Peace Lilly that was near the back door. I executed a final scan of all the rooms to ensure everything was locked before returning to the rental car to head to the airport. It was time for me to go home.

The flight to New York would take just over five hours so once settled in my seat I organized a drink coupled with a few complimentary packets of those measly serves of peanuts and I was set to commence reading. Happily there was no one assigned to the seat beside me so I didn't need to be concerned about being caught staring at a seemingly blank book.

*"Boys what's all the screaming about?" Said Vance as he and a couple of the other men entered the room.*

*Cletus was still bent over hurling the contents of his stomach while Eugene continued to scream.*

*Vance arrived at the foot of the bed saw Cletus, looked at the blade in my hands and finally what I had done to Leroy and Eugene, "Stand back men. Leave this with me."*

*He yelled at the men who followed him in. They hesitated, looked at one another then walked out.*

*Vance moved to be closer to me. I reactively shifted my hand holding the knife so it wasn't within easy reach.*

*"No, boy it don't matter what they done. It doesn't serve to be no better. Give me the knife."*

*I looked into Vance's eyes with stilled breath.*

*"I know what they did to you. I know. Vengeance affords no peace to the soul. Give me the knife." He said once again taking a step closer.*

*"I killed her." Spluttered Eugene as he coughed to dislodge the eyelids.*

*Vance's eyes squinted as his jaw tightened, "What did you say?"*

*He managed to swallow then took a deep breath and yelled, "I GUTTED HER LIKE A PIG," proceeding with manic laughter*

*Vance reached into his leather pouch, which had his prized hunting knife, concealed while Cletus wildly fumbled in the draw to select a tool. I swung around effortlessly gliding the knife in my hand across Eugene's throat splitting it open deep enough to convert the remainder of his moments of laughter into a gurgle.*

*I lent over Eugene so he could look into my eyes while he quickly fought to draw his final blood drenched breaths. I smiled and said one word, "Die."*

*Vance's knuckles were white as he clasped his hands together. Cletus released a curdling scream and began pounding on Eugene's chest while I stood there watching his ribs cave in under the multitude of strikes. The other men once again re-entered the room to see what was causing the commotion.*

*Vance turned to look at them, "My Adeline ... she's," his voice broke "She's gone. Evacuate the place. Remove every person here out on the lawn as far away from the building as possible. We are burning this God forsaken place down."*

*The men nodded their heads and changed direction to get the nurse who was slumped over the desk asleep in the room. I waved to Vance and shook my head at her being moved.*

*Vance looked at me while he called out, "She stays men. Move the others but these three stay."*

*I nodded my head. She was the one who always gave us the needle of sleep when they wanted to rape stilled bodies in the night.*

*Vance collected Cletus who was now slumped over Eugene's body hysterically crying and took him out of the room. I placed the knife into Leroy's unconscious hand with a smile knowing if he became conscious he would know he has a tool to help him escape but not able to use it with his arms bound tightly into position. He would burn alive just as she will. They deserved no less and had time been permitting I would have favored doing far worse.*

*Vance took Cletus outside and returned to the room with some jars in his hands and under his arms. "This is moonshine, spread it everywhere so we can get a strong flame going when it's lit. The men have spread out. They are climbing into the roof to get it going there."*

*I took a few of the jars and began pouring it on the beds and bodies Leroy and Eugene. As I walked across to the desk where the nurse was sleeping Vance called out, "York, are you certain?"*

*I opened a bottle of the moonshine and poured the entire contents over her. Vance never said another word. We completed emptying the jars and then went outside to meet the others. Once they were all returned we had two men re-enter to light the flames starting from the roof and then methodically room by room. Those who could were encouraged to leave to remove the chance of being caught.*

*In a flash I held an image of the innocent set to inadvertently burn. I picked up a length of twig and ran inside. Ignoring Vance calling me back I entered the main room. The smell of the smoke from the fire set in the roof was already starting to penetrate the halls. Bursting open the doors to the room of madness I grabbed the attendants chair carrying it across to the window. The babies were long gone but she was still there nestled in the corner behind the shield of her perfectly formed web. I couldn't leave her behind. Holding up the stick carefully underneath her I placed it near her abdomen. She used her legs to clasp the stick firmly and I carried her outside to safety. Vance watched without imparting a word as I found a spot to let her venture free.*

*Cletus was sitting with his legs crossed on the green lawn rocking back and forth staring at the building. My head turned to look at Huck as he released a bark. I walked across to grab him then froze in position. I read what was roughly carved into the trunk of the tree with tears streaming down my eyes. Looking down at the bed of freshly planted poppies in bloom I fell to my knees with the realization of a past puzzle called to light. All I could hear were the words Alphonse said in the room of madness 'Poppies up.'*

*I placed my hands into the soft surface dirt clenching handfuls tossing them aside. Huck started digging and barking as my heart raced speeding my motion. In the background I heard Vance yell, "Men get find some shovels."*

*Cletus skidded to the ground instantly planting his hands into the earth shoveling what he could over and over. Vance joined us on this knees until the men arrived out of breath with anything they could leverage as digging implements. They dug around the soft edges of the garden bed while*

*Greyhaven was thankfully still not revealing its flames of fury in any great proportion. It wouldn't be long before the fire was prevalent and attention drawn to the area.*

*"Here," Yelled a man with a deep voice.*

*It was Adeline's elbow.*

*Carefully they shifted the dirt to free her body from the shallow grave. In silence they helped to carry her to the car. Cletus had her head in his lap as he cried while stroking her hair. Vance without a word started the vehicle and drove directly home. By the time we reached the front door we could see the billowing black clouds of smoke in the distance.*

*The three of us carefully carried Adeline inside and placed her on the dining table.*

*The men who helped uncover Adeline shortly after came up the drive. When Vance heard the engine he walked outside to greet them part the way into the property.*

*"We agreed none of us are to meet for a while. It's too risky." Said Vance in a gruff voice.*

*They stopped the engine of the vehicle and the two men alighted taking their hats off. "No-one should have to bury their child let alone dig their grave. Pick the spot Vance, we're here to dig. Hortus has gone to let the others know there will be a service tonight for your Adeline. Once this is done we will all go our separate ways until it's clear, but you're not burying your child alone. Now pick where you want her to rest."*

*Vance glanced at the dirt, scuffed the surface with his foot making the dust rise, "Out the back there's the big old tree she and Cletus used to climb."*

*The man stepped forward placing his hand on Vance's shoulder, "I know the one. Come on Wilton." They walked around the house to the location to make a start.*

*I watched as Vance fell to his knees placing his hands flat on the dirt in front of him. He gripped the dusty soil then lifted it so the loose bits freely fell through his fingers. Shaking his fists in the air he screamed up to the skies, "Curse you God. Curse YOU." Then his body shook as he cried releasing the sounds of an ache in a man unlike anything I had ever heard before.*

*Vehicle after vehicle entered the drive. The men glanced briefly at Vance and then straight ahead as though he wasn't there. They parked their automobiles, fetched the shovels and picks looking directly at me. I pointed toward the back, without a word they left to join the others in the dig.*

*Vance didn't return to the house. He stayed outside smoking his pipe while sipping on his moonshine with Huck quietly sitting beside him. Meanwhile Cletus was inside propped up on the table holding Adeline's hand wailing with tears as he gulped the air struggling through reciting adventures they had together across their lives. I quietly walked out of the drive and down toward the nearby valley. Careful not to be seen I lowered down to break off a pile of the lavender stalks from the rows of bushes. I returned with a bundle, took some twining from the kitchen to fasten it together. Cletus didn't seem to notice me as I approached them. I placed it on her torso and turned to leave him to have his time with her.*

*"She loved yer York. I ain't seen her shine not fer me not fer any man like she shined when she spoke of yer."*

*I nodded my head and suddenly couldn't breathe. The tears streamed down my eyes as I walked out the door, calmly heading once again up the drive. When I was clear from their visibility I began to run. I ran so hard my lungs burnt from the pressure. I continued through blurred tear saturated vision until I reached the bridge and without a consideration jumped off the side all the way down into the awaiting river. The water hit my torso hard winding my already oxygen deprived body as I broke the surface of the water to catch the violent rift of a silent underwater current. My aching breathless lungs were now at the mercy of the river as it contorted my body throwing me upside down, left to right. Lashings to my face and hands were received in the rush of passing rocks jutting up. Scrambling in a blind panic my head managed to rise to the surface where I instinctively gasped deeply for breath. Splashing about I tried to aimlessly grasp the surface of the waters as the current pulled me under again. Flashes of white light pulsed in my eyes as I felt a hand grasp mine pulling me across the current to calmer waters. My upper body was propped to rest across a fallen partially rotted tree trunk. The only words I heard were "You must live York."*

*I whispered, "Adeline," then lost consciousness.*

*I woke to feel the sharpness of pain in my head. My body was shivering still half immersed in the waters. I went to place my hands down to push myself up, wincing at the shock waves of pain bolting up my arms. I looked at the palms of my hands to see they were shredded. I used my elbows to drag my body out of the water to prop myself to my knees and then to a stance. I turned to look at the river waters calm surface gently flowing and recognized a connection with the symbolism of its illusion.*

*It was close to dusk, as the red glow on the underside of the clouds was growing visibly more prominent. Except it wasn't the sunset's doing, this was Greyhavens raging flames causing the dance of light in the looming night skies. I walked back the whole way never taking my eyes off the glow. Just as I entered the start of the drive the last of the men arrived in a vehicle. I had wondered why these two had not joined the others to assist in the dig. All the men were present with the exception of them. Parking the vehicle, by the time I reached them they were unloading the rough cut handmade pine coffin. I opened the front door to the house for them so they could carry it straight in.*

*I didn't go inside. It wasn't long before I heard the bang bang bang of nails being placed in the lid of the coffin. Cletus was screaming out her name over and over until his voice faded. I assumed the men entered through the back door to get Cletus away from her coffin and try settle him before Vance was called to attendance. Wilton walked across to Vance lightly imparting a couple of words before Vance quietly stood up. Together they slowly walked toward the back. Just before they passed the front of the house Vance paused to look across at me. I shook my head. Vance blinked with a slight nod before proceeding to the back.*

*I waited a few minutes then quietly walked around to find a position with a clear view. In the shadows I crouched to sit on the floor of the porch. The men had lit a series of small fires around the area to provide light. I could see from the flickering flames a pair of legs dangling in the tree. I assumed they belonged to Cletus. One by one I watched, as the silhouette of each man would step forward where the underside of their faces were intermittently lit by the light before they stepped back past its reach again. When Adeline's body was being lowered into the hole only the sound of Cletus wailing out her name echoed into the darkness. Silent tears fell down my cheeks as my heart ached vowing never to say goodbye.*

"Excuse me miss are you okay?" I turned to see the air hostess bent down holding out a packet of tissues.

"Sure, it's allergies. They get inflamed when I fly." I said taking the tissues from her hand. "Thank you."

She glanced at me then the book nodding her head as she stood up to let someone pass by. I could tell she was going to ask some questions about what I was reading. I recognized the look in her eyes. It was the same one the waitress had the night I met Bahrain.

"How long until we land?"

"It's about two hours away." She said with her eyes fixed on the book.

"Thanks again for the tissues. I'm going to get some rest now." I said to encourage her to leave.

"Oh, you are welcome. Enjoy your flight."

"Thank you I will." I said watching her walk away with a hidden smile.

When the hostess had travelled clear to the end of the aisle out of site I looked to see if anyone else might be watching before placing the book in the waterproof body pouch I had hand sewn and attached to my torso. Once the book was secured flush under my left arm I stood up to open the overhead hatch. Fumbling about I made it look as though I placed the book away then returned to my seat. I folded my jacket into a makeshift pillow closed my eyes with a smile allowing myself to drift off to sleep.

I woke to the bump of the wheels connecting to the tarmac. When the signs signaled allowance to rise I unclasped my buckle and rose to pull my bag from the overhead compartment down. In an attempt to draw some attention I started mumbling, "That's strange, I wonder where it is," as I searched inside my bag looking for the book.

The little sprightly ginger haired boy waiting behind me pulled at my shirt. My smile widened as he gave me a sweet grin in return. "Maybe the lady took it." He said pointing.

I looked across to see the hostess watching from the other aisle. When she realized the boy was pointing in her direction her body language stiffened while she unsubtly attempted to shift her gaze.

"Excuse me miss, my book is missing. This little boy mentioned seeing you take it. Did you?"

The woman behind me scolded her son for pointing at the hostess. The queue forward was starting to gain momentum. The flight attendant shrugged her shoulders before stepping backwards disappearing behind the pre-drawn curtains.

I yelled out, "Its an heirloom so I need to find it. I have to get that book back," feigning concern.

Another hostess greeted me at the exit. "I'm sorry, we will search the plane and submit any property found to the lost and found department. If you register your details there they will call you if an item by the description you leave is found."

"I need to speak to the other air hostess, this boy said he saw her looking through my property while I was sleeping. The book's definitely missing so I need to talk to her."

The little champion nodded his head calling out, "Yep."

"I'm sorry, please take it up with lost and found. If we locate any items by this description they will be in touch. Now please you must alight as you are holding up the queue."

I glared at the woman before walking off the plane. In an overly dramatic huff I stormed down to the lost and found area to register. Once the paperwork was completed I grabbed my bags and left the airport terminal looking very flustered indeed.

It wasn't until I was in my car and well clear of the airport that I allowed myself smile to surface. There wasn't much left to read in the book. I hoped the fake copy the hostess pilfered would provide the Interferons satisfaction this time around. As amused as I was with my original prank I recognized their pursuit of this item would be relentless so it was in my best interest to have them believe they had the authentic item within their possession. I needed to finish reading the remainder of the book and then find a safe place to hide it. The added insurance of its safety was amplified if no one knew they still needed to look for it.

The time had passed for playing games. In less than two days the interferons would become aware of what they will believe is an integral part of my strategy. I held no doubts this would create bitterness and fuel their desire for retaliation, which was the point of doing it. The first taste of my mastery at the silent wars would draw a large degree of attention my way. It was critical during this portion of the journey I remained unencumbered. Vernon Wreath was their only attempter born of flesh during this life cycle and now he was gone. All they have left are the watchers and themselves. Zivah confirmed I'm untouchable in this life, if this is true then I possess free reign to do whatever the fuck I want. The interferons currently held invisibility as their default advantage but I held invincibility as mine. In retrospect, it seemed as though I had subconsciously spent my entire life acquiring skills and knowledge in preparation for this game and I was ready to engage in my first move.

# Pledge

When I opened the door to my apartment I welcomed the hints of frankincense, myrrh and rose into my lungs. They are the three scents I always burnt any place where I was going to be resident for a while. It was my way of becoming acclimatized to the familiarity of home, which always supported my belief of the concept of its ease of portability. Any place could be enjoyed when I had my creature comforts with me. In my case I gravitated toward conditioning myself to the presence of my favorite hat and those three scents. They held far more weight of importance to me than any of the items I had collected over the years.

This apartment is the only property I own. It took me a long time to settle into the alignment to societal normalities of purchasing a home, holding a mortgage. The idea of doing so always felt like a trap. I never wanted to be bound to anything. At the time I felt stumbling onto the availability of this property was a wonderful accident. I had my realtor assigned to look out for an open plan living space specifically a rental when she mentioned in passing this top floor warehouse conversion might become available. The property had not been advertised yet; her intel was sourced directly from the owner who she knew personally. He was an eccentric architect who purchased the building and had spent close to a decade personally developing each vacant allocation into a work of art. The man was a visionary who believed in amplifying the fusion of harmony between nature and its industrial surrounds.

The most spectacular aspect of my home when you first enter is the high cathedral ceilings with rows of thick walled full length self gradient polarizing panels of glass allotted randomly between the original industrial metal and wooden beamed panels. Stepping into this space I instantly felt connected yet protected from the sky. I knew the first time I came to inspect this apartment I was set to become a homeowner.

The total area is three thousand square feet of open plan expanse. One large room containing twenty-five foot walls made up of old bricks and spectacular large industry paneled windows. The kitchen has a tasteful commercial feel to it. I was attracted to the clever way the architect meshed stainless steel and various wood grains into the existing pipelines making it look intentional in design. He allowed for ample bench space for an aspiring cook such as myself to make an impressive mess.

There were only a few segregated spaces allocated. The cupboards for storage and the visitor's powder room facilities were some examples, even then the way he designed them made it feel as though I was living within an art piece. The rest of the expanse was visually sectioned by changing textured floor designs and the clever use of weighted industrial based material constructed into bookshelves for the purpose of make shift walls. He had them built on old railroad castors and had placed tracks embedded into the flooring for ease of movement. I imagined he must have been an avid reader for he allowed space for a sizable collection to be stored.

The main bedroom had some added pizazz because it was built on a suspended floor in mid air offset in the top left of the room. The access comprised of an old repurposed fireman's pole with a custom handcrafted, fully detailed wrought iron spiral framed staircase wrapped around it with polished wooden steps. I had the option to slide to the ground from my bedroom or walk down the stairs on days I wasn't feeling as heroic.

When I climbed those steps for the first time I recall looking up to the sky through the glass ceiling panel wondering what it would be like to sleep there as naked to the stars as they would be to me. The architect's one off hand made king size bed was set up for display. He had used steel and various other metals to formulate a collage of ideas which reminded me of something cross pollinated between scenes from Alice in wonderland and Dr. Seuss. It had broken glass pieces positioned into aspects, which caught the light refracting rainbow prisms on the soft textured white veils hung around the four-poster bed frame. There was not one aspect of this place I wasn't in love with. The architect was divined in his vision and design. I felt truly blessed to have been able to meet with him and be granted the privilege of acquiring the place I now call my home.

I propped my luggage on the table situated just inside near the front door as I entered and then did an immediate beeline to the lounge area executing an unimpressive belly flop onto my sofa. Glancing around, the place seemed to be in order. I was under no misconception that I was safe from them here. My new reality evolved around struggling to accept I would never feel alone again. The interferons possessed access to anyone vaccinated as a watcher. My landlord, my cleaner even my family were all unaware participants. Basically the only thing that altered was my illusion of privacy. In retrospect I could now appreciate without a doubt that I had been neatly held trapped within the confines of a petri dish for my entire existence and more importantly I wasn't alone. Anyone of interest was being silently watched, manipulated towards certain controls, situations and directions. The interferons it seemed could touch anyone with their puppetry of strings. It was almost time to test the extent of their mastery. They had a reliance on humans. I could use this to sway an advantage by setting actions in motion, which would leverage off a basic trait in human nature, fear.

The corner of the book was digging into my ribs. Propping myself up I reached down the front of my top pulling it out to place on the table. Visually I could see from the pages remaining there wasn't much left to read but I still felt as though there was so much of the story remaining. It made me wonder if the assumed untold portion was intentional or whether the author ran out of time, perhaps even lost a desire to complete it. All I knew at this point was my recognized self driven need not to feel the emotional depth of the story as it had unfolded. I was conscious of how my reaction to the discovery of Adeline's body, Cletus, Vance and York's responses were drawing on my latent anger, the feeling of insurmountable loss and a depth of sorrow that even if I chose to allow it to surface to full expression, I'm not sure I could. I shed tears but my emotional investment was clearly withdrawn. I had to trust there was a reason for this allowance of pent up frustration at all which had transpired. Thankful to be within the comfort of my own home I reshuffled into a sustainable reading position then reached across picking up the book to begin.

*The men had all headed off once the last of the soils were placed on Adeline's body. Vance left Cletus in the tree to mourn while he went inside to continue drinking. He made a small fire, sat in his old battered wing chair smoking his pipe and sipping moonshine. I continued to sit on the porch in the dark listening to the wind carrying the whispers Cletus was sharing. Every so often he would break into a wail and then the whispers would restart again. I still couldn't accept she was gone.*

*The next day I arose to the sound of footsteps to the door. I thought it was strange I heard the vehicle driving off but not arrive. When I opened the door there was the tail end of an automobile leaving the edge of curbed section of the drive. Whoever was here had delivered a newspaper leaving it near the entrance to the front door on the porch. The first page possessed a bold headline about Greyhaven. The article spoke of the search for the mystery heroes who pulled most of the residents out onto the greens. Only four bodies were found burnt and two others remained unaccounted for. The fires were still burning while some parts of the building were now deemed to be under containment.*

*My assumption that the four being referenced as dead were the doctor and the other three we left behind. I was unsure of who were considered to be the two unaccounted for. The photograph of the asylum's grounds filled with poppy beds depicted a beautiful image. The visual majesty of the gardens could easily inspire readers to lull into thoughts of enchantment. The article leant towards conveying* the tragedy of the fire's devastation on such a wonderful institution. It was calling for people to join in to assist in the restoration of the property to its former glory. The consumption of every word deepened my blood to boil.

How were they able to cover up the entire murderous activities taken place? The records must have shown something to account for other people's absence. Surely the fires would have unveiled the horrors which had been secretly embedded within those stonewalls.

Without realizing my fists clenched as I released loud elongated screams out into the air, "AAAHHHHHHHhhhhh.     AAAHHHHHHHHhhhhh. AAAHHHHHHHHhhhhh."

Vance jumped from his seat with his fists readied for a fight as he looked at me, "What is it York?"

I passed across the paper repeatedly tapping on the front page. He read it and then threw the newspaper onto the remainder of the previous nights small blackened smoldering coal in the fireplace. I held my arms tightly folded shaking my head pacing the room while the paper rose to ignite fresh flames.

"Leave it be York." Said Vance placing his hand on my shoulder to still me.

I looked at him and shook my head once left to right, "No."

Vance didn't flinch at hearing me speak. Instead he placed a half smile on his face and nodded, "I know, I recognize her look in your eyes. Tell me what you need and I will help you, so will Cletus."

I acknowledged his words with a blink and a nod before walking out the front door. I headed to the back fields, which gave me full access to the neighboring lavender grove. I needed time to think.

It was late afternoon when I returned. Vance was back in his chair and Cletus had still not come down from the *tree. I took pen to paper to write the instructions of my strategy in detail then handed it over to Vance.*

*He smoked his pipe as he read the words then out the side of his mouth said, "We will need Cletus for this and maybe Huck too. You have to stay here York. It's dangerous for you to go wandering. Someone might recognize you."*

*I nodded my head. I knew he was right.*

*Vance got out of his chair and walked toward the back door. "Might as well get a start, Cletus will need some convincing to get out of that darn tree."*

*I left Vance to speak with Cletus on his own while I went into the kitchen to grab some food to eat. I was famished. The whole time my mind was trying to think of clever ways to pin these people to the wall. I wanted them exposed and would not rest until it was done.*

*When the door swung open I had little time to brace myself as Cletus came running forward wrapping his arms around me in a tight embrace. He pushed the wind out of my lungs as he squeezed tight, "I'm gonna get em fer all us."*

*I placed my arms around him returning the intensity of his embrace. There were no words that could ever capture the gratitude I felt for his willingness to do as I am suggesting.*

*Cletus released me, picked up Huck and proceeded to the front door.*

*"Eat something first Cletus." Suggested Vance.*

*"I'm goin to lose light. I'm doin this now." Said Cletus shutting the door behind him.*

*Vance and I were left in the kitchen looking at each other. I was chewing on a crust of bread awaiting his thoughts.*

*"We don't ever need to talk about what you did in there York."*

*I popped the remainder of the crust portion in my mouth, continuing to chew.*

"Right, well help yourself to soup. I'm going to get some rest." With this Vance turned and proceed toward his bedroom.

Cletus didn't return until well after dark. I was already creating a slight wear to the surface of the porch wood panels where I had been pacing for hours. There was a risk in my plan, which could land Cletus into the wrong sort of attention if he slipped up in his words. A huge sense of relief washed over me when the vehicle came up the drive with him smiling and Huck propped up beside him wagging his tail.

"Yer did it boy." He said slapping my back hard as he jumped out of the vehicle and came straight toward me.

I smiled and turned to follow Cletus into the house. Vance was just entering the main room yawning while rubbing the back of his head. "It's done. They discovered them bodies and there out there still diggin fer more."

"Who did you get to do it?"

"Them Bakers boys are always playing pirates an such looking for gold so I dropped the treasure map near them whiles ther playin. It took no time fer them to be huddlin with whispers and then they were gone. I stayed at the inn across the ways like yer suggest and had me a drink while I watched the Greyhaven grounds through the winda. When the police arrived, then more came I knew them kids had been diggin fer treasure. I waited for a while before myself and a couple of the men drinking there went across to see what the fuss was about. One policeman held the map, another called out the spots and men were there with shovels diggin. By the time I was heading back they had uncovered nine of them poppy grave beds. I said what yer told me to say in passing to the fella with the camera. His eyes lit up and were off to talk to his fella which reports sittin in his vehicle."

*"Well done Cletus." Said Vance pleased. "Come let me fix you some supper."*

*I quietly walked out the back door to Adeline's grave. I took the knife I had found in the kitchen out of my trouser pocket and began carving into the trunk of the tree. It took me hours to complete my message but once finished I felt satisfied. It was the representation of my truth and vow to her.*

*This is all you need to know for now Harper. Yes I said your name. If the path has been set correct by now you would have already been guided to understand this book was unequivocally written by me for you, the soul key of wills. You have entered this life force of karmic flesh under the guidance of illuminarium in the process of evolving into the penultimate Harp player. You have one cycle set to Karmic flesh remaining, which if all bodes well is set immediately post this life. My imparting this knowledge share of my reincarnation into York is one of four I must tell and you must read.*

*Seek to find the others Harper and let no one know they exist. From here on you can trust only yourself. The vibrations of the illuminarium were activated the moment your hand touched the books surface. It set off an irreversible chain of events that must now be executed as foretold without you being engaged to know the future as you previously held capability to do. Feel the strength, knowledge, skill and fortitude you possess to make what you will possible. It all starts and ends with you. Are you ready?*

*The next book exists hidden in an open space where it belongs but would least be expected to reside. Find me within the pages, there is so much more we need to do together.*

*I miss you, Harper.*

I flipped the remaining pages in search for more but they were blank. I wasn't ready to stop reading let alone to see my name referenced. I couldn't help but feel as though information was being intentionally withheld. Who was this person writing to me? It's definitely a male. I can feel him very present and almost see the outline of what I perceive him to look like. Could he be my guardian angel guiding me? I hungered to know so much more.

"I miss you too." I whispered as I resigned myself to accepting there were no further words to consume. I sadly closed the book partly in disbelief that it ended so abruptly. I held it against my chest and breathed. There was no denying the experience had already been thought provoking. In actuality it was life altering for me and those whose path I was destined to cross. I didn't have any idea what the future would bring my only certainty was that it stood with no doubt to be a fascinating journey and mind blowing experience for those who dared to venture it with me.